PENGUIN BO

A PACK FOR WINTER

Eliana Lee writes character-driven romance with diverse casts and too many MMCs. After being repeatedly betrayed by love triangles, she now needs her heroines to have it all. She was born in Melbourne, Australia, to immigrant parents, and firmly believes food is a love language. Other titles include *The Scent of Us: Part One*; *The Scent of Us: Part Two* and *The Heat of Us*.

A PACK FOR WINTER

ELIANA LEE

PENGUIN BOOKS

PENGUIN BOOKS

UK | USA | Canada | Ireland | Australia
India | New Zealand | South Africa

Penguin Books is part of the Penguin Random House group of companies
whose addresses can be found at global.penguinrandomhouse.com

Penguin Random House UK,
One Embassy Gardens, 8 Viaduct Gardens, London SW11 7BW

penguin.co.uk

First published in the United States of America by G.P. Putnam's Sons,
an imprint of Penguin Random House LLC 2024
First published in Great Britain by Penguin Books 2025
001

Illustrations by AlexBrushes and Anna Vaughn Jones
Printed and bound in Great Britain by Clays Ltd, Elcograf S.p.A.

The authorized representative in the EEA is Penguin Random House Ireland,
Morrison Chambers, 32 Nassau Street, Dublin D02 YH68

A CIP catalogue record for this book is available from the British Library

ISBN: 978–1–405–98787–5

Penguin Random House is committed to a sustainable future
for our business, our readers and our planet. This book is made from
Forest Stewardship Council® certified paper.

For anyone who is overworked and overlooked,
wishing three men would come spoil them.
And teachers. You're pretty amazing.

AUTHOR'S NOTE

Welcome to Starlight Grove! If you picked up this book because of the super cute cover, I want you to know that this is a cozy, small town romance that's also *very spicy*. This book is for adults!

This book is intended to be a sweet, cozy, low angst read. However, there is some content some readers may find upsetting. Our character backstories include death of a parent via cancer and race-motivated bullying.

A Pack for Winter contains multiple explicit sex scenes, intended for audiences 18+. Ivy's HEA includes the intention to have children, but there is no on-page pregnancy.

It is part of the Cozyverse shared universe between Emilia Emerson and Eliana Lee. Our books can be read as standalones, but all take place in the charming town of Starlight Grove with shared characters.

Please visit my website for more detailed content notes and exclusive bonus content: https://www.elianaleeauthor.com.

INTRO TO OMEGAVERSE

A PACK FOR WINTER IS A WHY CHOOSE OMEGAVERSE.

Why Choose means that our female main character doesn't have to choose between her love interests for her happily ever after.

Omegaverse originated in fanfiction as MM (male/male) romance. It has evolved since then but remains a wonderfully queer-positive genre, which is reflected in the worldbuilding.

While every author has their own take on omegaverse, in general, it is an alternative world where society is composed of three designations: alphas, omegas, and betas. People are born into a designation, which influences their biology, personality, and instincts, but they do *not* shift into animals. Everyone has a scent that can change depending on emotions and stir up physiological reactions in others.

Cozyverse is our sweet, low-angst interpretation of the genre.

ALPHAS

Alphas are natural leaders, mostly male, and the most dominant designation.

Male alphas have knots at the base of their penis that swells during sex, allowing them to stay locked inside their partner. Female alphas have locks in their vaginas that serve a similar purpose with male partners.

When exposed to enough omega pheromones, particularly during an omega's heat, alphas can fall into rut, which is when they are overwhelmed by their instincts to sate and care for their omega.

Alphas can "bark," which means injecting their voice with a tone that omegas find difficult to resist. In this omegaverse, barks are used in trusting relationships where the omega consents to being put in a submissive state.

OMEGAS

Omegas are the rarest designation, and most are female. Typically, they are physically small and have a high need for physical touch. Omegas are often the center of pack life, the glue that holds the pack together.

Starting in early adulthood, omegas go into heat every three months. Heats last approximately one week, and during this time, omegas are ruled by their instincts. They have a strong urge to nest, gathering soft and cozy items into a bed for comfort.

Omegas must be knotted by alphas to avoid pain and physical harm during heat. If omegas want to prevent their heats, they can take a daily suppressant pill.

BETAS

Betas are the most common designation and what we would consider "normal" humans. They don't have strong scents and are least governed by pheromones but are not immune. Betas can be a part of packs, and alphas and omegas can bite them to form a bond.

PACKS

Polyamory is freely accepted and many people form packs, or chosen families. Romantic and sexual connections between pack members can vary.

SCENT MATCHES

Scent matches are people who are uniquely compatible with each other and have strong reactions to each other's scents.

BONDS

Bonds are initiated by a bite and form a permanent emotional link between two people. Alphas and omegas exchange bites, whereas betas simply receive them to create the bond.

Chapter 1

IVY

MY BOOTS CRUSHED THE REMNANTS OF AUTUMN LEAVES AS I drew closer to the house. Bob and Mary Russell were moving out and leaving their beloved fish tank behind. Mary had been regaling fellow Starlight Grove townspeople with descriptions of their new custom built-in tank. Long and detailed descriptions of how it would mold to the contours of their house while gesturing in a weirdly sensual manner.

No judgment here.

But if I played my cards right, that old tank was mine.

Bob's familiar egg-shaped head appeared from behind the moving van and I sped up to catch him.

"Excuse me! I'm so sorry to bother you, but do you have a moment?" I called out in a breathless rush.

"Ms. Winter?" Bob did a double-take. It had been a long time since I'd taught one of his children, but the name stuck, just as it had for most of the town. "What are you doing here?"

Come on, Ivy. You can do this. Assert yourself.

"I heard you were leaving your fish tank behind. Could I please have it for my classroom?" I asked politely.

Bob stared at me blankly. "Your classroom?"

"They make great teaching tools. Water chemistry, caretaking, teamwork," I explained earnestly. I tucked my hair behind my ear, neatening my short brown bob out of habit rather than untidiness. "Not only that, they help create a calming environment so—"

"Yes, yes, you can take it." Bob waved an impatient hand.

I did it!

"We have no use for it," Bob continued, before his chest puffed out. "Did you know the new tank we're getting is going to be *tailor-made* to the specifications of our lounge room? We worked with the most *fantastic*—"

I didn't have the guts to do anything except stand there and listen to him until I had turned into a desiccated husk.

"Thank you!" I finally squeaked. I shuffled sideways through the gap between the moving van and the front gate. "I'm so grateful!"

"Mary will give you a hand!" Bob called after me.

I left the Russells' old house with my prize in the backseat of my car. Mary had even thrown in the filter, heater and lights for me. Not having to buy them myself was a godsend. I would be able to afford substrate, decorations and test kits straight away.

And fish. I suppose they were an important part of it too.

It was a relief to know I would be able to get this up and running for my fifth graders sooner rather than later. I felt like we had limped our way into December. Budgets tightened, class sizes grew, resources drained.

I did my best with less and less every year.

That's why I was holding out for the Preston Eberhart Educator Empowerment and Excellence Grant. I'd spent weeks perfecting my proposal. I wanted art supplies for Tanner who drew the most amazing designs in his margins. A robotics kit for Riley who had a fascination for taking things apart to see how they worked. Books written in this century for Mona who had read and re-read every dog-eared paperback in my mini library. *No one* would make that $2,000 work harder than me.

But until we found out where the money was going, I would have to settle for begging for secondhand fish tanks.

I parked at my usual spot near the elementary wing of Starlight Grove School. I much preferred walking to work, but with the earlier nightfall and unpredictable weather it was safer to drive.

It quickly became apparent that getting the tank from my backseat to my classroom was going to be harder than I'd anticipated.

My omega designation was not usually something that held me back. I accepted that I would need a step ladder to reach things in high places. I took suppressants religiously to stave off my heats. Applying specialist deodorant was part of my morning routine to dampen my natural omega scent.

But as I stood there, staring at the giant glass box, the fat droplets of a chilly December rain began to fall.

Sometimes the idea of having a strong, manly alpha do physical labor for you just made sense.

Gravel crunched behind me. I turned to see Rome Chandrasinghe stepping onto school grounds. SGS's new music teacher and one hundred percent alpha. Even his big umbrella couldn't obscure that striking black gaze, warm tan skin and his neatly stubbled jawline.

It was a big cosmic joke and I was the punchline.

You wanted a strong, manly alpha? Here you go! Now make conversation like a regular human while your tongue decides to stop working.

Rome removed his headphones. He liked 90s RnB and lived close to the school as well, two facts that I should not have memorized but had anyway.

"Ivy! What are you doing here on a Saturday?" Rome called out. "Where's your umbrella? Here, come under mine."

I don't know why I found the thought of Rome seeing me so unprepared embarrassing.

"I usually have one on me, I swear!" I promised him. Rome jogged over and held the umbrella out over my head before stepping under it himself. I was immediately enveloped in the sumptuous haze of his mulled wine alpha scent. He was comforting. Complex. Designed to be held close and savored.

Scents were a natural lure between alphas and omegas. But after twelve years of being an omega, I was fairly practiced at not letting it go to my head.

Fairly practiced but not, you know, *immune*.

"Thanks," I said, feeling like I was protected by more than just the umbrella.

"Of course," he said softly.

My own gingerbread scent rose in a spiced, gentle swirl between us. Rome's tiny gesture of thoughtfulness pleased my omega. I looked up, caught the slight pulse of his pupils expanding and felt my face flush.

Let's side-step what my body is inconveniently doing, please.

Rome cleared his throat and both our scents receded slightly, the brief designation-fueled interlude forgotten. We were back to what we were supposed to be—colleagues.

"Is Jeff making you work on the weekend?" Rome asked, his heavy brow furrowed.

"No!" Our principal had nothing to do with this and I was a bit self-conscious that I had been caught going the extra mile. "I got hold of a fish tank and I'm putting it in my classroom," I explained.

"Got hold of . . ." Rome repeated.

"Not by stealing! I got it legitimately!" I assured him hurriedly.

Rome carded his fingers through his long, cheekbone-grazing strands of hair and side-eyed the tank in my backseat. "I didn't think you stole it," he said slowly.

My shoulders sank in relief. "Oh, good."

"But now I do."

"Rome!" I was indignant that he even thought I was capable of it.

His eyes crinkled with amusement. "Just kidding. Jesus, it's big. Do you need help with bringing it in?"

"Yes, please," I said gratefully.

Rome exhaled loudly. "Thank god. If you had said no I don't know what I would've done."

He pressed the umbrella into my hand and began taking off his coat. His movements were very graceful considering how broad his shoulders were. "Do you mind?" he asked, holding it out to me.

I took his coat from him, my mouth going dry as I fought the urge to press my nose into the wool blend. Rome began to roll up his shirt sleeves and I prayed all the claims the No-NonScent Deodorant ads made were legitimate.

Look at the ground instead of the strip show you've unwittingly initiated.

Rome lifted the tank with ease and began to make his way toward the school. I only let myself look at his taut forearms for a very brief moment. "Why are *you* here on a Saturday?" I asked, holding the umbrella over us both and trying to keep up with his long strides.

"You mean other than saving you a visit to the chiropractor?"

"Yes, that," I huffed.

"Robbie has the Tri-State Piano Competition coming up and is convinced he'll bomb," Rome said, somehow managing to hold the door open for me with his hip like a gentleman.

"Oh he'll do so well," I immediately assured him. Robbie O'Hara was a tenth grader and already playing at a pre-collegiate level.

"I agree," he said, flicking a quick glance my way. "The assembly hall is similar to the space where he'll be performing on the day. I suggested it to his piano teacher for an extra rehearsal. Hopefully it'll give him the boost of confidence he needs."

Rome had replaced the elderly, half-deaf Mr. Peters, who really should've retired twelve years ago rather than twelve weeks ago.

Starlight Grove was lucky to have him.

I held my classroom door open and pointed to the spot I had optimistically cleared for the tank already. Rome set it down easily, as if carrying it the entire way had been no effort whatsoever.

"Thank you, Rome," I told him sincerely. "That was nice of you to do that for Robbie, by the way."

He cocked his head to the side. "I can be nice."

"I didn't say you couldn't."

"It was implied."

"Was not."

Smiles played on both our lips.

My eyes narrowed slightly. "Are you still gunning for the Preston Eberhart grant?"

"You mean the PEEEEG?" Rome pronounced it like a long, dachshund-like version of *pig*.

"I think Preston prefers the Preston Eberhart Educator Empowerment and Excellence Grant."

Rome was unapologetic. "Lucky he's not here then and I can keep calling it the PEEEEG," he said smoothly before his expression flattened somewhat. "But yes. I am. You?"

"Of course."

"Good. If only the winner was determined by who could remember what the grant was called."

Was he rooting for me? "That *would* be convenient," I said shyly.

Rome took his coat from me and I reluctantly let it slip from my fingers. He made his way past me toward the door and laid his forearm against the frame. His chin pointed toward the tank. "If you need advice on setting that up, feel free to pop in and see James."

James Chen was a vet, Rome's longtime partner and from what

little I had seen of him around town—the perfect, charming counterpoint to Rome's darker intensity.

"I don't want to bother him, I'm sure he's busy at work," I said hesitantly.

Not that I was really looking forward to all the extensive fish research I would have to do now.

"Don't be silly." Rome pulled out his phone. "The clinic closes early on Saturdays. You can probably catch him as he's finishing up if you head over now. I'll check but I'm sure he won't mind. I'm stuck here anyway so he won't be in a rush to get home."

I laughed. "Are you implying that he won't have anything better to do because he can't be around you?"

Rome stopped texting abruptly. "Yes," he finally said.

"You think a lot of yourself, don't you, Rome?" I teased him lightly.

His answering smile made my chest flutter peculiarly. "You should try it sometime, Ivy."

A chirp sounded as his phone went off. Rome's expression brightened seeing the response from his other half.

"He said he'd love to . . ." Rome paused. "And used every fish-related emoji there is." His lips pursed with equal parts exasperation and affection.

I don't know why I suddenly imagined what it would be like to receive texts like that throughout my day to make me smile the way he did.

"Tell him thank you and I'll see him soon." I gave my next words some serious thought. "And add a seal emoji."

Dogs of the sea. Friendly and capable of waving. It would hopefully please someone like James.

"He'll think I've had an aneurysm."

"I'll reassure him of your good health."

Rome sent my reply and pocketed his phone. "You're a bad influence, Ivy Winter," he said, his voice like velvet.

It was the first time in my life anyone had called me a bad influence. It was . . . ill-fitting and a badge of honor at the same time. I met his dark eyes and swallowed loudly.

There it was again. His rich, enticing alpha scent.

I stared at the bare brown skin above his collar and pictured running my nose along it and breathing him in.

For a brief, mortifying second I wondered what it would be like to be his pack's omega.

Don't bother. It's not like anyone ever shows interest.

You're just Ms. Winter. Wrangler of children, and—I glanced down at my shapeless woolen sweater—*sexless caterpillar.*

The razor of negative thought sliced along a well-practiced path.

My palms smoothed down my pants. "I better go. Don't want to keep him waiting," I said perfunctorily.

"Of course. I'm sure Robbie's wondering where I am too," Rome said with a quick glance at his watch.

I watched him leave my classroom, and waited until I was sure his scent had dissipated from the doorway before I made my exit.

Chapter 2

IVY

"HI, MS. WINTER!"

Naomi Allen may have been sixteen and working her first job as Whiskers Vet Clinic's junior receptionist. But to me, she would always be ten, trying to lead the class in a mutiny against fractions.

"Hi Naomi," I greeted her, closing the door firmly shut behind me and shivering off the blustery windchill.

"Have you read the latest *Runeweaver Knight* yet? Can you believe—"

I shushed her quickly. "No spoilers! I'm a third of the way through."

Naomi scraped her nails over her face and let out a silent scream.

"I'll finish it soon and we can discuss," I laughed.

"*Thank you,*" she moaned.

It was rewarding to see the nudge I had given her toward epic fantasy had grown into a full blown addiction.

"Did you forget your pet?" Naomi's forehead creased as she glanced down around my feet, looking for a furry companion. "*Do* you have a pet?"

I grinned. "No, but class 5W is about to get several."

Her eyes rounded with surprise. "No way! That's why you're the best, Ms. Winter. What are you—"

"Ivy! You made it!"

I'd heard him speak at the last town meeting but I did not remember him sounding so . . . *lush.* A husky baritone that strummed something fundamental within me.

James strode out of the exam room, his appearance even more devastating than his voice. He filled out his blue scrubs like they were designer threads and probably missed his calling as a runway model. His hair was thick and dark, in a slight wave up from his forehead and rounded glasses framing expressive brown eyes. A single dimple adorned his left cheek.

He was a beta, the most common designation. But there was absolutely nothing *common* about him.

"Here I am," I said, tucking my hair behind my ear nervously.

"Come with me." James flicked his head toward the consulting room. "The computer's in here."

Was I allowed to be alone with that blinding smile without a chaperone? I gave Naomi a wave good-bye and followed James into the office.

James settled himself easily into the swivel chair and gestured for me to sit at the chair beside the desk. As he leaned back casually and steepled his fingers together at his waist, my eyes dropped to his exposed toned forearms.

These are the second pair of arms you've stared at today, Ivy. What's the matter with you?

"Seal emoji. That was you, wasn't it?"

My eyes shot back up to his face, hoping he didn't notice my detour. "Yes. Rome would like you to know he didn't have an aneurysm," I informed him seriously.

James threw his head back, rewarding me with a laugh that was genuine and bright. "It's good that you told me, it was a very real concern of mine," he teased.

His manner was so open, inviting me into his world. I didn't really want to start discussing fish just yet.

"How are the two of you settling in?" I asked quickly. Was that a silly thing to ask? They'd been here for several months now. "I know Starlight Grove is barely a blip on a map compared to New York but—"

He let out a sheepish huff. "Do you know how Rome and I met?"

I shook my head.

"We were waiting in line for a croissant."

"That's a cute way to—"

"For two hours."

"Oh."

I couldn't imagine anything worse.

James seemed amused by how badly I was hiding my thoughts. "We chatted almost the entire time and by the time we got to the front of the line there was only one left. Made sense to split it."

"Was it worth it?"

"Yes. Definitely." He pushed his glasses up the bridge of his nose, suddenly shy. "But not because of the croissant."

I inhaled sharply, feeling my heart expand.

Would I ever find a love like that?

"Point is," James continued, "Rome and I are happy to find a home where a two-hour wait for a viral croissant is not a thing."

"I'm glad," I said softly.

His scent was subtle—all beta scents were—but suddenly the whispers I'd been picking up didn't feel like enough. Hot chocolate with a hint of marshmallow. It was such a tease, a mug passing by in the hands of a waitress for someone else. I wanted to hug it between frozen hands, lift it to my lips and let it warm me from the inside out.

God, imagine our scents together.

Imagine our scents with Rome's.

I got the briefest flash of how that would look—clashing lips, an escaped whine and whitened knuckles—and swallowed hard.

Inappropriate, Ivy! So inappropriate!

There was a loose yarn between my fingers, accidentally yanked free from my sleeve. When did I do that?

James' jaw was tense, a stillness in his limbs reminiscent of a beast poised to strike.

And then it was gone and the dimple returned.

"So . . . ready for Fish 101?"

I LEFT WITH A stack of printouts with meticulously detailed notes of recommended fish and a list of reasonably priced accessories that worked with my budget. James even scribbled out a classroom feeding schedule and gave me tips on how to best involve the children in the maintenance.

"Just name one of them after me!" was all he said when I thanked him profusely.

I was determined to find the prettiest betta fish possible in order to do him justice.

The image of a beautiful swirling fish wearing tiny glasses popped into my head. I pulled my scarf a little higher around my face to hide my goofy smile.

After leaving Whiskers, I'd driven to Main Street, needing to stop at Mariposa Market and pick up a bottle of wine before heading to dinner with my parents.

I'd lived in Starlight Grove my entire life, but the way she adorned herself for winter would never lose its magic. Wreaths of various sizes and gaudiness hung from doors, neighbors trying to outshine each other like male birds seeking a mate. My steps slowed to a stroll despite the brisk early evening air, admiring the fairy lights and paper snowflakes that had gone up in shop windows. I stopped in front of the toy shop and giggled at the felt mice wearing Christmas sweaters, positioned like they were hard at work setting up the display.

A plaintive meow drew my attention. Felix slunk out from around the corner and stretched himself up, pressing two cotton-white paws on the window edge. His little pink nose squashed on the glass and left a heart-shaped mark behind.

"They're not real mice, Felix," I explained. "Won't be a good mouthful."

He blinked golden eyes at me.

"Yes, I'm very sure," I assured him.

Felix was a fixture in Starlight Grove. A riot of black, white and orange fur. His imperious attitude masked how good a listener he was.

I didn't want to call him a stray. He was far too majestic for that.

Felix was just . . . ours.

Plus he was invaluable at town meetings for settling debates when our mayor Stanley droned on for too long. We liked to think of Felix as our mayor too, to Stanley's great consternation.

"Have you picked your house for tonight?" I reached down and gave his head a scratch. "Not yet? You can come with me but I'm visiting my parents first."

Felix scrunched his nose with distaste. I shouldn't have said that. Mom and Dad's chocolate labrador was in love with Felix and it was a torrid one-sided affair.

"Oh, he's not that bad!" I recalled the way Teddy had chased Felix through my parents' yard and winced. "Ok, maybe for you he is," I conceded.

The sky was darkening quickly, the amber glow of the streetlamps illuminating the rain-soaked sidewalk. My pale cheeks were already ruddy from the cold. "Well, don't stay out here too long. All right?" I instructed him, sticking my hands even deeper into my pockets.

My reflexes barely kicked in as Felix barreled toward me without warning.

"Oof!"

I struggled to hold him *and* maintain my balance as he scampered up my front. He nuzzled his head into my neck with such an aggressive, burrowing motion I squealed.

It was sadly the most action I'd gotten in years.

"Sorry, you *do* want to come with me after all?" I wheezed as his big bottlebrush tail batted at me.

Then he was gone, like a demented poltergeist, leaving me flustered and confused.

"What on earth . . ."

I stared down at my woolen coat, now covered with cat hair. I sighed, brushed the orange, white and black off me as best I could and continued on my way.

Chapter 3

ROME

I ARRIVED HOME TO A CAT ON MY DOORSTEP.

James and I didn't have a cat.

Surely it belonged to someone? It looked extremely well-fed. Shiny gold eyes and glossy multi-colored fur.

I stared at the overgrown hairball.

He/she/it stared back.

I couldn't fucking believe I was stuck in a staring contest with a stray cat and about to lose.

"Shoo," I commanded.

The cat's nose twitched and I was certain that was the equivalent of it laughing uproariously in my face.

Our front door swung open suddenly and I jumped.

(The cat didn't).

My bonded beta stuck his head out and smiled when he saw me.

"Rome! I thought I heard you," James beamed. He noticed our unwanted visitor and his eyebrows flew up to his hairline.

"Oh my god, it's happening, I can't believe it," he muttered urgently. "Rome, it's *Felix*."

"Who?"

"Please tell me you haven't been *that* unobservant."

I couldn't because clearly I had been.

"Felix is the mayor, Rome," James said slowly. As if that explained everything instead of being even more confusing.

"What? Then who the hell is the guy we met when we first moved here? What's his name, er—"

"Stanley."

"Yeah, him."

James waved his hand. "He's mayor too but Felix is really the *people's* mayor if you know what I mean. Don't you remember him at the town meeting we attended?"

If James thought I was able to process anything during that cluster-fuck of new faces and names, then he would be sorely let down.

"He was there?" was all I said.

"Yes! They couldn't come to a decision about the width of the parking spaces. That's what that laminated sign is for—so he can cast the tiebreaker vote. But he couldn't because he was sleeping. Don't you remember?"

I rubbed my eyes furiously with my knuckles. "I thought they were referring to the old man who was snoring under his hat."

"No, babe, that's Hank Prescott."

Sometimes I was very grateful for the way James adapted so easily to new situations and tried his best to help me keep up. Even if sometimes I felt like I was being buffeted violently trying to hang onto a speeding car.

"Ok," I sighed. "So we have the cat mayor on our doorstep. What do we do about him?"

"He's chosen our home to sleep at tonight. Marisol told me about it when she brought her bulldog in for a check-up. Apparently he's been missing all autumn and only recently started house-hopping again. It's a *big* deal, Rome," James emphasized, adjusting his glasses.

I stared at him aghast. "So we're supposed to let a strange cat rub itself all over our furniture?"

At that moment, our neighbor's door opened. Logan Bennett was such a huge alpha his shaggy head almost scraped against the top of the frame. There was a neatly wrapped present in his hand. He noticed the three of us and gave a polite wave.

"Hey, you got Felix tonight," he observed. "Congrats."

"So this is just *widely* accepted, is it?" I questioned.

James ignored me. "Hey Logan, do you know if he's been fed?"

"Oh, we're feeding him now, too?" I crossed my arms.

I may as well have been talking to a brick wall.

"Beats me." Logan shrugged. "But he'll meow like he hasn't either way. Do you need his food? I always keep some cans for when he stays with me."

"Thanks Logan." James pushed past me. "I might take you up on that, we weren't prepared at all."

"What the fuck is happening," I hissed under my breath.

Felix was watching me. Looking outrageously smug. This was getting out of hand. I bent down, getting eye to eye with him so I could lay down the law. Man to . . . cat.

Only to be hit with a burst of Ivy Winter's delicate gingerbread scent.

Fuck.

It had been months since I first scented her and it hadn't lost its allure. Not one bit. In fact, I think it was getting worse.

My alpha was driven to the point of distraction by it lingering in the halls of the school. Being able to help her with the miniscule task of carrying her fish tank today was like a feast for my caretaking instincts.

I almost scent-marked her when we stood under that umbrella together today. My fist curled, nails digging into my palm as I held myself back from running my cheek along hers and shrouding her in my scent.

I wanted to say it was just biology. But there was nothing *biological* about why my eyes always tried to find her telltale brunette bob in a crowded assembly. Or why my heart and lungs felt crowded whenever I saw her going the extra mile for the students, whether they were hers or not.

I didn't know how to explain why her periwinkle blue eyes felt like a lightning strike every time they met mine.

Ivy was empathetic, thoughtful and so goddamn brilliant. How could I make sure her shine would never be dulled? I almost pulled out of the Preston Eberhart grant when I realized she had applied as well. The principal admonished me for that. Something about maximizing our chances.

I got the most irrational surge of jealousy that Felix had been cuddling with her. And judging by his implacable expression, he knew how I felt and did not care.

"The bed is off-limits," I ordered him crossly. "And no scratching the new couch. Capiche?"

Felix yawned with his whole body, stretching nearly the entire width of the porch. He shook it off before striding purposefully through the open door with his tail regally in the air.

James returned with the cat food. "Where is he?" he asked.

I flicked my head inside. "I laid down some strict ground rules first," I added.

James' kiss might have had a tinge of exasperation to it but the way his palm slid down my back was all love.

"Regrets?" he asked after we broke apart.

I loved having a bond with him. Loved the insight it gave me to his emotions. I understood exactly what he was asking, his thoughts settling on the town and our decision to move.

"Never." I smiled.

Despite the strange cat that was now eating from a bowl that I had to remind myself never to use again, I was content.

I'd grown up in a pack. An omega mother, four fathers and

enough siblings that our first home had extensions on the extensions. My Sri Lankan father may have given me my last name but I was lucky enough to be raised in a wonderfully chaotic mix of cultures and influences. It was normal to see feijoada next to mackerel curry at the dinner table. The sound system bounced between the rhythmic samba of Brazilian pop and 80s power metal. Sunday football bled into T20 cricket matches. Our backgrounds were all so family-oriented my childhood home was always brimming with extra people.

My dads said that one day my mom put me on her lap while she played piano and I grew up stuck to the keys. It never felt like enough and I picked up a guitar soon after. Dabbled in brass briefly. Music gave me calm, my family gave me love and the small town they raised me in kept me safe.

Then we moved. I was thirteen. Two of my dads had jobs so lucrative it was worth taking the whole pack family along like a great big traveling circus. Their contracts ended and we moved again. And again, until I didn't know where home was anymore.

I spent a lot of my teenage years lost and angry. Angry that my fresh starts always seemed to come with the grime of judgment—my name, my skin, my interests. College in New York was deliberately chosen, yet it didn't make it *right*. I eventually grew, uneven and odd-angled, out of whatever childish whim drove me. I finally let go of the feeling I was chasing that had no name.

Along came James. Right on cue, the way everyone said it happened when you stopped looking. The same, strange jolt of fate struck me again when I saw the job listing for a music teacher in Starlight Grove.

I had never even heard of the small town before.

When my offer came through, I made sure to check they had a vet clinic before I told James about it. It wouldn't be a home for me if it wasn't also a home for him.

"You wanna run away with me?" I had asked after I finally shared the news.

James didn't hesitate. "Yes. Always."

I bonded him that night. Kissed and loved that bare spot on his neck before letting my teeth mark him as mine.

The moment I set foot in Starlight Grove, I felt like I could breathe. The static in my head went quiet.

James and I settled ourselves on our couch in front of the TV. Felix hopped up easily and rolled himself into a furry puddle between us. James did a double take as he smoothed down Felix's patchwork fur.

"Is it just me or does he smell like . . . gingerbread?"

Betas took a little longer to pick up scents compared to alphas and omegas. I was surprised James could detect Ivy on a freaking cat.

I wasn't sure what possessed me to send Ivy James' way this afternoon. Maybe I was desperate to know what he thought of her.

"Sneaky bastard must've snuggled with her before he came here," I muttered.

James gave me a meaningful look. "You know, we've never courted an omega together."

Knowing we were on the same wavelength lit a spark of satisfaction in me. I *did* want a pack to call my own. So did James. Our relationship had always felt like the first links to something greater than the two of us.

But not yet.

"I want to be more established first." I heaved a sigh, my fingers plucking restlessly at the edging of the couch cushion. "We've only recently settled in. If we're going to do this, I want to be able to do it properly. Provide her with everything she needs."

James didn't look convinced. "Ivy doesn't strike me as someone who wants *stuff*, Rome," he said reproachfully.

I didn't know how to explain it wasn't just about *stuff*. It was my alpha not wanting to settle for anything less than the absolute best for her. I'd grown up seeing how my dads doted on my mom, and how much her happiness meant to them. How was I meant to do anything less for my own omega?

Ivy needed dates tailor-made for her. An extravagant nest. Courting presents.

Probably another alpha too, especially when she decided to have heats.

"Let's just see what happens," I mumbled.

James went silent but I could feel a yearning, complex emotion weighing on his heart. "She's beautiful, Rome," he finally said.

"Yeah, I know."

She's everything.

At least . . . I think she could be.

Felix began to purr, the soft continuous hum hitting some magical frequency that loosened all the tension from my limbs.

"So, er, did Marisol mention if Felix ever chooses a house twice in a row?" I whispered.

James laughed, the feel of his delight bubbly in our bond. He leaned over and kissed me. My hand curled around the nape of his neck, pulling him closer as his lips perfectly fitted with mine. "Love you," he said, before settling back onto the couch.

I guess I would have to wait until tomorrow night to find out.

Chapter 4

IVY

MARIPOSA MARKET SAT PROUDLY ON ONE OF MAIN STREET'S prized corners, opposite the square. It took its central position quite seriously, showing off its emerald green awning and wooden crates lining the front laden with brightly colored produce. The excess continued as I stepped inside, every available surface bursting with clusters of fruit, a selection of spices and chutneys or cellophane-wrapped baked goods.

It was owned by Marisol and Carmen, Dominican sisters who took great pride in expanding Starlight Grove's palate and waistlines.

Carmen greeted me from her usual spot—the little raised table where she doled out free samples. Her neat braids were aptly formed in a crown on her head, her shimmering eyeshadow catching the light as she looked me over.

"Ivy! You and Felix! When's the wedding?" she gushed effusively.

"He attacked me out of nowhere, Carmen," I said exasperatedly, patting down my coat some more.

"Darling, that doesn't sound like him. Don't worry, I know what will make you feel better." Carmen approached me, plate in hand. "Try some jalao."

"Mmffhgh!"

Suddenly there was a honeyed, coconut confection in my mouth. It was almost too sugary, but the more I chewed the more I craved a second.

"Aisle four." She swanned away, no doubt looking for more victims. "Thank me later!"

Giving an omega a single sweet was *mean*. I meandered down aisle four and tucked the tray of sugared candies under my arm. I seriously debated eating the whole thing during the ten minute drive to my parents' place.

Not that I would actually do it. Turning up to dinner with a full stomach was far too rebellious.

I turned into the wine aisle and crashed directly into a solid, extremely large male chest.

"I'm so sorry!" I winced and held up my hands, shuffling away like an apologetic crab.

Logan Bennett bent down to pick up my candy. "Did Carmen make you get that?" he asked shortly.

"N-no. I wanted it," I stammered, taking it back from him.

He grunted in reply. The language I was most familiar with from him. Logan was a silent, aloof grizzly bear of a man. He was Starlight Grove's electrician and very good at his job—not so much with people. I think he preferred hiding. Hunching his shoulders in an attempt to minimize his size. The rugged growth of facial hair masked most of his features and he compulsively tugged his flannel shirt over his thick waistline.

Logan turned back to the wall of wine. He was standing in front of the one I wanted but I was too scared to ask him to move. I hovered instead, pretending I was examining bottles on another shelf.

A bitter scent hit me. I wrinkled my nose. Soured sap and hardened resin, murky and brittle on the bark of an old pine. Logan was tense, his alpha scent betraying him. My eyes drifted to the side and watched him run a harried hand through his hair.

I could feel my omega wanting to help. Responding instinctively to the stress pheromones he was exuding.

"Are you . . . having trouble picking one?" I asked tentatively.

Logan's face clouded over. "Didn't realize there were so many ways to bottle grape juice," he muttered.

He reminded me of my students, lashing out from frustration when they felt lost.

"What's the occasion tonight?" I kept my voice light and conversational.

Logan tugged at his beard. "Dad's introducing his . . . girlfriend to me."

There it was.

I had noticed Chester Bennett with an extra spring in his step around town. Suddenly taking lots of trips to neighboring Briar's Landing. He deserved it. The alpha had raised a barely teenage Logan entirely on his own. Considering Logan was pushing forty now, it had been a long time coming.

Seeing the sharply dressed older man holding a bouquet of flowers ready to woo his lady love had almost made me weep.

A deep line appeared between Logan's brows. "This is the happiest he's been since Mom passed and I need to make a good impression."

Oh. He was nervous because he thought he could somehow mess this up. Not because he didn't approve.

I wanted to hug him around his middle. Squeeze him extra tight and tell him he was going to be wonderful and there was no need to worry.

Instead, I gestured at the gift he had tucked under his arm. "That was very thoughtful of you."

He turned away from me, clearing his throat into his fist. "Trying to be . . . I guess."

"Let me help," I offered. I walked slowly down the aisle, surveying the labels. Logan hovered at my back.

Despite living in the same town our whole lives, I'd never been close enough to scent him properly before.

It was different to getting a flash when passing someone on the sidewalk. Logan's tension was subsiding and with it the bitter edge to his scent. Slowly it invigorated. A pine forest rose up protectively around me, my breath dissipating in the frost-laden air.

It took me a moment to remember what I was supposed to be doing.

If you perfume, Carmen will never let you hear the end of it.

I pointed out a dark bottle with a burgundy capsule. "Well, you can't go wrong with a great red with dinner. This winery is only a few hours from here." My fingers trailed across and stopped at one wrapped in yellowed parchment. "But if you want something that feels a bit more important and fancy—"

"Don't make me try and pronounce extra French words in front of them," Logan implored.

I didn't laugh. It was a legitimate concern if you weren't familiar with wine. I chewed my lip thoughtfully. "What are they serving tonight?"

"Dad's showing off his lobster."

Oh, that clinched it. I pulled a greenish bottle off the shelf, its label depicting a sprawling vista. "New Zealand sauvignon blanc. Sorry, I can't avoid French entirely," I apologized ruefully.

Logan took the bottle from me, staring down at it and then back up at me. "No, this is . . . thank you, Ivy," he said quietly. "I'm . . ."

His eyes were the loveliest shade of forget-me-not blue.

"You're nervous. It's natural," I said. Why did my hand itch to stroke through his burnished bronze hair? "I'm sure she'll be equally as nervous wanting to make a good impression with you."

He gave a little huff like the thought was preposterous. "I doubt it."

"Well, I know for certain there's one thing you're both fans of." I smiled. "Your father. Talking him up will definitely win you points."

The faintest pink hue colored his cheeks. "I can do that. Thank you. Again."

"Of course. Anytime." I grabbed the red wine Logan passed on. Mom's favorite and Dad was guaranteed to be cooking something that came from a cow.

Logan watched me, his face unreadable. "Have a good night, Ivy."

The low timbre of his voice rippled down my spine. I blinked, shaking it off and returned his well wishes.

"You too."

THE USUAL GARDEN GNOMES lining the brick path to the door of my parents' home had been swapped out for equally garish Christmas elves the moment the calendar flipped over to December 1st. I was sure Mom had something extravagant planned for the rest of the charming gray home that Dad would inevitably be roped into helping her pull off. She'd already hung a humongous wreath on the cherry red door, embellished with dried orange slices, red berries and cinnamon sticks she had tied on herself.

I pushed open the unlocked door and was immediately hit with the smell of a roast that had been cooking low and slow for hours. Teddy came bounding up to me, his nails clicking on the floorboards.

"Hello, you big dork," I said, affectionately rubbing his floppy ears. Teddy's expression was extra goofy as he sniffed me. "I know I smell like Felix but I haven't got him stuffed in my pockets, I swear."

Teddy ignored me and conducted a thorough search with his wet nose.

Mom's head poked out from the kitchen and lit up.

"George! Ivy's here! And she's brought the Moonfall Valley merlot, bless her."

I hung up my coat and fussed over my unruly windswept hair

in the hallway mirror. Entering the kitchen was like being folded
in a warm, nostalgic hug. I kissed both my parents on the cheek
and went digging in the cupboards for wine glasses to add to the
table.

"Try."

Dad pressed a spoonful of gravy into my mouth. Why were people feeding me against my will today?

Not that I was *mad* about it but still . . . boundaries and all that.

"More salt?" Dad asked quizzically, looking at me over the top of
his glasses perched on the tip of his nose. Our blue eyes were twins,
just as my dark mahogany hair was a match for Mom's, though hers
was streaked with a dignified gray now.

I smacked my lips thoughtfully. "Maybe just pepper, actually."

He clicked his fingers and returned to the stove.

Mom was busy beautifying the dishes Dad had cooked—swirling
the top of the mashed potatoes just right, a flutter of parsley over the
brown sugared butternut squash.

"I can't believe it's almost winter break, Ivy." Mom shook her
head. "Golly this year has gone by fast!"

I risked stealing a green bean behind Dad's back. "I know, it always creeps up on me," I said, chewing rapidly. I thought about the
updates to policy documents and assessment plans I still needed to
make before next year.

Maybe I should do a version that factors in the grant money.

I nixed that idea almost immediately. Getting my hopes up
would only make the disappointment even more crushing.

"Marisol told me she saw your car at the school today, Ivy Noelle," Mom said warningly.

I only got middle-named when a lecture was about to come
my way.

"Does Marisol have some sort of hidden camera network set up
in this town?" I grumbled.

Mom ignored me. "You already give so much of your time to that school, going in early and staying late. You don't need to give them your weekends too."

I sighed. "I was only there because the Russells—"

The crash of the front door opening was heralded by Teddy's excited yowl.

"Teddy, at least buy me dinner first!"

My younger sister Caitlin blew in like a hurricane, shedding her coat, hat and various layers in piles over the furniture. She yanked at her hair tie, freeing her long brown hair with a vigorous shake.

She recoiled when she noticed the wine in my hand. "God, it was my turn to bring that, wasn't it? Sorry Ivy."

"It's ok, I don't mind." I smiled. After we had gone wine-less the last few dinners, it seemed better to play it safe.

Caitlin hugged Mom hello as we took our seats at the table. "Sorry I'm a bit late, my car was making a funny noise so I thought I'd better drive a bit slower," she said breezily.

Dad froze halfway through carving up the roast. "What kind of noise?"

"I dunno, like a—" Caitlin proceeded to make a sound that I could only describe as an angry cat fornicating with a clanking robot.

"Caitlin Georgie Winter."

Oops, guess I wasn't the only one getting middle-named.

"When was the last time you had it serviced?" Mom admonished her.

Caitlin made the exact face she used to make whenever she was about to lie about her grades.

"Please don't say that time when I took it in for you before you moved out," Dad said warningly.

"Ok, I won't," she said a little too quickly.

"*Caitlin.*"

"Sorry. I'll take it to Gavin's garage straight away. Promise."

Mom and Dad sighed in unison. I knew they wished Caitlin still lived at home so they could keep her wrapped up in cotton wool. She'd come to me quietly last year and asked for advice on moving out. With my help, she avoided three rental scams and she now lived in Briar's Landing with roommates. When she wasn't making the most of her twenties, she worked as a hostess at a local upmarket seafood restaurant.

"How's work?" I asked her.

Caitlin gasped sharply, her eyes alight with excitement. "Want some goss, Ivy?" she asked with a suggestive raise of her brows.

"Sure," I agreed cautiously.

Caitlin and I's idea of gossip was very different. I wanted to know who stuck 'HONK IF YOU LOVE CAKE' signs in Stanley's front yard and Caitlin . . .

"Sean came in with his wife the other day. They ended up arguing and left before dessert. Sounds like he's having some regrets, Ivy," she said gleefully.

"Oh." I couldn't even force any enthusiasm.

"Oh? Ivy, I thought you'd be glad to know your douchebag alpha ex is realizing he got the short end of the stick." Caitlin waved her fork at me, the limp green bean in danger of flying off. "Isn't that like, I dunno, omega crack for you?"

I knew Caitlin thought she meant well. As the only omega in a family of betas, my designation was a conundrum they never quite understood. Not that they didn't try. Mom and I waded through an agonizingly awkward conversation about omega heats and alpha ruts right after I presented at eighteen. I don't think I would ever wipe the memory of her explaining that one day I would not only crave group sex but require it for my health.

We mutually and silently agreed on rug-sweeping after that.

My knowledge of pack life subsequently came from books, movies and gawking at the few who had made their home in Starlight

Grove. Several alphas, sometimes a beta or two, all focused on an omega like spokes on a wheel.

The idea of finding *one* boyfriend was already far-fetched, so several was incomprehensible. Maybe that's why I was so quick to accept Sean's offer of courtship when I was twenty-three. He was an alpha who had also grown up in Starlight Grove. He professed to have waited for me while I 'did my college thing' and I was relieved that life had presented me with an option so easily on a platter.

But it was also my first year teaching and I threw myself into doing the best job possible. I guess I could understand why Mom chastised me for going in early and staying late because that's exactly what I did.

Sean didn't really understand why I couldn't just turn up and then leave when the bell rang. Resentment grew and he eventually broke up with me, marrying a beta woman from Briar's Landing and moving there to start a family with her.

I couldn't even blame him. I felt like I was waiting our entire relationship for my fabled omega instincts to kick in and show me what I was supposed to do. But as my twenties passed by, it became clear that I was not wired that way. Now here I was at thirty-one, no closer to finding an alpha, let alone a pack. No closer to experiencing that all-consuming, head-in-the-clouds kind of love.

Tick tock, went that biological clock. I would be on suppressants forever and never experience a proper heat at this rate. Sean did ask me to go off them, of course, but there never seemed like a good time. Now I was on the merry path to spinsterhood one daily pill at a time.

But thanks to my bleak love life, I'd watched hundreds of kids in my classroom discover what made them spark. If that was my legacy, then so be it.

I let Caitlin's comment about my designation slide and took a little longer than I needed to chew my mouthful.

Later as I helped Mom wash up in the kitchen, she enfolded me in a side hug, her cheek resting on my hair.

"Do you know how many parents come up and tell me how wonderful you are with their children? It's a relief that all I worry about with you is that you're *too* good at your job," she laughed lightly, giving my arm a squeeze. "Caitlin struggles a little more to find her way than you ever did. I'm glad that you're doing so well."

I don't know if that's true.

I pushed the thought aside and returned her smile. "Thanks, Mom."

I returned to scrubbing a particularly stubborn bit of grease and never did end up telling Mom and Dad about my fish tank.

Chapter 5

IVY

THERE WAS SOMETHING IN THE AIR ON THE LAST DAY OF school before winter break. Attention spans shrank to nothing, excited chatter was at an all-time high and every classroom clock seemed to move at a snail's pace.

Rather than try and corral a herd of manic ten year olds, I embraced the chaos instead. We did a handmade secret Santa gift exchange, watched *Elf* and ate cupcakes I had baked the night before.

I also invited James to come visit. He had been a fantastic guest speaker and the kids were ecstatic to learn they had been taking great care of the fish.

"Wait, Dr. James . . ." Tanner scrunched his face up in thought. "*You're* called James. And Ms. Winter said the betta fish is called James too."

James caught my eye and winked. "Funny that." He grinned.

I felt my cheeks heat. Fish James was by far the most beautiful, elegant creature in the entire tank.

While the class was poring over some X-rays James brought, he sidled up beside me.

"How are you going to tell us apart?" he asked, nodding down at the bubbling water.

I blinked. "One of you is a fish and one of you is a human?"

"You're very smart, Ivy," he said, managing to sound completely sincere.

"Are you teasing me?"

He clutched at his chest. "Never." I got a hit of melting marshmallows and hot cocoa as he leaned close. "Only Fish James would do that."

I could feel myself breaking out in a sweat. His manner flustered me so easily.

Maybe it made the kids a bit too comfortable with him. After a few vet-related inquiries during the Q&A segment at the end, my gremlins went full-on boundary-stomping.

"I've seen you around town with Mr. C," Madison said with her hand still in the air. "Are you and Mr. C bonded?"

"You don't have to answer that," I cut in quickly.

"No, it's ok." James waved my concern away. "Yes, we are."

Oh, he was in for it now. Give them an inch and . . .

"But you're not an omega."

I nipped that in the bud as quickly as humanly possible. "Madison, people can bond whoever they wish regardless of designation."

Another student piped up. "Does that mean you and Mr. C are a pack?"

"Well, there's only the two of us for now, so I guess you could call us a very small pack," James answered.

"For now? Does that mean you're looking for an omega?"

"Is that why you moved to Starlight Grove?"

"Where are you from?"

I silenced the class with three sharp claps, clearing my throat so they knew I meant business. I didn't miss the immediate pinch in James' expression on the last question.

"5W, let's thank Dr. James for being so generous with his time today," I said firmly.

My students applauded dutifully and thankfully did not ask any more questions.

Rome stuck his head in right before lunch, just as James was gathering his things. His class must've gone to the cafeteria already. He always managed to look chic, dressed simply all in black. Small touches accentuating his style, like the signet ring on his finger and the glimpse of a fine chain at his neckline.

The alpha tapped his knuckles against my door. "Your door is squeaky. Have you asked Bruce to fix it?"

Our maintenance man had a very sophisticated system for job requests—he did what he felt like whenever he could be bothered.

I shrugged. "It's been like that for ages. I'm sure he'll get on it soon."

"Hmm." Rome did not sound convinced.

James threw an oversized jacket on over his scrubs. His face lit up when he saw Rome and my knees went weak from secondary exposure to his dimple.

"How did it go?" Rome asked.

"Terrible," I catastrophized.

"Fine," James chuckled. "Your students were great, Ivy. Precocious even. I gotta get back to work." He waved at the tank. "Bye Fish James." Then at me. "Bye Ivy." Rome got a squeeze of his hand, James' voice going tender. "I'll see you at home."

It was a good thing I was leaning against the door so I didn't melt entirely into the floor of my classroom. I was extremely grateful when the bell rang.

Principal Jeff scampered into the room like an opportunistic little rodent right before the rush of students fleeing to the cafeteria.

"Ivy, *so* glad I caught you."

"Here? In my classroom? Right when class ended?"

Jeff showed no signs of detecting my sarcasm. "Larry can't do bus duty today. Do you mind, Ivy?"

But I did it yesterday.

My brief moment of hesitation did not go unnoticed by Rome.

"I'll do it, Jeff," he stepped in.

Jeff almost jumped out of his skin. "Rome, don't lurk in the shadows like that," he wheezed.

Rome gave me a pointed look over our principal's shoulder.

Was I lurking?

I bit my lip and gave a tiny shake of my head.

"I'm sure Ivy doesn't mind, right?" Jeff gave Rome a wink.

Even *I* knew that was an extremely dumb move.

"I'm good with doing it, Jeff."

There was a definite increase of alpha energy in the room and it certainly wasn't from our beta principal wiping his suddenly perspiring forehead.

"Great, Rome. Knew I could count on you." Jeff strode out of the room, head aloft as he pretended he had gotten his way. "Make sure you two pop into the cafeteria for a *special treat*."

Rome and I watched him leave.

"Why did he have to say it like that? *Special treat*." Rome shuddered. "Any idea what it is?"

"Kenny's House of Hotdogs," I said automatically.

I giggled at the bewildered look on Rome's face. "It's always Kenny's House of Hotdogs," I explained. "It's terrible and I suspect the only reason he turns up at all these school things is because he has some sort of dirt on Jeff. That and Kenny is his brother-in-law."

Rome snorted. "I guess this is what small towns are like, huh?"

"Yep. Regrets?"

His expression was odd. "Never."

We had almost reached the cafeteria when we were intercepted. Robyn taught sixth grade and I was privately concerned the bow of her blouse would eventually consume her whole neck.

"Ivy, can you send me your IEP for Tanner?" she asked, clicking her fingers. "I have a new student starting next semester with autism too. I thought I could just repurpose yours."

I stared at Robyn and her bow. "They're *Individualized* Education Plans," I emphasized heavily.

Robyn tutted. "I don't have time to start from scratch, Ivy."

There was a numb, hollow sensation, the pit in my chest widening. It felt wrong, but Robyn was waiting expectantly. "I'll send it to you," I finally said.

"Do you mind looking over it for me when I'm done? You're doing *really* well with Tanner," Robyn said a little too enthusiastically.

"Oh, um, sure. Happy to help."

She had already wandered off. "Thanks, you're the best," she called over her shoulder.

Rome was watching me, his mouth set in a thin line. "Why did you do that?"

I scratched beneath my collar, his intense stare making me itchy. "Robyn is going away for winter break. She probably doesn't have time to get it ready before they start."

"So your time doesn't matter?"

I really didn't know what to make of his question, nor the way the muscle in his jaw tensed. "I-I'm staying here for Christmas, Rome."

"Not what I meant," he muttered but we continued on to the cafeteria without further comment. He pushed the door open for me and our eyes immediately landed on the garish red and yellow cart set up in one corner.

"Ivy, I don't know if I want to eat mystery meat served to me by a guy wearing a wiener hat." Rome sounded so adorably despondent I almost hugged him.

Almost but didn't.

"What could go wrong?" I said brightly.

I really shouldn't have tempted fate because twenty minutes later I was throwing up into a trash can. In front of Rome of all people, who was pacing back and forth on the verge of tearing his hair out. We'd left lunch together and I was caught off guard in a thankfully empty hall.

I didn't even want to think about what was in that hot dog to make it come back up so fast.

"Please don't say I told you so," I said weakly. The queasy topsy-turvy sensation was still careening around in my gut.

"I would *never*," he growled. Rome pressed three bottles of water into my hands he'd managed to magic up from somewhere. A bit excessive but appreciated nonetheless. I opened one and drank it in slow sips until that awful acrid taste went away.

"Then why do you look so upset?" I asked, wiping my mouth with the back of my hand, feeling my nausea subside.

"Because I want to sue the living daylights out of this *Kenny*," Rome hissed, lacing the name with acid. He was back to wearing a hole in the floor. "But I only have teacher money, not *fuck you* money," Rome muttered to himself. "Maybe I should've become a doctor or lawyer like my dad wanted after all."

Despite logic telling me his reaction was really out of proportion with Kenny's supposed crime, his outrage felt . . . nice. Like a secret, vengeful flame in my chest.

"Are New Yorkers always so litigious?" I asked, trying to calm him down.

Rome came to an abrupt stop. "Should I go fight him instead?"

The tiny flame became a roaring inferno.

What on earth?

At least my tummy was settling down now that the cursed hot dog was out of my system.

"I know you're trying to make me laugh and feel better but don't joke about that," I said reproachfully.

His back was to me so I think I imagined hearing him say *not joking* under his breath.

"Well, I think I'll be able to get through the rest of today. I really do feel better," I tried to reassure him.

Rome looked me over to confirm my words and then suddenly the back of his hand was against my forehead.

I was so aware of his touch, the feel of his fingers tracing down my temple and cheek. My breath grew shallow. Partly as a defense mechanism, because I couldn't risk getting drunk on his spiced citrus scent right now.

He didn't seem anywhere near as affected, merely dropping his hand and stepping away once he was satisfied.

"If you need anything, send a student to me with a note," Rome insisted. "I'm finishing the semester with the third graders. *Recorders.* You'd be doing me a favor."

I ducked my head to hide my smile. That did sound torturous. "I'm ok," I promised. "You might be on your own with them."

The bell rang, its sharp metallic clang startling us both.

"I better—"

"Yeah, me too."

Neither of us moved. Rome held my gaze and it felt impossible to look away. "Well, since I have bus duty, I guess this is it until next year."

The heaviness in my stomach had absolutely nothing to do with Kenny's unfortunate hot dog. "I guess it is," I agreed.

"Merry Christmas, Ivy."

"Merry Christmas, Rome."

Chapter 6

LOGAN

"THE USUAL, LOGAN?"

I nodded and made a sound that was a cross between a hum and a grunt. Char had already scribbled my order down and was gone from my table in the next second.

Efficient. Straightforward.

Char understood that small talk before ordering was a painful ritual I was happy to forgo. Tall, blonde and sharp as a tack, she was the pragmatic owner of Rosie's Diner, Starlight Grove's proverbial watering hole. I'd been a regular for years and our interactions had barely changed since the first week when she clocked me.

I scanned the diner, shifting my weight in the plastic chair. It was packed to the gills tonight thanks to the start of winter break. So much so that Rosie herself was helping out, the bubbly omega manning the register with her kilowatt smile. Char doted on Rosie like any good alpha did, heavy plates disappearing from the omega's hands every time she tried to help deliver orders.

The familiar chime of the door rang out and Ivy Winter stepped in. Or rather, was blown in from the buffeting wind outside. For some reason my ass was almost out of my chair to do god knows what— shield her? Help her get her hair off her face? Punch nature itself?

I was a goddamn moron.

"Oh heya Rosie," she greeted the other omega.

"Ivy!" Rosie blew a brown coil of hair out of her eyes. "It's a madhouse in here," she said apologetically.

Ivy was busy stuffing her mittens into her bag. "It's ok, I don't mind sitting at the . . ."

She trailed off when she noticed every stool at the counter was taken.

Rosie winced. "Like I said. A madhouse."

I stared at the empty chair across from me. My alpha instincts yanked at me to the point of pain, the sensation like needles behind my eyelids.

The hell?

I jumped as a hand landed on my shoulder.

"Easy, big guy," Char said quietly. "Do you mind if I sit Ivy at your table?"

Mind?

Did I want her to sit so she could eat instead of waiting? Absolutely.

Did I trust myself to not fuck up small talk with her? Hell no.

"If you have to," I huffed.

Char caught Rosie's attention and waved them both over. Sweat immediately formed on my back. I instinctively pulled my arms close to my body and managed to knock the pepper shaker over with my elbow.

"Are you sure, Logan?" Ivy asked. She stood politely to one side, one hand clasped over the other. Trapping me with her wide-eyed gaze.

I was shitty with words. I could never be a man who compared a woman's eyes to the sky or the sea or rain or some other force of nature and have it make sense.

All I knew was that when Ivy looked at me, I didn't feel the need to hide.

"Of course."

I watched her sit, smiling up at Char as she recited her order. Her cable knit sweater and scarf swallowed her. I liked how bundled up it made her look. Made me imagine ways she might steal clothes and huddle blankets around her to make a—

Jesus, what the hell is the matter with you?

The last thing I needed to be thinking about was Ivy building an omega nest.

She removed her scarf and inadvertently sent a wave of her gingerbread scent my way. It woke my cock up *immediately* and I hunched over even tighter, willing it to go back down.

That's it, I'm becoming a hermit.

My body's reaction felt downright disrespectful. She had no control over her scent. Well, apart from applying deodorant to mask it slightly like most omegas did. Despite my best efforts not to inhale, it settled deep within my pores. Reminding me of sunlit kitchens, the sweet torture watching baked goods expanding through an oven door.

Thankfully, Ivy turned our conversation toward my dad and nothing killed a boner faster.

"I never got around to asking how your dinner was. Did it go well?" she asked kindly.

"Yes." I scratched nervously at my beard. "Glenna loved the wine, thank you. How was your last day of—"

"I'm *telling* you, you old fruit loop, it's going to happen tonight." Marisol slapped her hand on the table.

Hank was just as worked up, gesturing with his walking cane and in danger of braining somebody with it. "The big storm's coming but"—Hank put his hand on his hip, eyes fluttering as if he were divining wisdom from it—"not until tomorrow. My bum hip doesn't lie, young lady," he insisted.

"Well, neither does my bad knee!"

"You want two bad knees?" Hank said threateningly.

Marisol scoffed. "*Hilarious* that you think you'd get anywhere near me."

"Well, that's because my hip is playing up because of the storm tomorrow!"

"*Tonight!*"

I caught Ivy's eye and we had to look away immediately, otherwise we were both in danger of bursting into laughter. Hank and Marisol's arguments over whose dodgy body part could best predict the weather were legendary. Every time there was a slight drop in temperature, you could bet these two would be found somewhere arguing loudly.

The only thing certain about their predictions was that they would never agree.

"What do you think, Logan?" Ivy whispered. "Storm or no storm tonight?"

I whistled low. "My money's on Marisol's knee. Starlight Grove's gonna be white tomorrow."

"All right, I'll bet on Hank's rickety hip. No storm." Her hand came up to hide her giggle.

The sound jolted my instincts like a livewire. My alpha urged me on, needing more of it, more of her, more of *everything*.

I glanced at the glass display where several pies sat and got a brilliant idea. "Winner owes the other a slice of pie," I challenged her.

Ivy's teeth caught on her pink lower lip, the blue of her eyes sparkling. "You're on."

This feeling was just . . .

If I could bottle it, I'd be a millionaire.

Char arrived and dropped two burgers in front of us. Ivy perked up, wasting no time as she grabbed a french fry.

"I'm *starving*." She popped it in her mouth and hummed appreciatively. "I haven't eaten since Kenny's bad hot dog came back up at lunch."

"Kenny's hot dog did *what*?" I snapped.

Who the fuck did he think he was? Health and safety was the bare minimum for a food business. I was going to have to find Kenny and cut some strategic wires in that stupid cart of his.

"Oh sorry," Ivy said quickly, misunderstanding me. "I shouldn't have said that right before we're about to eat, that's gross." She moved on to her pickles next. "I swear Char gives me more every time," she laughed. "I'm not mad about it but I worry one day she'll give me a plate that's just all pickles."

"You like pickles?"

"They're my favorite."

I pushed my plate toward her. "Take mine too."

You would've thought I'd offered her a vault full of coins to dive into. "Are you serious?" Ivy asked. "You don't like them?"

It would be better if I didn't look her in the eye when I said my next words. "Can't stand them," I said gruffly, munching on my own french fry.

Ivy helped herself to all of my pickles. "Lucky me," she beamed.

I ate slower than usual, wanting our time together to stretch that little bit further. Ivy spoke excitedly about her Christmas plans, what she hoped to achieve with her students next year and books she had been reading. I always knew she was an amazing teacher and hearing her speak only cemented that further.

She asked what my winter break plans were. The question gave me pause. Apart from spending the holidays with my dad and now Glenna, what else did I do? Made sure I was available if there were any outages due to snow. Taught Hank *again* how to fix his heating when it iced over every year. Single-handedly continued to keep Char in business.

There wasn't really much else I did.

God, that was depressing.

"Think you'll make it to the rink this year?" Ivy asked me brightly.

Starlight Grove set up a temporary rink in the town square every year and I couldn't think of anything worse. I would be as graceful as a yeti stuffed in, well, ice skates. It would give the town a year's worth of ammunition to make comments.

No thanks.

"Definitely not," I grunted.

"Oh." I saw the light dim in her eyes somewhat. Why did that gut me? I'd fucked up somewhere and I didn't know how to fix it.

It was probably for the best that I'd never felt the urge to find an omega or join a pack.

"Tell me more about your fish," I said quickly. "Have the kids named them?"

Ivy's smile returned and I breathed a sigh of relief.

Chapter 7

IVY

I OWED LOGAN PIE.

He had surprised me. I expected him to silently tolerate me sitting at his table but he had been a wonderful dinner companion.

Also, how often did I get double the amount of pickles? I should try and eat with him at Rosie's more often.

I'd only just made it inside my home when the few snowflakes that had begun to fall during my drive seemed to multiply a thousandfold in an instant. It clung to the evergreen trees outside my house as the sidewalk disappeared in a blink of white.

I changed into an old sleep tee, leggings and fluffy socks and began to collect all my blankets to wrap around myself on the couch in a makeshift nest.

Minimal clothes, lots of layers. Very omega of me.

I had my marshmallow-loaded hot chocolate and a riveting baking competition on my television. The newest episode of *The Grand Sugar Rush Showdown* had just dropped. Big Friday night for me, indeed.

I was a bit teary over Oscar the long haul truck driver talking about his dreams to be a baker and stay close to his family. Just as he was about to reveal if his caramel apple upside down cake was as perfect as it needed to be, he stuttered, warped and flickered off my screen.

My lights went out two seconds later.

I was devastated that I wouldn't know if he'd made it to the next episode.

Then I panicked, because if my house lost power then the school might have too. I had no idea if Fish James was going to be all right when all the contraptions attached to the tank grinded to a halt.

"No," I whispered.

I'd only gotten him and his fishy friends a few weeks ago. My class loved them. *Loved them.* I couldn't have them return after winter break to an empty glass box and a whole lot of traumatizing questions about life and death.

I didn't even think. I threw on a thermal long sleeve, a sweater, snow pants and my long puffer coat over it all. Hat, gloves and scarf went on while I was already halfway down my drive.

It was hard not to rush over to the school, but I kept my steps measured and sure. Only my familiarity with the route kept me going as visibility worsened into a white blur in front of me. I could feel my muscles straining as the wind picked up, threatening to throw me off balance.

God, what are you doing? This is stupid.

Still, I pressed on.

You just need to see they're ok. Then you can turn back around and go home.

I reached the entrance, fumbling with the key in my gloved hands. The violently strong winds blew open the door and I only just managed to close it by leaning hard against it. *Made it.* My fingers scrambled around for the light switch.

"Please, please, please," I whispered right before I flicked it on.

Nothing.

"Ok." I turned my phone's flashlight on. "It'll be ok," I told myself. "Maybe your classroom has its own generator you had no idea about and it's magically kicked in."

My classroom did *not* have a magical generator and was as devoid of power as the rest of the building. Luckily the building's gas heating was unaffected, the soft whirr audible as I made my way to the tank. Fish James and his friends were completely oblivious to their impending doom, much like the dinosaurs before the meteor hit.

"No ice age for you," I promised them firmly. Time to check if the next building had power. Maybe they were on different grids. Was that a thing? If there was power nearby all I would need was one, two maybe ten extension cords and—

"Are you out of your fucking mind?"

I screamed. Screamed at a decibel so high I was surprised the windows did not shatter and swamp us in freshly powdered snow.

Us being myself and one extremely pissed off alpha.

"Rome, w-what are you—"

"I should ask you the same thing." He stormed up to me, eyes ablaze. There was still snow dusting his shoulders and it peppered the ground with each deliberate step. "I saw you through my window rushing across town. I thought, surely not. *Surely* Ivy would not wander off in the middle of a blizzard to the school to do *god knows what*."

"I-I was," I stuttered, eyes darting as I tried to explain. "The fish, you see, I didn't want them to—"

My ass hit my desk as he backed me up against it. A tiny gasp escaped as I inhaled sharply.

Big mistake. Huge, colossal, monumental mistake.

His mulled wine scent plumed hot and dizzying down my throat. Spilled into my lungs and the heat of it billowed through my entire body. The brandy was sharper, a delicious fire with a burn I chased. Demanding my attention while cloaking me in its protective warmth.

"I was . . ." I stammered as I tried to find my voice again. My scarf felt so restrictive. I ripped it from my neck with an agitated tug. "I wanted to check on my fish."

My head felt too hot. Hands too. I let out a cross *hmph* as I pulled my hat and gloves off.

"Ivy, what are you doing?" Rome's voice was low and barely controlled.

I was only half listening to him. Did I really need to put on so many layers when I left? Suddenly my thermals and two pairs of pants didn't make any sense at all.

The sound of footsteps coming down the hall startled us both.

"Jesus, Rome, you could've waited for me to catch up," James grumbled, his flashlight whirling as he tried to find the entrance to the classroom.

Rome and I flinched as the beam shone in our eyes. "Shit, sorry," James said, hurriedly lowering it. His mouth turned down in a frown. "I'm glad you're ok, Ivy. You really scared us."

I felt stupid. I *had* been needlessly reckless. "I'm sorry," I whispered. "The power went out at home and I-I couldn't have my kids come back in the new year to an empty tank."

"They'll be fine for a few hours," James reassured me. "I'll run back and grab Logan. I'm sure he'll be able to figure something out to get everything back up before the fish even realize something is wrong."

I sagged with relief. I really wanted to hug him close for some reason. "Thank you, James."

His smile was back and made me feel like everything was going to work out.

After the fuss I had caused, I might as well make myself useful while we waited. There was a stash of battery-operated tealight candles in my storage cupboard. I'd bought them when we learned about Diwali and I reused them just this week to make my classroom feel more festive. Rome took one of the boxes from me and we silently placed them in clusters around the classroom until we were bathed in a golden glow.

The candles were tiny. Incapable really of giving off any sort of warmth against the cold of the blizzard that seeped into the walls of the school. Yet the heated itch beneath my skin seemed to grow rather than diminish.

"You should put your scarf and hat back on, Ivy," Rome said, picking them up from where they lay discarded on my desk. "I know we're inside but it's still cold."

I couldn't imagine anything worse. "I'm really hot actually," I said, my voice sounding strained. My coat felt claustrophobic even after I unzipped it so I removed it entirely.

"Are you getting sick?" Rome swept his fingers across my forehead and cupped my cheek. "Ivy, you're burning up. Shit, I *knew* I should've stopped you and brought you inside sooner." His distress made the citrus of his scent stronger, sour with an edge of bitterness.

Before I realized what I was doing, my hand carded through his hair. The effect on him was instantaneous, a shudder running through that tall, alpha body of his.

"Have to keep you warm," Rome muttered. His eyes were unfocused and glassy as he removed his coat. *Yes.* That made so much sense. In fact, it was probably better if he took even *more* clothes off.

Rome draped it around my shoulders and I pulled the thick fabric up to my nose and breathed it in. God, it smelled so much like him even though it hadn't been directly on his skin. If his coat smelled this good, then what about his sweater? I eyed it greedily and caught hold of the hem in my fingers. I was rewarded with a glimpse of ink, black against his dusky brown skin.

He's tattooed. I never knew.

I couldn't help lifting his sweater higher, taking in the way the sleek tiger wound along the hard lines of muscle of his abdomen.

Was there more? How far up did it go?

"Ivy," he groaned. His hands coasted down my waist and gripped me firmly on my hips.

I could count every eyelash framing his black eyes.

"Alpha."

It was as if I had physically struck him. He reeled back, shaking his head like he was trying to clear it. I didn't understand. I wanted him closer, I wanted his hands back on me.

"Shit. Oh *fuck*."

I didn't understand, I didn't understand any of this.

A noise slipped out of me. High-pitched. Needy.

I'd never ever made a noise like that before in my *life*.

"Baby, listen to me, I think you're in—"

The scrape of my classroom door sliding open cut him off. James and Logan appeared. Their hands were full of . . . tools? A box of some kind? It was irrelevant and uninteresting to me. I wanted them closer, all the layers peeled off them so I could—

Another one of those *sounds* left my throat. Rome's coat fell off my shoulders and my sweater was unbearably warm. I tore it off and sighed with relief as the chill hit my bare skin.

"What the fuck is going on?" Logan snapped. His chest was heaving, taking in air in big lungfuls. "Her scent, it's . . ."

James stared at Rome, then me. "Is she—"

"I think so," Rome gritted out.

The beta stepped decisively between me and the alphas. He tore his gloves off with his teeth and I sighed as he held my face between his hands.

He was so very pretty and smelled wonderful.

"Hi sweetheart." James was smiling as usual but there was a tightness in his eyes this time.

"Hmm?" I blinked.

"Are you on suppressants?"

Why was he asking me this? Almost every omega was. "Mmhmm," I answered anyway.

"Is there a chance you might have missed one?"

I made a disgruntled noise. I was very diligent with my suppressant use and resented the question.

"Not trying to upset you, gorgeous. But I think there's a chance something has gone wrong. Rome told me you were sick today at lunch. When do you normally take them?"

My mouth suddenly went dry. "Right before lunch," I croaked out.

Logan hissed. "How can one missed pill cause—"

Rome was staring at his coat I had stolen so readily from him. "One missed pill and a fuckload of compatible alpha pheromones," he cursed.

The realization collided with me in one dizzying rush.

I was going into heat for the first time in my life. Likely not a full-blown, days-long heat as I had only missed one dose of my suppressants. But clearly Rome's scent had affected me enough to throw me into a spike. A short mini-heat that could last anywhere from a few minutes to *hours* and there would only be one thing I would want during that time.

I whined, torn between panic and need.

"Ivy, look at me," James ordered me firmly.

I whined again, clawing at his arms. He was steady. I let myself sink a little deeper into the warmth of his gaze.

"I'm scared," I whimpered. "I've never . . ."

James stroked my hair. "I know. You say the word and I get both these alphas out of here."

"No!" I cried out.

My lower abdomen seized with pain. I doubled over and saw Logan and Rome visibly sway, needing to get closer to help me.

"I-it hurts, James," I gasped. "I need—"

I need to be rutted until I'm limp from coming so much. I need to be
stretched with a thick alpha knot, right before I'm filled up with cum.

Not only was I having these thoughts for the first time in my life,
but it all seemed like an incredibly good idea.

"You want to be helped through this heat spike?" James asked,
caressing his thumbs across my cheeks.

"You don't have to. You can just leave me."

The alpha growls grew louder.

"Safe to say if you want them to stay, that's not happening."
James searched my face. His bottom lip looked very inviting. Plump
and slightly peachy and I wondered what sound he would make if I
bit down lightly on it.

"*Ivy.*"

Whatever look I gave him made him curse low under his breath.

"I need to hear you say it, Ivy. Do you want them to ease your
heat?"

Them?

"I want you all," I corrected him.

James was caught off guard that I'd included him but recovered
quickly.

"Good girl." His voice sank into that deep, velvety pitch that
made my thighs clench in response. I could feel wetness soaking into
my panties.

Slick.

Getting me ready to take an alpha knot.

I was caught up in the embrace of Rome's strong, steadying
arms. Forearms overlapped at my back, the fit of him filling every
touch-starved inch of me.

"Baby, I have to—"

His face turned toward mine, his stubbled jaw grazing the rounded
apple of my cheek. *Oh.* He was scent-marking me.

I'd seen alphas do this to their omegas. I always thought it was the equivalent of a cheek kiss. A perfunctory good-bye gesture. At least that's how it always felt with Sean.

I was wrong.

It was *so* much more than that.

There was an intimacy in sharing our scents that was hard to describe. Rome was leaving his mark on me but I was doing the same in return. Spice on spice, my earthy ginger with his brandy fire.

His eyes were black when we parted, his alpha rut creeping up as quickly as my heat. I wanted to build my nest, pull him down into it and find out exactly what his knot felt like.

"It's probably best if I leave."

What was this? There was tension in the room, a disagreement sparking in my periphery.

Logan was pacing in agitated circles. "Rome looks like he can handle it."

James frowned. "If you don't want her that way then—"

"Jesus, that is absolutely not the problem."

"Then what? She asked for all of us, Logan."

Logan turned away, dragging his hand through his hair. "Because I don't know the first thing about omegas. Except that you're meant to court them before . . . *shit*."

I needed him to stay with me. I disentangled myself from Rome and made my way over to the others.

Logan flinched when I reached up to touch his face.

"Ivy. I have no idea what the fuck I'm doing," he confessed hoarsely.

"Me neither."

He smelled so good. Like a quiet breath in a deep forest. I buried my nose in his neck and he shuddered.

"Please stay with me."

My face was tilted back roughly and his mouth was on mine in an instant.

Logan kissed me like we had forever, sweet and careful. As if there wasn't a reddening flush sprawling down my neck and chest. As if my head wasn't growing woozy and lightweight as my hormones went haywire.

I didn't realize how demanding they could be. My *omega* instincts. I fisted his neckline to bring him closer, needing more.

As soon as Logan and I broke apart, Rome was there. If Logan had kissed me like we had forever, then Rome kissed me like he was going to *keep* me forever. He was possessive and hot, bearing down and encompassing my whole body with his. The crush of his mouth to mine was desperate, and I rose up to meet his heat with my own.

I was disoriented when it was over. The need to taste and beg and fuck them was so confusing and foreign. Yet it was all I wanted, all I craved.

"Ivy."

James. He was trying to ground me once again as I felt my lucidity waver like a mirage.

I tilted my face up to meet his lips. They were incredibly soft and gentle. He was tender but determined and the way his tongue stroked mine melted down my spine.

"I will look after you no matter what," James promised in a whisper only for me.

I believed him.

I trusted him.

I sucked in a sharp breath and all their scents hit me. James first, of course, but the alpha scents were a tidal wave I stood no chance against.

And then I was gone.

Chapter 8

JAMES

FOUR MONTHS AGO, I WAS ON A NEW YORK SUBWAY. I WAS utterly drained after a shift in a toxic work environment. Trying my best not to make eye contact with the passenger opposite me wearing a carrot costume, loudly crunching on baby versions of himself.

Now I was moments away from a four person, heat-induced fuckfest with what I was almost certain was my future pack.

Life certainly was strange.

I always dreamed of having a pack. First in secret, because the last thing I wanted was for my single mom to think I resented my upbringing. Then uttered out loud to Rome after meeting his family. He'd agreed wholeheartedly with a caveat—nothing as big and crazy as his parents' pack and all the extended family they came with.

So this right here? Felt destined.

I'd never experienced Rome's bond like this before. Alpha ruts were a response to an omega's need during a heat. And he sure as hell was *responding*. He was driven and territorial and doting all at the same time. Wrapped up in an urgent energy that I could only describe as *primal*.

If this was a taste of the more carnal side of pack life then sign me the fuck up.

Ivy had no idea how fucking beautiful she was. How enthralled we all were by her. Her usually neat hair was disheveled from being caught in the alpha's grip. Lips already reddened from kisses. I could barely see the sea glass blue of her eyes, her pupils were so wide as her hands burrowed beneath clothes searching for skin. Her gingerbread scent was so vibrant and demanding I swore I could taste every individual spice on my tongue.

Needless to say I was hard as a fucking rock.

While Ivy was making quick work of the alphas' clothes, I ducked out to ransack the nurse's office.

I wished I could do better than scratchy, gray blankets. I wished we were somewhere other than her classroom. But with the blizzard worsening, it was safer to hunker down. At least our winter layers were a blessing in disguise. Ivy collected each piece of clothing from us and laid it in a circular pile. She wrinkled her nose at the blankets but eventually took them too.

Even in heat she was meticulous. She built her nest carefully—clothes with hard buttons and zips were on the bottom and the softer sweaters and heavily scented t-shirts sat on top.

I knew there was etiquette around an omega's nest but it went out the window when we were all stripped down to our trunks, being pulled down into her safe space.

"Now you," I told her gently. I pulled her shirt off and revealed a little bralette, her hard nipples peaked against the lace. "Fuck," I swore. I couldn't resist pulling a cup down and sucking one between my lips. Ivy's hold on my hair tightened.

I could see Rome tucking his thumbs into her waistband and easing her leggings off her. I kissed my way back up to her ear. "Turn around," I whispered. I leaned back against her desk for support and settled her in my arms, her back pressed against my front.

My palms coasted along her thighs and slowly eased them open. The scent of her slick perfumed the air—sweet, delicate and so desperately needy.

I did not expect Logan to release a low growl and lunge straight for us.

He looked mad, feral and completely instinct-driven as he yanked her soaked panties to one side. One look up at Ivy—waiting, wanting, hoping. A small arch of her back and a caress through his hair was all he needed.

Logan lapped at her pussy like a man starved and the effect on Ivy was immediate. Her breath came out in short little pants as she writhed in my arms.

"Look at him, Ivy," I murmured. I cupped her perfect tits and kissed along her fluttering pulse. "Look at what you've reduced this alpha to."

"Feels good," she moaned, closing her eyes and rocking against his face.

Logan let out a pained groan. He lifted his head only long enough to pull her panties down her legs before pressing deeper between her thighs. Rome knelt down beside us. We both kissed and nuzzled the sides of her neck. Traded rough kisses between us so she couldn't catch her breath. Her desperation knocked my glasses askew and I laid the foggy lenses aside.

She was so responsive to all of us, seeking mine and Rome's touch all while Logan was making her fall apart.

"You're driving Logan crazy, you know," Rome chuckled.

"Does that please you, gorgeous?" I asked. "Knowing he'll never want to go a day without tasting that perfect pussy of yours?"

Ivy whimpered and began to move faster and faster against Logan's mouth.

"Come on his face and soak that beard," I spurred her on, flicking her nipples lightly with my thumbs.

"Oh god," Ivy cried out, her body going tight. Fuck, I could get addicted to watching her come. I loved the feel of her trembling in my arms, the involuntary roll of her hips as she chased her pleasure. She threw her head back against my shoulder and Rome stole her breathless cries with his kiss. Logan snarled, swiping his tongue in long strokes to catch the slick that poured out of her.

His snarls turned into cursing. "Oh, fuck. I'm—" Logan swore, his hand reaching down as he let out a low, frustrated moan. A few pumps and then he sagged, going still as he pressed his forehead against Ivy's thigh.

"Did you just . . . ?"

"Yep."

I wasn't going to judge. I was sure eating Ivy's pussy was as life-changing an experience as it looked.

"Alpha," Ivy said gently. Logan rose up and kissed her as I ran the backs of my fingers up and down her arms. I could feel Rome's need pounding like a heartbeat in our bond. But if Logan's handi-work was enough to break Ivy's heat then his need was secondary to hers.

I turned Ivy around, pulling her into my lap so I could check in with her. I did my best not to think about how my cock was prod-ding right against her spread pussy. Or how perfectly her ass fitted in my palms. Her gaze was unfocused as she wound her arms around my shoulders and nuzzled her cheek against mine.

She's scent-marking me.

Just when I thought my dick couldn't get any harder.

"Mm, I want . . ." she hummed, drifting off as she marked me again.

"Do you need more?" I asked, stroking her back. Her skin was still radiating heat. "You want a knot, gorgeous?"

Her head dipped a couple of times in the tiniest nod.

Logan was leaning against the wall, watching us. "You're good with her," he observed.

I raised an eyebrow as if to remind him that he ate her pussy to orgasm moments earlier. He gave a little scoff, turning his head away, embarrassed.

Rome moved up behind her and guided her legs off me gently. "On your knees for me, baby. Let James keep cuddling you."

Ivy obeyed immediately. I slid down onto my back, letting her rest her bodyweight on top of me instead of holding herself up. She seemed pleased by this, burrowing against me.

"Kiss, please," she asked simply.

Her omega was so fucking sweet. I kissed her and she melted against me with a soft little sigh. The sound was so utterly addictive that I suddenly understood why omegas were the natural center of packs.

Watching Rome fit his toned, hard body against Ivy's was mesmerizing. The ink sprawling up his side was so stark against the pale cream of Ivy's skin.

Please don't let this be the last time I get to watch them together like this.

"You're going to love the way he fucks you. He's so good with that thick cock of his," I promised her.

Ivy's forehead dug into my chest. Her scent got impossibly sweeter and another one of those demanding little whines slipped out of her.

It was hard to describe the way they were with each other. All I knew was that it made sense. Rome went to kiss her shoulder and Ivy had already turned her head to scent-mark him with her cheek. I drank in every change in her expression as Rome teased the tip of his cock against her entrance before slowly pushing in. He was losing his mind from the feel of her tight and wet around him. I kissed her hair as she babbled incoherently into my neck.

"Fuck, baby," Rome groaned.

"You're taking him so well, aren't you? All the way up to his knot." I brushed the silky brunette strands away from her ear so I could lean in close. "Look how hard he's rutting you. I can hear how wet your pretty little pussy is—"

My words died as Ivy wrapped a hand around my cock. *Fuck*.

Had to go and rile her up so much she put me firmly in my place.

Logan chuckled at my predicament and I managed to give him the finger.

"Nothing to say all of a sudden, James?" Rome's voice was strained but he was smirking. "Don't worry, Ivy. He talks a lot but there's a lot of ways to shut him up. I can't wait to show you," he purred.

"I want him," Ivy hummed.

Rome chuckled. "I don't blame you."

Ivy was teasing the head of my cock with her thumb. That sensitive spot on the underside that made my hips kick.

Suddenly she was out of my arms, yanked back hard against Rome's kneeling form. "Go on, baby. He smells so good but I promise you he tastes even better," he said before guiding her head down to my aching length.

I bit back a moan at the first lick of her curious tongue. Ivy stroked me, watching fascinated as precum dribbled from my tip. She quickly darted forward to lick it up, made a small noise of appreciation before taking more than half of me deep down her throat.

"Jesus fucking Christ," I hissed.

"Fucking . . . knew she'd love it," Rome growled. "She's squeezing me so—"

Something snapped. A fresh burst of Ivy's heat-sweetened scent exploded, drowning out everything in Rome's head except the alpha instinct to sate his omega. He fell into a rut, fucking her hard and deep while my cock muffled her tight screams.

I knew the instant he knotted her. Mind-numbing euphoria and satisfaction in our bond.

Ivy popped off my length, her eyes wide. "Oh my god," she whimpered. "Oh my *god*."

"Yes, Ivy." I began to stroke myself furiously, wanting to get there at the same time as them. "He's got you, sweetheart. You can let go for us."

Ivy pleaded for us both as she came and it was too much for me. Watching her ignited something deep and I erupted hard all over my tensed stomach. My hand eventually slowed, the last of my release still oozing from my slit.

Ivy was staring at it.

"You want his cum, baby?" Rome purred into her ear.

"Mmhmm."

Every single second I'd lived before that point barreled through me. Bringing me to this exact moment where *my* omega—because she sure as fuck was going to be mine—was happily licking my cum from my cock and belly. I twitched and jerked and groaned at every swipe of her hot tongue. When she was finally, *finally* done, Rome leaned forward and pressed us all together in a loving, sated mess, kissing me hungrily.

I glanced over at Logan. He'd managed to find his boxers again at some point and he had a wistful expression on his face.

"I think she'll want you close," I told him.

Logan shook his head. "You two have it covered," he mumbled.

Rome and I shared a look and we shuffled slightly. Well, as much as we were able while Rome was knotted with a content, relaxed omega. "Come on," Rome encouraged him. "Don't let her get cold now."

We knew we'd done the right thing when Ivy immediately nestled her face into his wide chest. Logan swallowed hard, unsure of where to place his hands and eventually settled awkwardly on her shoulder.

"Do you think it's over?" he whispered, unable to take his eyes off her.

Rome smoothed her hair back and felt her forehead. "Hard to say."

The storm outside was a dull, constant roar, punctuated by the occasional rattle of glass as the wind picked up. "We're stuck here until the storm passes, anyway," I said. "We may as well try to get some rest."

"Will the fish be ok? I can't set up the generator while she's—" Logan looked down at Ivy sleeping peacefully against him and back at me.

"They'll be fine till morning," I reassured him, unable to resist tracing the soft dip of her waist.

IVY NEEDED SATING TWICE more overnight.

I noticed Logan never knotted her. Finger fucked her, yes. Ate her out, definitely. But he always guided her back to Rome afterward. In a way I understood because I was the same. What mattered was that she was being cared for, not us getting off.

Logan became her personal pillow for most of the night. I found bottled water in the staff lounge and got her to drink, even though she was much more interested in getting a second taste of me.

It was impossible to deny a determined, eager omega for long though.

I woke as the first rays of sunlight began to seep into the classroom, the snowstorm finally subsiding. The others were still sleeping. Ivy's forehead was feeling cooler now, even though her skin was still luminous and blush pink. By now the room smelled like slick and cum and *all* of us. I was very aware that we were lying on top of our own ruined clothes and there was a hand-drawn "Flags of the World" poster right above my head.

Yet I could stay here forever.

The others began to stir slowly. Rome grunted as his knot loosened and slid out of her. Ivy lifted her head off Logan's chest, taking in her surroundings.

She blinked rapidly.

The dreamy look in her eyes vanished in an instant.

"Oh god."

Ivy stared down at her naked body and then around at all of us.

"Oh my god."

"Ivy," I said, slow and steady. "Don't freak out."

She patted the pile of clothes beneath us. Feeling around and searching. "I-I can't believe . . ."

"Ivy," Rome tried.

Her panic rose and I could see her spiraling hard. "In my *classroom* of all places," she said, growing more and more distressed.

"It's ok—"

"In front of the fish!" Ivy exclaimed. "I can't believe they're all going to die because we were too busy—"

"They're not going to die," I promised her.

"I brought a generator," Logan added lamely, still rubbing sleep out of his eyes.

Ivy found her coat and gave it a hard pull to free it. "That's good, that's really good," she babbled. "What a good solution to a terrible problem, thank you so much." She grabbed a shirt—Rome's—realized it was, er, *wet* and flinched. "Oh my god," she muttered again and found another one (mine) along with her snow pants.

"Ivy, you don't have to—"

"Thank you all for helping me," she said, suddenly formal. She put her arm through the wrong sleeve of her coat twice before getting it right. "I'm sorry my heat pheromones made you feel like you had to."

"Wait a minute," Rome interjected. "You've got this all—"

"I can assure you I am on birth control and all my tests were clear," she charged onward. "I mean, it was years ago but it's not like there was any need to test again."

She went bright red at her admission.

Shit, we didn't even think about any of that.

"Same with Rome and I," I blurted at the same time as Logan stammered his own agreement.

Ivy backed away further. "Wonderful. So we can forget this ever happened. I will pay to launder all your clothes, of course. Send me the bill." She grabbed her boots and put them on without socks. "Or you can just leave it here and I'll come back and get it all. But not in a blizzard! I won't be stupid and go running off like that again. I promise. I'll wait for the plows before I go anywhere," she promised.

We all glanced at the twenty inches of new snow outside.

"Err . . . except for right now."

Then she disappeared out the door.

Rome swore and leaped up, digging at the pile. "I'll follow her and make sure she gets home safe."

"Don't overwhelm her," I warned him.

"I will watch her from an appropriate distance," Rome promised as he hurriedly dressed and ran after Ivy.

Logan stared dumbly at the tools and equipment he had carried in before things went south. "I'll . . . get the generator set up, I guess."

I collected up the remains of Ivy's nest, separating the clothes into piles for each of us. The blankets we would probably have to burn.

She was scared. Overwhelmed. It was understandable.

But Rome was the perfect alpha to show her how a pack could love an omega.

I could already see how devoted Logan was to her. He'd love her so hard once he moved past whatever hang-ups held him back from going all in.

And me? Hopefully she'd see a place for me with them too.

Chapter 9

IVY

I HAD NEVER FELT THE NEED TO MOBILIZE THE GIRLS IN MY group chat before. Not that I ever begrudged the others for doing so, no matter how trivial the reason. I was equally happy to help Summer pick the right bank for her business loan or which of her five sneaker purchases she should return. Or answer Lucy's urgent need to try Beans 'n Bliss' new syrup flavors. Olive had certainly leaned on us all when she was being courted by her alphas this fall.

Olive, Summer and Lucy were three of the best girls I was lucky enough to call my friends.

But of the four of us, *I* was the one that gave the advice. Kept the *what if* scenarios from growing too outlandish. Occasionally googled statistics mid-conversation and cited relevant articles or research papers.

Now my cooler head had gone up in flames thanks to my first ever heat.

I arrived home, peeled off what clothes I had managed to throw back on (including, to my great humiliation, James' shirt) and quickly realized I could not bring myself to wash their scents off.

I rolled myself up in a blanket until I resembled a human cannoli and opened the group chat named *Felix's Sugar Mamas*. There were a whole bunch of new messages from last night I'd missed during my . . . interlude.

> **LUCY**
> Summer

> **SUMMER**
> Yes babe

> **LUCY**
> I forgot to tell you I saw your dad today
>
> Walking lil Tofu around town
>
> sort of

There was a picture included of Summer's father that had been taken from a distance. Victor Pham was holding a fluffy white dog in his arms, having what looked to be a very serious conversation while he fed Tofu treats.

> **LUCY**
> Btw tell him sorry for the stalker picture I didn't have time to say hi

> **OLIVE**
> I thought he didn't want a dog

> **SUMMER**
> he's a liar and won't admit Tofu is his best friend
>
> Dad decided the ground was too cold for Tofu's feet and carried him the whole time

OLIVE

I'm not sure you can count that as a walk

I began typing quickly.

I need help

Serious help

Emergency meeting, please!!

The girls, bless them, replied almost instantly despite the early hour.

LUCY

WHEN WHERE I WILL BE THERE

SUMMER

Do I need to get stabby or huggy

Mainly huggy

SUMMER

MAINLY

So there's a chance I'll need my kitchen
knife is what you're saying

LUCY

Gosh whatever it is, you know we're here for you, Ivy!!

OLIVE

Beans 'n Bliss at 11?

Summer please don't bring a knife

Their support was both heartwarming and frightening. I told myself I was only going to snuggle a bit longer before drifting off, wrapped in comforting scents.

I dreamed and for once, I didn't feel alone.

MY FRIENDS WERE SEATED around the table, clutching their steaming beverages and waiting expectantly. Olive with her bangs and swoosh of long brown hair beneath a cute beret. Lucy, blonde and beaming in her jacket covered in her own hand embroidery. Summer was effortlessly cool with gold safety pin earrings, perfect eyeliner and her silky black hair up in a bouncing ponytail.

Then there was me in my giant pom-pom beanie and usual swath of wooly knits. And underneath it all, James' shirt a secret close to my skin. I was feeling sorry for myself because I forced myself to shower and smelled only of gingerbread again. I felt like my hot chocolate was mocking me, an unsatisfactory replication of what I actually wanted. The marshmallow melted onto the surface of my drink and I felt a kinship with the sad helpless pile of sugary goo.

"So," Lucy began, as if it was completely normal that I had summoned everyone and then . . . said nothing. "What's going on, Ivy?"

I stirred my spoon and the marshmallow disappeared into the little whirlpool.

"Did something happen last night?" Summer prompted. "Our house lost power overnight but it was back on this morning."

Ah yes. The power outage that started . . . everything.

"This is about a boy, isn't it?" Olive asked, astute as ever.

I winced.

Everyone noticed.

"It is!" Lucy gasped.

Logan, between my thighs, groaning as he—

I covered my face with my hands, my cheeks hot enough to fry an egg.

"Who?" Summer was looking around as if they were possibly in the shop with us.

Rome, stretching me out on his knot until I—

"It's not just him, is it? I think this is about boy*s*," Olive said, emphasizing the *s*. "Plural."

James, talking me through everything they were doing until I was a complete and utter slick puddle in his hands.

And then you licked up his—

I let out a tiny but agonized scream and alarmed my friends even further.

Lucy was tugging at my hands. "Ivy Noelle Winter, you tell us and you tell us now!"

"IhadaheatspikeandRomeJamesandLoganhelpedmethroughit," I squeaked.

They stared at me.

"Could you repeat that at human speed? My chipmunk is a bit rusty," Olive requested kindly.

I took a deep breath and recounted what happened to me last night. The power going out. Rushing to the school. Rome and James turning up . . . then Logan.

The remaining details were kept light but they got the picture.

I fiddled compulsively with the fringe of my scarf, twisting the loose strands. "This is so embarrassing," I said, squeezing my eyes shut.

"It's *not* embarrassing!" Lucy immediately countered. She gently pried my tattered scarf from my fingers. "Your first heat and it hit you out of nowhere. I'm so sorry it happened like that."

Summer scratched her head. "I've missed suppressants before," she said sheepishly. "But that's never happened to me."

"It's being around scent compatible alphas," Olive said sympathetically. "Those pheromones go straight to your head."

Lucy's blonde hair whipped as she turned to face the other omega. "I think it worked out pretty well for you?" she teased.

Olive pulled out her phone and turned the screen to face us. She swiped through an ungodly amount of text message notifications considering we had been out for less than an hour. "It's like having a vibrator in my pocket," she sighed.

"Oh come on, you love your obsessed boys!" Summer laughed.

Two spots of color appeared on Olive's cheeks. "I do," she mumbled.

"See!" Summer gestured at Olive, who was now happily bonded to three alphas after a whirlwind courtship. "Maybe they will want to court you like Olive's pack did with her!" she told me excitedly.

I shook my head. "They're not a pack. Logan's a stranger to Rome and James."

Lucy tried a different tack. "Were they nice to you, erm, *during* and after?" she asked.

"Yes and . . ." I shrank a little further into the big collar of my sweater. "I don't know, I ran away," I said in a small voice.

"You ran away?" Summer repeated incredulously.

My head started to descend into a mad panic. "What if they only helped me because they couldn't resist? What if I *forced* them?"

The girls exchanged a look. "I don't think . . . you just said James asked if you were ok with them helping before it started fully. That he even offered to get the alphas out of there," Lucy said carefully.

"Yes, but I never asked *them*." I rubbed my chest furiously, certain there was an invisible rhino sitting on it. "Oh god, is that entrapment? What if I get arrested? Or worse, Jeff finds out and *fires* me?" I said aghast.

Summer very carefully took my hands in hers. "Breathe in," she instructed.

I inhaled shakily.

"And out. Good job." Summer gave me a little pat. "You are focusing on the wrong thing. I think they cared for you and didn't want you to ride it out alone." I opened my mouth to argue and she shushed me. "Yes, Ivy. All three of them. You are a catch and I am not the least bit surprised you had three men falling over themselves to help you."

My first instinct was to correct her on me being a catch but I did not think Summer would be amenable to that. But as I thought about this morning, I vaguely remembered some protesting on their part when I was rushing to leave.

What a mess you've made, Ivy.

"What am I supposed to do now?" I said miserably.

"Well, you might have to figure it out quickly because isn't that one of them?" Olive piped up, pointing out the window.

Everyone's head swiveled. No tact, no discretion. No chance of pretending we were doing anything except gawking at Logan as he walked past.

Logan must have felt the prickle of four sets of googly eyes on him.

He looked inside.

Made direct eye contact.

Flinched and strode off hurriedly the way he came.

"I think you're made for each other," Olive said brightly.

My forehead made a loud thunk as it hit the table. "This is a disaster," I mumbled.

Chapter 10

ROME

I checked my watch for the third time in two minutes.

"How can he be late? He lives next door," I said crossly.

James grabbed my arm with the wrist-watch and tucked it behind my back. "Maybe he misjudged how many steps it would take and only budgeted for ten instead of fifteen," he said lightly.

I gave him a long look. "Do you feel clever?"

"Yep," James said unrepentantly.

My leg bounced restlessly as impatience gnawed at me. I'd made sure Ivy made it home safe this morning. From a distance, mind you, even though it rankled my instincts. It would have been *better*, retorted my alpha, if I had followed her inside. Spent the day feeding her, making sure she was well-rested after her heat spike. Kissed her until we tumbled naked into bed.

Maybe if she squirmed off my knot in the middle of night I could fuck her back onto it to remind her that she was mine.

Instead, I had trudged home where James and Logan followed soon after. We agreed to meet later that day with cooler, less scrambled heads.

Then I let James lick the remnants of Ivy's slick off my cock before I stole it back with my kisses.

"Goodness, Rome, what on earth are you thinking about?" James asked with false curiosity.

I sighed wistfully.

A heavy fist knocked on our door.

"Finally," I said, standing up and going to let Logan in.

"I fucked up," he said as soon as the door swung open.

I had no idea what Logan had done, but if he had upset Ivy in any way I was going to shut the door in his face.

James stepped between us and dislodged my white-knuckled grip from the handle.

"Hello," James said with exaggerated slowness. "Please come in."

Logan ran a frazzled hand across his bearded face. He had three takeaway coffee cups in a cardboard holder balanced in one hand. "I went to get coffee for everyone," he said, kicking off his wet boots. "And I saw her."

"You saw her?" I prompted. "How did she look?"

"Yes." James nodded encouragingly. "What did she say?"

"Is she all right?" I urged.

Logan pinched the bridge of his nose like he was trying to dispel the memory. "I ran away," he grimaced.

He fucking did what?

No. *Calm down.* I forced myself to see reason.

Ivy likes him and he brought you coffee.

Plus if you hit him he will absolutely crush you with that wrecking ball he calls a fist.

"Thanks for the coffee, Logan. You didn't have to do that," I said once I was zen.

James looked at me like I was a psychopath from how quickly my mood had changed in the bond. "Maybe tell us what happened from the start," he said, taking the coffee from Logan and guiding us to move into the living room.

Logan sank into an armchair. "I didn't even make it into Beans 'n

Bliss. I was walking past the window and she was in there with her friends. They were all staring at me. So I turned around and took the long way around to go to Rosie's instead," he explained.

"Ok, that's not that bad," James said diplomatically. "Right?"

"No, not that bad," I agreed grudgingly.

I wanted to say that in his shoes I would've marched confidently into Beans 'n Bliss. Called Ivy mine in front of all her friends and all the townspeople. Then dipped her into a swoony kiss to the sound of rapturous applause.

But that would be a lie.

Clearly our courtship of Ivy required a little more . . . finesse.

James patted my hand. "All right, blood pressure down?"

"Yep."

"Good."

I leaned forward and looked at the two other men in the room. I'd known James was pack somewhere during that two-hour conversation when we met. It was a feeling that was independent of the romantic love I had for him.

Logan, I was still trying to figure out.

Nevertheless, the fact that Ivy had wanted him for her heat meant something.

"I think Ivy is our omega," I declared. Saying it out loud made my alpha purr with delighted possessiveness.

Logan's shoulders dropped and he expelled a resigned breath. "Yeah, I thought that might be the case seeing the way you were with her," he said quietly. "I get it and I wish you the best. She deserves the world so—"

James interrupted him before I could. "Present company included, Logan," he said with a wry smile.

"What?" He looked genuinely shocked at the thought.

The familiar stirring instinct was back.

It shouldn't have made sense that hearing someone insist he

didn't belong with us only cemented my belief that he did. Logan wasn't even considering his own happiness, only Ivy's. So much so that he needlessly fell on his own sword for it.

I was almost afraid of how unstoppable he would be once he won her love.

I made a circular motion with my finger to encompass all of us. "I think Ivy is *our* omega," I repeated.

Logan's gaze ping-ponged between James and I. "You want me in your pack?"

James tilted his head in my direction. "I think he's finally getting it."

"Yes, I was getting a bit worried there," I agreed.

"But . . ." Logan shifted his weight and adjusted the way his shirt sat around his stomach. "She's so smart and pretty and everyone loves her. Why would she look twice at someone like me?"

"I can recommend some TikToks for you if you think women do not like a gruff man who's good with his hands," James offered.

"*What?*"

But then James grew serious, a small frown forming behind his glasses. "Is that why you never tried to court her? You thought she didn't like you?" he asked.

Logan managed to look even more uncomfortable if that was possible. "It's not that I never tried to court her. I've never tried to court anyone."

"Anyone?"

He looked away instead of answering me. I suppose he wasn't ready yet.

"She wanted you there last night just as much as she wanted us, Logan," I said quietly. "We should court her together as a pack."

Logan took his hat off and ran his hand nervously through his dark blonde hair. Each movement leaving him more frazzled than the last. "Don't let me fuck up," he pleaded finally.

I honestly didn't think that was possible.

Unfortunately for Logan, James spoke up before I did. "I will *personally* sit in on every date you have with her and—"

He yelped as I elbowed him.

"I mean . . ." James cleared his throat. "We won't."

The way Logan nodded was almost like he was trying to convince himself.

"So . . . how are we doing this?"

I'D READ THE GRANDIOSE banner hanging across the town square several times already trying to make sense of it.

"The Christmas Eve Eve Festival," I recited slowly. "Why is 'Eve' on there twice?"

Logan let out a deep sigh. "Well, it's the 23rd today, isn't it? It's not the Christmas Eve festival. It's the Christmas Eve *Eve* festival."

"Do you have another festival tomorrow for Christmas Eve?" I demanded.

"Yes." Logan's mouth formed a harsh grim line. "I'm just as mad about it as you are."

I gestured curtly at the vendors and excited crowd milling among them. "Is it all the same shops and activities all over again?"

Logan crossed his arms over his chest. "Nope. Stanley insists on an entirely new line-up."

"Yeah, Rome. Christmas Eve Eve and Christmas Eve are very different events, why would they have the same vendors?" James said incorrigibly.

"I think he even tried to insist that the decorations should be taken down and replaced too but Felix vetoed that. But Stanley gets around it by adding more on top so it looks different enough for him." Logan drew our attention to the mayor pointing at the bunting while a nervous woman holding a clipboard followed him taking copious notes. "Everyone tells Janice that being secretary only means taking notes at town meetings, but she insists she's happy to do it."

We all stared at Janice squinting as she counted street lamps. Stanley had already walked off, chattering away.

"Felix would never make her do that," James sniffed.

Why did a cat mayor make more and more sense? This town was rewiring my brain faster than I thought it was possible.

I shook my head to clear it. "Well, shall we go find her?" I asked.

My pack—*still adjusting to that*—stepped beneath the banner and entered the Christmas Eve Eve festival.

Chapter 11

IVY

"Ivy. *Psst.*"

My sister looped her elbow with mine and hauled me close.

"What did you get Mom and Dad?" Caitlin asked out of the corner of her mouth.

I raised my eyebrows at her. "Do you still need to get their presents?" I asked, surprised. I'd sorted out mine more than a month ago during the Black Friday sales.

"Shhh. Just . . . help me pick, ok?" Caitlin said, marching me along.

Luckily, the Christmas Eve Eve Festival was tailor-made for last-minute shoppers. Starlight Grove's town square was lined with crafters, makers and designers selling their wares. Caitlin and I wandered past ceramics, jewelry, leather goods and candles and only barely scratched the surface. Tomorrow's Christmas Eve Festival would focus more on food and events like the Ugly Sweater contest, the Snowman Building competition and the live nativity scene.

I mean, we all made fun of Stanley when he first came up with the idea to turn the Christmas Eve festival into a two-day extravaganza, but it really did make sense.

Two feather-plumed horses clopped by and I waved to Mom and Dad astride the ornate carriage. As children, Caitlin and I used to join them. Held tightly in their laps for those first few years and then with our little butts squished in whatever space we could find on the seat. Despite long outgrowing the tradition, we still attended the festival as a family every year and Mom and Dad got their carriage ride.

"Have you seen him yet?"

The question was like an unwanted spray of muddy rainwater in the face. I was annoyed by Caitlin reminding me *yet again* of my ex. Sean returned to Starlight Grove every winter break to visit his parents.

"No," I said shortly.

That was a lie. I'd spotted him at the reindeer petting zoo with his wife and kids and steered Caitlin over to the market stalls.

We passed a vendor selling cutting boards and I seized the opportunity to distract Caitlin from her line of questioning.

"What about those for Dad?"

Caitlin perked up. "Ooh, good idea. Thanks Ivy," she said, wandering over.

I hugged my arms around myself and watched the unhurried passage of gray clouds across the wintry sky.

"Hey Ivy."

The screech that escaped me was proof I was the furthest thing from an elite predator on the food chain.

It was Rome who had spoken but he wasn't alone. All three of them were in front of me. Together.

Rome had on his usual long coat. Wide lapels perfect for grabbing onto and pulling his head down to me. He wore black on gray on black like a dark prince.

James was cheery in a khaki puffer and orange beanie today. I wondered how many different colors he had. I also wondered what state his hair would be in if I pulled his hat off and entangled my fingers in it.

And finally Logan. Logan, Logan, Logan. His beard had gotten even thicker since I saw him last and I wanted to feel it scrape against my . . . cheeks. He had a sherpa-lined jacket that I wanted to crawl inside. I could probably wrap myself around his chest and belly and fall asleep a very happy, warm omega.

It was two days away from Christmas, the town a white wonderland of snow and I was burning up into a crisp.

James made a motion like he wanted to reach for me but held himself back instead. "How do you feel after . . . you know," he said wryly.

Like I'm wondering why you're not throwing me over your shoulder and carrying me off for round two.

"Good. Thank you. I have *two* alarms on my phone to remind me to take my suppressants now," I admitted.

"This is for you!" Logan cut in, eyes wild with panic. He stepped forward, revealed a large gift bag he had tucked behind him and pushed it into my hands.

"I-I didn't realize we were exchanging Christmas presents," I stammered.

Even the fresh, biting air couldn't sweep away the sudden acidic edge to Logan's scent. He dragged his collar away from his neck. "I told you not to let me fuck up," he hissed at the others.

James stifled a laugh and clapped Logan's shoulder. "You're ok, man."

"It's not a Christmas present," Rome clarified.

Logan found his voice again. "It's a courting present. From all of us."

"The first of many," Rome added.

"Many . . . presents?"

My omega was absolutely *preening* at this. Practically frolicking out of my chest and demanding that I scent-mark all these delicious-smelling men.

"What happened at the school was . . . unexpected. But none of us have any regrets being there for you when you needed us." Rome's expression softened. "We would only have regrets if we never got the chance to court you properly."

Court me . . . properly?

I would have to process that later because I was still dealing with the wave of relief that they were not reporting me for inappropriate after-hours classroom use.

James gave me a little nudge. "Why don't you open it?"

We had managed to draw a bit of an audience. Well-meaning but the nosiest of townspeople doing a terrible job of pretending they weren't watching us. I spied Stanley deep in discussion with the roasted nut vendor on the corner (funny because he was allergic) and Carmen hovered nearby petting a display of scarves like a cat.

"In front of everybody?" I whispered.

Rome's head slanted to one side. "What do you think we gave you that's not appropriate to be opened in public?"

I didn't, that's not what I—

"I don't want to answer that!"

James looked thoughtful. "That does give me some great ideas for future courting presents though."

"No." I shook my head vehemently. "No, nonono."

"Too late."

I envisioned a giant rubbery dildo in my future.

It was a relief when I opened the bag and there was absolutely nothing phallic inside. "It's a . . . puffer jacket," I said, removing it slowly. Similar to the one James was wearing but in a lovely cerulean blue. It seemed a lot bulkier than a regular coat. "I feel like there's an underlying message here."

"There is," Logan grunted.

"Don't go running off in blizzards but if you insist on it, wear this?" I guessed.

"Yep."

Rome helped me out of my coat so I could try it on. His touch lingered on my shoulders and I could feel the heat of his gaze skim across my body. The flash of our eyes meeting before we quickly drew away betrayed our darker thoughts.

My perfume was spiraling wildly out of control. I could see Logan's nostrils flare, James' weight shift and Rome's fist go tight.

But they didn't say anything. Not out here, not like this. I let Rome zip up the jacket before he finally stepped back.

It quickly became apparent what was different about this coat.

"I feel like Violet Beauregarde in *Willy Wonka* after she ate the three course dinner gum," I said, rotating my limbs to show my limited range of movement.

Logan nodded crisply. "It's perfect."

"Is it normally this big?" I had no idea where they could've gotten this monstrosity.

"We took it to your friend Lucy's tailoring shop and she helped us stuff it with extra feathers so it would be warmer," Rome explained.

"Ah." I would be having some choice words with Lucy the next time I saw her.

"Do you like it?" James asked earnestly.

They were waiting so attentively for my answer. "I . . . feel like I am in a giant sleeping bag and could lie down and nap right here," I said truthfully.

Especially when the winter sun hit me *just* right. They'd essentially given me a portable nest. I could see myself sitting on my front porch, toasty warm with a hot drink enjoying the view.

I *loved* my giant new blueberry coat.

I think they knew because they looked extremely pleased with themselves.

Rome stepped close and stroked his thumb lightly across my cheek. Out of the corner of my eye, Carmen spasmed and a flurry of scarves went flying. But then Rome started speaking and that silken cadence made the rest of the festival melt away.

"I know it's Christmas and you probably have plans over the next few days. But after . . ." Rome cleared his throat nervously. "Each of us would like to take you out. Then all of us together, as a pack."

"A pack?" I echoed. Obviously he and James were bonded but Logan . . . I glanced over at the other alpha. He smiled at me, nervous but filled with hope.

Suddenly the responsibility of meeting those hopes felt daunting.

"Don't expect too much," I blurted suddenly.

They were taken aback but I couldn't stop. It was only fair that they knew exactly what they were getting into.

"I work a lot. Watch reality shows that make me cry. See my friends and family every now and then." My voice dropped to a small whisper. "I don't really do anything else. I'm not very interesting."

"Was that meant to deter us?" James grinned.

I stuttered. "No, maybe, I don't—"

Rome shrugged. "Makes us want to court you more, if anything."

It didn't seem real. This couldn't be the path that fate eked out for me. Lit with burning attraction and paved with a careful kind of affection I could already feel growing between us all. It was meant for someone more notable, more fascinating, more beautiful than me.

Yet when I blinked, the three men before me did not waver and disappear.

For what felt like the first time in my life, I let myself be brave.

"Yes. I'd like that," I said. My heart staccatoed wildly, nerves jangling knowing the town was watching. Before I could overthink my way out of it, I leaned forward and brushed my cheek lightly against Rome's. A small gesture that spoke volumes, my omega accepting their courtship and marking her claim. His sharp intake of breath gave me a dark thrill as I left my scent on him and stole a taste of his own in return. I didn't stop there, moving over to Logan.

"Princess, you don't have—"

I rose up onto my tiptoes at the same time as I reached for his fleeced collar. His beard was so much softer than it looked as I scent-marked him. I forced myself to stop before I nestled in and made myself at home in it.

James was already waiting for me. "Fuck yeah, Ivy. Lay it on me, I'm ready," he said, tapping his cheek with his finger.

I laughed and yanked him to me with a little extra force. "You're trouble," I whispered. He turned just in time to graze the tip of his nose against mine as I was pulling away.

"And opportunistic," he murmured.

I thought I deserved a medal for not tumbling into a full-on makeout session with him in the snow.

The blend of their scents on my skin was like a homecoming. Our days apart since my heat vanished in an instant. Tension I didn't even realize I was holding in my neck and shoulders cascaded out of me.

I could see Caitlin was wrapping up her purchase. Mom and Dad were disembarking from the carriage.

"I need to get back to my family. Merry Christmas and I'll see you soon." I smiled, trying to contain the flutters in my stomach.

Caitlin eyed me quizzically as I fell into step with her as she left the stall. "Why do you smell like you raided some sort of Christmas candle booth?" she asked me suspiciously.

"No reason," I said, praying Caitlin did not see Carmen giving me an enthusiastic thumbs-up as we passed her.

The handful of other town busybodies had reintegrated themselves into the bustling crowd of the festival. A flicker of trepidation skittered along the back of my neck. I searched the crowd, and caught Sean's eyes for the briefest moment. The next blink he had turned back to his family, pointing something out to his son.

Caitlin stopped abruptly, grabbing my arm.

"Waitaminute, were you wearing that coat the whole time?"

I SPENT CHRISTMAS EVE with Olive, Lucy and Summer. Olive hosted us at her beautiful home by the sea and we exchanged presents excitedly. The only caveat was that it had to be handmade. I cherished my lumpy-looking hand-built mug (Olive), enormous box of cookies (Summer) and crocheted flower coasters (Lucy). I made them friendship bracelets and they put them on immediately.

Felix joined us and eventually chose *my* house for Christmas. I didn't expect it and may have cried a little. On Christmas morning, we watched *The Holiday* in pajamas (well, at least I did) while he spread himself out in the lone patch of sunlight that streamed through my window. A tiny sliver of peace before I'd see Mom's side of the family tonight and Dad's tomorrow.

My phone buzzed. I expected to see a text from Caitlin asking if she could come over and steal some wrapping paper, but it wasn't that at all.

LOGAN
Merry Christmas Ivy

ROME
Look outside

I laughed as James' addition to the conversation was every Christmas and snow emoji. I peeked out my window and there were three boxes on my front porch.

My heart was in danger of jumping out of my chest as I brought them inside and unwrapped them. Rome had gotten me a new book bag in leather so extravagant I couldn't help but hold it up to my nose and sniff. James' present was a new scarf and enough candy to take down, well, an omega. I could tell Logan had gotten me a book but I was stunned when I peeled off the paper to reveal a special edition of the first *Runeweaver Knight*.

Logan, where on earth did you get this?

LOGAN

I asked Naomi for help

You'll get the rest. I won't leave you with an incomplete set

My former student probably had a field day helping him pick which edition to get me. I ran my fingers across the silver foil and admired the sprayed edges depicting a set of blades.

You know that could be years, right?
The series is still ongoing.

LOGAN

That's ok with me

First Felix and now this. I did not anticipate tearing up to be a regular occurrence this Christmas.

JAMES

Does my present fit?

I giggled.

Maybe not after I finish the second
part of your present

JAMES

Hmm, I didn't think this through

And Rome, I love the bag, thank you.
I'm already excited to move everything
from my old bag across.

ROME
You're welcome, Ivy.

By the way, have you checked your letterboxes?

The replies came in thick and fast.

ROME
What

LOGAN
Hold on a minute

JAMES
Aaaand they're both outside. Wanna bet who gets back inside first? Quick Ivy!

I snorted, picturing the two alphas rushing to their letterboxes.

I didn't have much time so I baked for you

Not sure if I was being presumptuous by baking you gingerbread but I do really love my recipe regardless of it being . . . you know

I hope it's ok

There was no reply for the longest time. My mind began ticking over, measuring my measly cookies up against the expensive, thoughtful gifts they got me. What was I thinking? Baked goods was what you got relatives you saw once a year, not the pack who wanted to court you. Why didn't I at least get something different for each of them? They hadn't even taken me out yet and I'd already—

LOGAN

I almost don't want to eat them

That doesn't make much sense, does it?

God, the way I wanted to hold him until that deep dull ache in my heart went away.

JAMES

They look amazing Ivy. Thank you. Rome's . . . having a bit of a moment being reminded of your scent with something you made him.

A warm flush spread through my entire body.

Oh.

My throat went dry as I saw someone was typing.

ROME

Merry Christmas Ivy

Enjoy today and tomorrow with your family

But come the 27th, you're all mine

Suddenly I couldn't wait for Christmas to be over.

Chapter 12

IVY

I heard Rome had lived practically everywhere in the country growing up. His previous home before coming here was New York. I was worried he would eventually chafe at living in our small town.

But when he turned up on my front porch with flowers and excitedly announced he was taking me ice skating in the town square, I suspected he might be a Starlight Grove townie at heart.

He took my gloved hand in his as we walked over. "I wasn't expecting this at all," I said honestly. "I look forward to the rink every year."

Rome spun suddenly, facing me and walking backward. "Did you think I was going to serenade you?" he asked with an incorrigible smile. "Take you to a karaoke bar where I'd blocked the first ten songs for myself?"

I shoved his chest and he stole my other hand too. "What sort of establishment would allow that?"

Rome laid my hands around his neck and pulled me close by my waist. "Maybe I should've hired those horse and carriages," he mused, guiding us to continue in step together. "Pulled out my guitar and played for you while you were trapped. We could ride around town and everyone could hear and see us."

My feet faltered. "Rome, if you did that to me I would die."

He leaned in and whispered in my ear. "How would you know? You haven't even heard me sing."

"Can you sing?" I managed to ask.

Rome released me at once. "I guess you'll never find out." He shrugged. I made a noise of disapproval and he laughed, his hand instantly finding mine again.

We arrived at the rink and I knew the rest of the town were watching us. I quickly realized I didn't care. Let them gawk at my gallant attempt to avoid spinsterhood.

But as Rome and I lined up for our skates, I got a covert elbow to the side.

"He better treat you right, Ives. Or he'll answer to us," Char whispered loudly before making a slicing motion at her neck. The female alpha was perfectly innocent again, wrapped up with Rosie by the time Rome had turned around.

I glanced around, looking at familiar faces in a new light. The town weren't gawking, they were . . . looking out for me.

Tears pricked at the corner of my eyes and I blinked rapidly trying to dissolve them.

"You all right, Ivy?"

"Mmhmm," I said, letting Rome guide me gingerly onto the ice. I skated this rink every winter and it always took me a few rotations to find my stride.

I found it much quicker this time, hand-in-hand with the gorgeous alpha steadying me.

"How does this compare to the rink at the Rockefeller Center?" I asked innocently.

Now that I was certain he was not measuring Starlight Grove

against his old home, it was easier to tease him. Rome gaped, aghast that I would compare the two.

"Do you know how tiny and overrated that rink is?" he spluttered. "How many tourists and how expensive—"

"I thought you would make a point of visiting it every year as soon as it opens," I cut him off, my lips pursing seriously. "Make James take a photo of you in front of the tree pretending to hold the star between your fingers."

I slid to a stop and demonstrated for him, pinching the air above me. Rome did *not* stop, guiding me out of the path of the other skaters and caging me against the wall of the rink. Our breaths fogged and mingled in the icy air, our scents rising through all our winter layers, wanting to blend.

"You're messing with me." His fingertips found their way beneath my coat and pressed against my hips.

"A little bit," I said breathlessly.

"I deserve it though."

There was a glint in that bottomless gaze of his, right before he scent-marked me. Chilled skin burning hot with the first touch. Hints of citrus, a burst of spice before settling into the smooth, warming aftertaste.

I was so close to turning my head and kissing him. So close to fulfilling the promise his scent left with me, consuming his lips and drowning in the taste of him.

But there was an exquisiteness in waiting. Resting on the knife-edge between need and want while something titanic built between us.

It was crazy because . . . he had been inside me. Knotted me. If we kissed it wouldn't even be our first.

But that belonged to a pheromone-fueled version of us.

This moment right here had nothing to do with our designations.

"Come on." Rome grinned, skating backward until only our hands were linked. "We haven't even had a proper race yet."

I was tunnel visioned. Twitterpated. Goopy on good feelings.

Char would recount the whole thing days later for me, saying I was completely oblivious to the panicked teenager flying toward me screaming *Ms. Winterrrrr*.

All I knew in the moment was that I lost equilibrium, Rome reached for me, and suddenly I was staring at a slash of red across the white ice.

JAMES WAS DRIVING US to the nearest hospital twenty-five miles away.

I sat in the backseat with Rome, pressing a gauze pad against his brow to stem the flow of blood. He scraped back the longer strands of his hair and tied it in a knot so it was out of his face.

"I'm sorry," I babbled. I repeated it several more times, wincing as I pulled the pad away and examined the wound.

"Why are you sorry, Ivy?" Rome blinked at me.

How deep did the cut go? "Because I sliced your head open with my skate?" I answered.

"Don't feel bad. I think he'll look really hot with a scar through his eyebrow," James piped up.

Rome waved my concern away as if it were an insignificant little mosquito. "I should be the one who's sorry because now we won't make our dinner reservation," he sighed.

"I'm a bit worried about both of your priorities here."

There was a dreamy look in Rome's eyes. "It was a really nice place, Ivy," he assured me.

James adjusted the rearview mirror and shrugged. "It was. We managed to find a restaurant with authentic Sri Lankan food about two weeks after moving here. There's actually a bunch of places I have saved that I'd like to try as a pack."

I choked a little at his casual use of *"as a pack."*

"I do miss New York hot dogs though," James continued. "Somehow I don't think Kenny's is gonna cut it for me."

"You are *never* to eat there," Rome told him sternly. His hand squeezed my knee and *stayed there*.

The vending machine sandwiches at the hospital's waiting room were a definite downgrade from the dinner Rome had in mind. We made it through to the frazzled ED doctor after a couple of hours who introduced himself as Dr. Patel.

"Not my first ice skate injury tonight if you can believe it," he said wryly as he examined Rome's brow. "It's deep enough that it will require stitches though. Probably about five or six."

Rome shook his head vigorously. "Nope. No needles."

"We can glue it but your scar will be more visible and may not heal as cleanly," Dr. Patel warned him.

"That sounds great, I'm on board."

"No, stitch it up and make it clean," James interjected, ignoring Rome's protests. "*Yes*, Rome. It's on your goddamn face, this is not the time to cut corners."

Rome turned to Dr. Patel. "I will pay you to knock me out. Because if you come at me with a needle, it will be like trying to cross-stitch a fish, just—" He flopped his hand around gracelessly before suddenly gesturing at me. "I was on a date with *her* tonight. Can you fucking believe, I mean, just *look* at her. I can't even pretend I'm not afraid of needles to try and impress her so you're gonna have to give me something, doc."

I had no idea what to do with his impassioned plea and neither did Dr. Patel. "I . . . won't be bringing an anesthetist in for this procedure. But I can give you some nitrous oxide to calm your nerves," he offered.

Rome threw up his hands. "Ok fine, let's do that."

I sidled up next to James while Dr. Patel fussed around with a mask and tube.

"Nitrous oxide. Isn't that . . . ?"

"Laughing gas? Yep," James confirmed for me. "Don't worry, he'll find out soon enough."

Rome held the mask over his face and sucked a few deep breaths. He relaxed, his expression taking on a euphoric quality. Dr. Patel quickly numbed the area with local anesthetic and got to work.

"Ivy."

I took Rome's outstretched hand. "Mmhmm?"

"I wish I *had* serenaded you," Rome confessed.

"Oh . . . no."

"The night is still young."

"No, it's really very ok," I said, panicking slightly.

"Ok. No singing."

I breathed a sigh of relief.

"But how do you feel about poetry?"

James turned away from us and his shoulders started shaking. *Traitor.*

"Your eyes are so blue like . . ." Rome scrunched up his face and thought for a long time. ". . . the sky."

Dr. Patel cleared his throat with a stuttering croak that sounded awfully a lot like a smothered guffaw.

"Thank you, Rome, you really don't have to continue."

"No but I want to."

I was strapped into a carnival ride with no exit. "Ok," I agreed, giving myself over to the experience. "Lay it on me."

"The sky," Rome orated. "Limitless. Unknown." He gave me a knowing look. "Blue."

James let out a heaving sound like he was dying.

"Is it a surprise that it reminds me of you?"

I was paralyzed, unsure if I should answer. After a beat, Rome continued his spoken word . . . performance.

"So bright, so bleak. With stars complete. The change is the constant, the unpredictability its truth. This endless feeling, despite the ebb and flow."

It was better for all involved if I focused less on the words and more on the way he was looking at me. I wondered how much of that hopelessly smitten expression was a result of the gas he inhaled.

Rome stared at me expectantly so I had to assume he was done.

"Thank you. That was wonderful," I said with as much sincerity as I could muster.

"And I meant every word."

"Good job, babe." James took his other hand. "There was something almost profound in here. *Almost*."

Rome gave him a dopey smile. "You have a nice face."

James shrugged at me. "Guess he's poetry-ed out. At least he said *face*."

I just . . . adored them together. Adored how they were with each other and felt lucky that they let me be a part of it.

Dr. Patel declared he was done with the stitches and affixed a fresh bandage over his handiwork.

"Go home and get some rest. Tylenol every four hours if needed. And schedule a follow-up appointment with your PCP to get the stitches out in a week."

Rome's head drooped sleepily on my shoulder on the drive home, crashing hard after the adrenaline had run its course. I followed behind James as he helped his alpha to their bedroom. He tucked Rome in carefully, adjusting his arm so it wouldn't rest against his wound.

James' hand came to rest on the small of my back as he led me to the living room. "I'm sorry your date ended up badly. He'll be beside himself tomorrow."

"Tell him not to beat himself up. I had the best time with him," I told him honestly.

James frowned. "I have to stay with him. Otherwise, I would take you home."

"Of course you should stay, you don't have—"

"So I've asked Logan to do it. He'll be here soon."

It was a small gesture but it made a million butterflies come alive within me. Beating tiny wings that fanned my instincts. Automatically showing care and support when things went wrong. Letting it bring us closer, leaving no one out.

Is this what having a pack is meant to be like?

I turned away from James' dark, astute eyes and allowed my gaze to drift around the room. It was lived in but not messy. An open book laying facedown on the coffee table. Rome's beautiful piano in the corner with a stack of sheet music on top. I itched to take a closer look at the photo frames lining the mantelpiece overhanging the brick hearth.

"Hey," I said shyly. "I'm in your house."

The corner of James' mouth lifted. "Yes. You are."

"It's nice." It was. In so many ways. The small details I began to notice that made it theirs—a dropped guitar pick, an art print of dogs playing poker.

Not to mention the blend of their scents lingering over everything like a warm blanket.

James chuckled. "I'll bring you back here tomorrow as part of our date and you can snoop to your heart's content. How's that?"

I couldn't wait.

The way my gaze dipped to his lips did not go unnoticed.

James' eyes narrowed. "Are you thinking of kissing me, Ivy?"

"Maybe a bit," I admitted.

He groaned and the sound traveled instantly *south*. "We can't. That would be . . . rude of me."

"How so?" I asked. The way his jaw clenched was slowly dismantling me.

"Tonight was Rome's date." Every ragged breath lured us closer and closer. "I can't kiss you after his date," James insisted weakly.

All it would take was a single snowflake to break the avalanche of his control. My tongue carefully traced my lower lip, leaving my mouth slightly parted. "Why not?"

"If Rome asks, tell him I put up more of a fight."

Then he plastered me against the door frame, crushing his lips to mine. Our bodies were flush together and he was everywhere. The taste of him on my tongue, his scent in my lungs. I moaned into his mouth as my hands fisted his thick dark hair.

"So fucking sweet, gorgeous."

Me? What about him? He was the most luscious spoonful and I knew I would crave him forever.

The three hard raps against the front door were deafening. I gasped as we broke apart. James' pupils were blown, his hair and clothes awry and his full lips a vivid shade of pink.

Did I do that?

"That'll . . . that'll be Logan," James said with obvious strain.

"Ok."

I was kissing him again. I don't know why. It just made sense. James swore, kissing me back feverishly before pulling back with a low hiss.

"I will see you tomorrow," he promised me. James laid a firm hand against my throat and I whimpered. He feathered kisses along my jaw until the frenetic beat of our hearts slowed. "Now, are you ready for Logan or do you need a moment?"

Another three knocks.

Breathe, Ivy.

Don't open the door and scare the alpha with an explosion of perfume and risk leaping into his arms.

"I'm good," I croaked.

The influx of frozen air as the door swung open helped immensely. I gulped it greedily, letting my head clear as James greeted Logan.

"Thanks for taking her home."

"Of course. Ready to go, Ivy?"

Well, if I was trying to feel *less* worked up then the appearance of an alpha smelling like an enchanting pinewood forest was not helping. Logan hadn't bothered with his jacket or hat so I got the full brunt of his bronze, tousled hair and broad chest. The top button on his shirt was undone and *god help me* that dark fuzz of hair peeking out made my knees weak.

"Yep," I said, my voice extra high pitched as I put on my coat. "Night, James."

"Night, gorgeous."

Logan walked me down the drive and next door to his car. He tucked my hair behind my ear carefully and an observant smile graced his lips. "You seem really happy for someone whose date ended with a hospital visit."

"Yeah, I am. It was still a great date." I smiled up at him. "I can't wait for ours, Logan."

He immediately went pink beneath his grizzled beard. An adorable, low, rumbling sort of sound escaped him and he coughed into his fist to mask it.

Was that a purr?

I'd been thoroughly spoiled tonight with Rome's flirtations and James' kisses. But as Logan opened the passenger door for me, I couldn't help but lean against him a little. He pulled me close and kissed my forehead and it was like the final piece falling into place.

Chapter 13

JAMES

Dinner and a movie.

Probably one of the most classic date nights, right?

I picked up Ivy like a gentleman and then the universe delivered me a swift kick downhill from there.

It made sense to start with a movie—something to talk about at dinner. Very logical decision. We turned up to Starlight's Hollywood Cinema and I'd never heard of the film spelled out in black letters on the marquee.

"*Ephemeral . . .*" I recited stiltedly.

Ivy peered at the poster in the window. I fought to keep my eyes from wandering downwards because she stirred something feral inside me with her tights and skirt combo. "From soil to soul," she said, reading out the tagline.

What the hell? It was a single-theater cinema. Why wouldn't they show something to get as many butts in the seats as possible?

"I thought they would be showing the new *Operation: Blackout* film." Now I felt like an idiot for asking if Ivy liked the action/thriller heist franchise.

Ivy shook her head with a laugh. "They haven't even shown *Operation: Phantom* or *Operation: Vortex* yet."

I looked at her in disbelief. "But they came out two and four years ago."

"Yeah but the explosions are too loud for Missy and Herbert."

"Missy and . . ."

"The DeWitts, who run this place."

I double-checked the signage plastered across the overhang. "But it says Hollywood Cinema," I said blankly.

Ivy shrugged.

"All right. *Ephemeral* it is."

I told myself a runtime of almost three hours was normal for an arthouse film.

It was not and it absolutely should not have been allowed for this one.

After thirty excruciating minutes of watching the moon-faced actor make brooding faces at a succulent plant that wouldn't grow, I had to say something.

"Ivy." I leaned over our long-empty popcorn bucket. "How do they stay open showing films like this?"

Ivy, inexplicably, remained glued to the screen. "Mostly because of them," she said, jabbing her thumb backward.

I turned around and saw the vague shapes of teenagers . . . not watching the film. Now that I was aware of it, all I could hear were the ghastly sounds of slurping alongside the movie's depressing soundtrack.

"Ok, that's it." I sat forward in my chair, ready to stand up. "Come on, Ivy, let's get out of here."

"But I want to know if he manages to replant it in his garden," Ivy protested.

Her pouty lower lip was suspicious.

"Do you really?"

"Yes."

She was fucking with me and it was cute.

But I also *really* needed to get out of here.

"What's the main character's name?" I asked her, unable to keep the accusing tone out of my voice.

Her giggle was a devious little sound. "I have no idea," she gasped.

I grabbed her hand and pulled her up. "All right, we're going," I muttered.

Once we were finally free and back outside, I checked the time and wondered how I was going to salvage the evening. "Do you mind having dinner a bit earlier at La Dolce Vita?" I asked.

"La Dolce Vita?" she echoed. "It's the last Friday of the month, isn't it? Antonio won't be opening the restaurant today."

I was a house of cards and her words the lightest flick of a finger. "What do you mean it's not open today? I checked Google."

Ivy gave me a sympathetic sort of grimace.

I was an idiot for relying on Google—got it.

"Antonio takes his Nonna to visit her grandkids and great-grandkids once a month. Her house is too small to host everyone so they go to his sister's."

That was very lovely for Antonio's family but where the hell did that leave me? Literally out in the cold. I scrambled to come up with a solution, any solution, and was left with nothing.

"Hey."

A mittened hand slid down my back and Ivy's chin came to rest on my shoulder. I automatically wrapped my arm around her.

"You said you'd bring me back to your place yesterday." Her big blue eyes were practically glowing. "Does the offer still stand?"

"Jesus, of course, yes."

She gave my sleeve a gentle tug. "Ok good. But drive us to the market first and then yours."

I dug around in my pocket for my phone. "Let me give Rome a heads up."

Did I want to reveal to Ivy that the three of us had a group chat separate from her? No, because if she saw how much we had overthought every facet of our courtship of her she would run for the hills.

> Date is a disaster

> We're going to Mariposa's and then bringing Ivy back to ours

LOGAN
Is she upset?

> Not in the slightest, I'm the one freaking out

ROME
I'll make myself scarce

> You don't have to do that

ROME
This is your date, babe

Logan, you free?

LOGAN
Yeah come by

ROME
Excellent. I think we should find out if you're a better sous chef than James at Overcooked.

> Ok sure. Good luck with not getting your head put through the TV when you yell CUT MY CUCUMBER over and over

ROME

Good-bye I'm done with this conversation

LOGAN

I take that back I'm not free

ROME

Already outside man

After we parked, Ivy had a little extra bounce in her step as we walked hand-in-hand into Mariposa Market. She meandered down the baking aisle. "Mm, I feel like crepes."

"For dinner?" I knew omegas liked sweet things but dessert for dinner seemed to be taking it to extremes.

"Why not?" Ivy shrugged. "Do you have any flour at home?"

"Probably not."

"Eggs? Butter?"

I tried to think of when we last did a proper planned grocery shop instead of buying only what we needed for dinner that night. "How about you assume Rome and I live under a tarp," I finally said.

I was very, very lucky that Ivy found that funny but we would have to get our act together when we lived as a pack in the future.

Woah, jumping the gun much?

But once I started to imagine coming home to Ivy it was very hard to stop. Maybe she would be cuddling on the couch with Rome and Logan. Baked buttery goodness, pine and mulled wine heavy in the air. Her cheeks slightly rosy, a knowing smile on the alphas' faces and when I lifted the blanket draped over them I would find—

"Oh my gosh, look how big this jar of Nutella is!"

Ivy wasn't kidding. It was so big she was cradling it like a chocolatey child. The need to touch her overwhelmed me and I closed the gap between us with a quick pull of her hips.

"Get it," I said, my voice gravelly.

"You'll never be able to finish it." I watched her lips part slightly, the gradual expanse of her pupils.

I was spiraling dangerously off the deep end. "Maybe I could if I put it on something I really wanted to lick."

That earned me a light smack, bringing me back to reality. "James, no!" she chastised me with a giggle. Why did that tone make my dick hard too? "That's not sanitary."

"I meant a spoon."

"You did *not*."

I really wanted to kiss her there and then. In the middle of that fluorescent-lit aisle, surrounded by jars and risking anybody seeing.

But I second guessed it for a beat too long. The moment passed as she turned to swap out the comically large Nutella for a smaller one.

There was something about driving home together with groceries in the backseat. It ran a neural pathway in my brain that lit up and made me want to traverse it again and again. Small things to a big life.

She let me lay my hand on her thigh the entire way. Tracing circles with my thumb and fighting the urge to explore higher.

Ivy looked right at home searching our cupboards for a mixing bowl and spatula, drifting around the kitchen in stockinged feet. I bent over to show her where the hand beaters were and I was pretty sure she ogled my butt.

I got to work washing and cutting up strawberries when I heard her gasp behind me.

"James, why do you have an entire cupboard section filled with spicy ramen?"

Sometimes I forgot it was there. I had long surrendered that part of the kitchen to it.

"When we first moved, I mentioned *in passing* to my mom that I liked that particular brand and flavor," I said, continuing to chop strawberries. "She sent me a wholesaler-size box the next day."

Ivy's demeanor softened, her palm splayed across her chest. "She missed you."

I nodded. Every word was trapped in a tangle of emotions. "My family is just my mom and I. I feel like she put her life on hold having me. Not that she would ever admit it," I said, plucking the leaves off a strawberry aimlessly. "The week I started college she told me she went on a date which . . . I was happy about but also horrified by."

"That's a completely understandable emotion. What about your dad?"

There was no judgment in her question. Only a tender sort of curiosity that came from years of knowing how to create a safe place for children to voice their vulnerabilities.

"I never knew him," I admitted. "Mom was originally from Singapore and moved to New York for work. Met my dad and made me, I guess. That's about all he contributed to who I am."

A sperm donor, nothing more.

Sometimes I wondered about the other half of my genes. I hated that I wanted to know, as if I was somehow incomplete by not knowing. Then came the guilt for the implication that my mother—who had sacrificed so much yet never made me feel like I wasn't worth it—hadn't been enough.

"Mom had her tiger mom tendencies." I suppressed a shudder when I remembered trying to hide that I'd gotten a C on a pop quiz. "But she was fully supportive when I told her I wanted to be a vet," I continued. "Even so . . . it was lonely growing up. I think that's why I've always . . . always wanted a . . ."

I'm sure the fact that I always wanted to be part of a pack was making a therapist's pen itch somewhere.

"I've only ever known pack life looking from the outside in too," Ivy said softly.

Too. I don't know how she offered so much grace and understanding in a simple word. She was an omega, sweet as anything and the perfect heart of a pack. I was a beta and the jury was still out on whether that life was meant for us. Yet right here right now, we were the same, the ache in my chest a twin of hers.

"My family are all betas except for me." Ivy hugged her delicate frame tightly. "I was always fascinated by how different packs lived. Wondering how they all fit together. I never felt like I understood it." She stared at the floor, one foot swinging back and forth aimlessly. "Maybe that's why I'm still unbonded after all these years."

I couldn't go another second without touching her. A brush of her arm and she unraveled like a fine thread, clinging to me.

"We can figure it out together," I said against her hair. "I think you were meant for us."

Her breath caught like a snapshot and embedded itself in my memory. Ivy lifted her head off my chest and I was ensnared by the deep endless blue of her eyes.

I wasn't ready for them to flutter close as she closed the distance between us for a kiss.

Chapter 14

IVY

I LIKED ALL THE DIFFERENT KISSES I'D HAD WITH JAMES.

The promise-laced one during my heat. The impulsive reckless-ness of last night's.

This one started off tentative, exploring the taste of each other. Our bodies slipped and clicked into what felt right—his thigh be-tween my legs, the twist of his sweater in my fist to bring him closer.

James nudged his leg against me and I could feel myself grow slicker. There was a hungry sort of push and pull between us. Fric-tion building friction despite the layers separating our skin.

It was impossible to ignore his cock thickening against me, hot and hard and trapped.

I reached for the button of his jeans and popped it open with my thumb.

"Help me take it off," I managed to say in the gaps when his lips weren't on mine.

"Yeah, good idea."

James twisted my request completely, a trickster finding loop-holes for his own benefit.

He slid his palms up the outside of my thighs. Under my skirt.

His thumbs hooked over the waistband of my tights, tugging them down and undressing *me*.

There was nowhere to hide, no way that James didn't know that the gingerbread scent bomb that just detonated was because of my slick-soaked panties.

I yelped as he lifted me onto the kitchen counter and fitted himself between my spread legs. I tore off my sweater and my skirt rode up higher and higher until his bulge was pressed against my damp center.

"Do you still want your crepes?" he asked, moving down to kiss my neck.

"How can you, why would you . . ." I couldn't even think. It wasn't just the kisses but the way he was bracing my throat and jaw in his grip, holding me in place with just the right amount of pressure. "Crepes can come *after*, James," I scolded him.

He laughed.

I thought it was quite rude that he found my desperation funny.

"There's something else I've been dying to taste anyway," James said, kissing his way down my front. "Well, at least properly. Licked off Rome after the heat doesn't count."

The visual image set my entire brain ablaze.

"You *didn't*."

"Why would I lie?"

Oh jeez. Dig me a hole and put me in the ground already.

James was frighteningly efficient. One rough push and my skirt was around my hips. A quick pull and my panties were in his fist. I was spread, displayed wantonly for him and he stared at my pussy with a dark determination.

Then all that carefully crafted tension snapped the second he playfully reached for the Nutella.

"No!" I gasped, slapping his hand away.

"Next time," he promised impudently.

"*Never*," I ordered him firmly, pulling him in for a kiss. It didn't last long because we were smiling too hard. I loved that he was like this, wanting to make me laugh just as much as he wanted to make me . . . well, *not laugh*.

The pleasure hooked me again as James grazed my inner thigh. I could feel slick gathering at my entrance from the anticipation alone.

My head grew light and I couldn't get my breathing even when he traced the crease of my inner thigh, exploring me slowly. The dark brown curls I'd trimmed this morning just in case. Lightly down one of my outer lips and then back up the other. His knuckle grazed my clit and I bucked hard against his hand, soaking it.

"Is this all for me?" he asked.

I could only manage a shaky nod.

His touch changed, growing more aggressive as he circled my entrance, gathering slick and swirling it around my clit. He was watching me and adjusting his movements, the pressure. Calculating how it affected me.

I started to think about how long it would take to come and it was the wrong move. The fixation and awareness sank claws into me, the contradiction of trying to reach for an orgasm pulling me further away from it. Suddenly the overhead light felt too bright. The kitchen counter was hard on my ass. The more I tried not to overthink the faster the moment slipped from my grasp.

"Ivy."

My eyes squeezed shut and I realized he stopped touching me. He closed my legs, pulled my skirt back down and massaged my thighs lightly.

"Do you want to stop?"

James asked so gently without any judgment. For some reason that made me even more embarrassed because there was no reason I should be feeling this way.

"I . . . started thinking about whether I would come soon. Then that turned into wondering if I should be getting there faster and why I wasn't coming yet. When I tried to stop thinking about it, the light got distracting and the counter wasn't comfortable anymore and . . ." I trailed off, feeling like a complete idiot.

James brought my hand up to his lips and kissed my knuckles. "You're a bit in your own head, aren't you?"

The self-consciousness and sticky feeling of shame wouldn't go away. I remembered flashes of what I was like in heat. This instinctual being who sought her own pleasure and took what she wanted.

It felt like a version of myself I wanted to find but didn't know how to access.

"Is there anything else that's on your mind?" James asked.

Only the completely irrational fear of him judging my naked body even though he had already seen it.

"My butt's kind of flat," I said instead.

James shrugged. "I have enough for the both of us."

I put my head in my hands and laughed despite myself. "You do."

"I noticed you staring at it earlier."

Of course I had. There was a fucking peach stuffed down his jeans. Two fat loaves of sourdough. The curvature of the Earth as viewed from the moon times two.

I couldn't mask the anguish in my voice. "It's *so* round, James."

His impertinent smile lit up his entire face. "I know." He dotted light kisses on my cheek and lips until my scent sweetened again. He made me feel light, the present moment alive between us.

It was apparent that James wasn't going to push me. If I wanted the night to continue down the direction I was craving I would have to ask for it. My pulse rocketed wildly as I forced myself to speak.

"Can I see your bedroom?"

He went very still. I prayed he wouldn't ask me if I was sure because there was a good chance I would overthink my reply like everything else I'd been doing.

"Come on."

I breathed a sigh of relief.

James led me down the hall and opened the door at the end for me. I'd already gotten a glimpse the other night but I could take a good long look now. Wooden furniture with hints of metallic accents and sheets the color of wheat. James steered clear of the overhead light and turned on one of the softer bedside table lamps instead.

I sat myself right on the edge and placed my hands on my lap.

James didn't join me. Instead, he stepped close, nudging my legs open with his knee, standing in the space he created between my spread thighs. It was impossible not to imagine what would be within my grasp if he were unclothed. The top button of his jeans was still undone and I flicked the zipper with my finger.

"Show me," I whispered.

James took his time undressing and I felt that familiar ache building. Each discarded item of clothing making me want to squeeze my thighs together. His body was lean but strong, muscles rounding out his shoulders and shadowing down his abdomen. Hints rather than cut lines of definition. Somehow I knew if I traced them with my tongue they would twitch and tighten hard.

He straightened up after removing his jeans, and I could see the shape of his hard cock pressing against his boxers.

"Stop."

I really, really wanted to uncover it with my own two hands.

James ran a finger along my neckline. "Can I?"

I fell back onto the bed and dragged him down with me. He kissed me against the sheets embedded with the scent of him and Rome, undressing me layer by layer. Every newly revealed bit of skin seemed to unravel him a little more. He told me that the freckles that dotted my decolletage were beautiful. He caressed my straight figure like he was memorizing my shape. The fear that I lacked the curvaceous dips and swells usually found in an omega vanished. The urge to make excuses and cover parts of myself diminished with every appreciative noise that escaped him.

My hand lowered, searching for him and he moved out of my grasp. "Not yet," he whispered, before sliding down my body. Further and further south until—

I lost my everloving mind when his hot mouth closed around me. He released the most ungodly noise of pleasure and ripped himself away.

"I'm starting to understand how Logan could come just from eating this pussy," he groaned.

James licked me several times. Messy and unfocused, like it was entirely for him just to get a taste. But when he did find his rhythm, a light flicking of his tongue against my clit, I jolted with every cry he coaxed out of me.

"Don't you dare come, gorgeous. Give me a reason to stay down here as long as fucking possible."

I couldn't think because my head was filled with the sounds he was making. They were obscene and should've been illegal. Moans and a low, dirty drawn out *fuuuck* as he pulled back for a breath before diving back in. The room echoed with the filthy lap of his tongue through my slick, wet on wet and so unbelievably hot.

"Oh, god. James I'm—"

I dug at his scalp and fucked his face like a compulsion. I flew apart, shattered beneath his hungry mouth. Shards of my pleasure flashed bright behind my eyelids as I panted through the orgasm.

You did it. You came. There's nothing wrong with you.

I covered my face with both hands, relief making me giddy.

James didn't seem so pleased. "I told you not to come yet," he practically purred against me. "I wasn't done eating your pretty little pussy. I guess you'll have to give me another one."

Another one? Was that even—

I cried out as his tongue found my clit again. This time, he pushed two fingers deep into my fluttering entrance as well, stroking in and out of me. The second orgasm almost caught on the end of the first one, like a rising tide, a chain reaction I couldn't fight against. I came a second time, squeezing and pulsing around his thrusting fingers.

"Do you want to go make crepes now?"

I sat up and stared at him incredulously. "What?" I rasped.

The crazy thing was I think he was serious. He stuck slick coated fingers into his mouth and licked them clean before laying back casually. Completely ignoring his dick still trapped in his boxers. There was a small wet patch right at the tip where he had leaked precum just from eating me out.

If I don't get him inside me I will scream.

I leaned over and shoved down his briefs. His freed cock smacked against his abdomen and I actually licked my lips at the sight of it. The smooth skin of his shaft was a shade darker than the rest of him, culminating in a reddened tip. The fluid oozing from his slit spilled over, running a rivulet down the length of his cock. I darted forward, chasing it with my tongue. All the way up before taking the head of him into my mouth. I lowered my lips, trying to see how much of him I could take before gagging.

A surprising amount. I sucked and savored his length until it was wet with my saliva.

James' head was thrown back against the pillows, one arm banded across his face like a Renaissance painting. "If you want me to last longer than twenty seconds inside you, you have to stop," he bit out.

Knowing I had this effect on him gave me the bravery to move up his body and straddle him. My pussy was perfectly positioned on top of his cock, hugging and slicking his shaft. I gave an experimental rock of my hips and whimpered as his tip massaged my clit.

"Fuck, Ivy. You're going to make me embarrass myself," James said, his hands flying to my waist.

I leaned down and kissed him. "You could never."

My hips lifted slightly and I reached down to angle his cock at my entrance. I was so slick he notched easily, his tip already sliding half-way in. A whine escaped as he pushed up into me and I felt myself opening up to take him.

"More, please," I begged.

"You're beautiful." A kiss and I sank down further. "Perfect."

He felt so good inside me. But more than that I loved the way he looked at me. The dig of his fingers into my hips. The strained, corded muscles of his neck and hard swallow of his throat. We rocked together, finding the perfect surging rhythm punctuated by the loud slap of his thighs against my ass.

"You're so pretty riding my cock." James pulled me down for a heated kiss, bracing the back of my neck as he fucked up into me. Rough, relentless and all I could do was hold onto him and take it.

He rolled us suddenly, his cock hitting me deep and ripping a screamed gasp from me. I didn't think his ass could get any more perfect but feeling it flex beneath my hands as he fucked me was al-most a religious experience.

"You feel so fucking good," he breathed. His hand snaked be-tween us and found my clit. "You'll stay tonight, won't you?" James began to stroke it gently. "I want to sleep wrapped around you. Not ready to let you go, in fact, I don't know if I ever will."

I wanted that. So much. But I was aware there was another per-son who slept in this bed.

"Wh-what about—"

The bump of his nose against me was like a tease of a scent-mark. "I think Rome will lose his mind when he gets home. But the ques-tion is . . . what do you want to be doing when he comes in?"

I pictured Rome finding James buried deep inside me. Maybe he would kneel down, unzip himself. I could open my mouth eagerly, ready to—

My climax took me by surprise, my whole body seizing up. James cursed loudly, before devolving into an incomprehensible stream of expletives about how hard I was squeezing him. His strokes grew longer, harder. He slammed into me with a groan and I shuddered, feeling his cock pulsing with each warm burst of cum. It unearthed a feral kind of possessiveness within me and I locked my legs around him long after he went still.

"It's never been like this before, James," I admitted, feeling intensely vulnerable.

He dotted kisses over my face. "I told you, Ivy. You're ours."

My tummy chose that exact moment to rumble.

"Is it finally time for crepes?" James laughed.

"In a minute."

I held him close, wanting to enjoy the feel of being in his arms just a little bit longer.

Chapter 15

ROME

"THROW ME A FISH."

"Here."

Logan and I were perched on the edge of his couch, controllers in hand and eyes glued to the screen. Our chef characters raced around in-game, trying to fulfill the mounting restaurant orders appearing on the corner of the screen.

"Oh fuck, I threw it in the trash instead."

"Try again," I encouraged him. "It's ok, it's gonna be ok."

"Got it," Logan muttered. "I got it, I got it."

We were absolutely nailing this. Logan was an excellent sous chef at Overcooked. He'd picked up the game quickly, kept his cool and—

"LOGAN THE NOODLES ARE BURNING!"

"FUCK!"

When the timer sounded we collapsed back in unison onto the couch. Against all odds, three stars popped up triumphantly on screen.

"Rome. I've never been so stressed about anything in my life," Logan complained.

I threw him a sidelong glance. "But are you having fun?"

Logan hesitated. "Yeah," he finally admitted. "How many people can play at once? We could get everyone to help."

I shook my head. "Logan, we want to bring this pack together, not tear it apart."

"That's true."

My skill level began dropping noticeably during the next couple of levels and Logan got upset with me.

"Rome, stop throwing mushrooms in the ocean!"

Fuck, I was doing that, wasn't I? I scraped my hand through my hair. "Sorry," I grunted. "You might have to accept that I'm not going to be very good at this for a while."

"What do you mean?" Logan asked quizzically.

"The bond," I said shortly. "James and Ivy's date is going well."

Logan looked confused, before going pale then a bright red as he processed what I had implied.

"This early?" he whispered. "It's not even 8:00 p.m."

I shrugged. James could be very irresistible when he put his mind to it.

Logan set aside the controller, the game long forgotten. "Fuck, how much can you feel?" he asked.

"I can sort of mute it a bit. To give him a bit of privacy," I explained. "It's like I'm . . . in the house with them but not in the same room if that makes sense."

Logan nodded slowly, processing what I'd just said. "What's it like having a bond?" he asked.

I understood why he was curious. But no matter how many ways you could be told what a bond was like, there was nothing like actually experiencing it. It was a living, ever-changing connection. The strongest emotions could catch me off guard and other times I almost had to go searching for it.

"Imagine having insight into the person you love where you know exactly how to make them happy. And in return, they do the same for you." I looked over where Logan was staring at the floor, tracing the seam of his couch distractedly. "Is that something you would want?" I pressed.

Logan was quiet for a long time. When he finally spoke, his gruff voice was subdued. "My dad's an alpha. And my mom was an omega. We lost her . . . almost twenty-five years ago now. Breast cancer and then it spread to her bones. Dad was bonded through it all and I thought I would lose him too."

It happened sometimes in tragic circumstances. Bonded alphas and omegas unable to live without their other halves.

Logan steepled his fingers, knuckles tight with tension. "Sometimes we're absolutely fine. And some days it feels like it happened yesterday."

Suddenly Logan's closed off demeanor made a lot more sense. I could read between the lines of that tightly clenched jaw and wall of grief. I couldn't imagine what it would've been like to witness his father losing his bonded. Twenty-five years ago . . . it would've been the keystone to his formative years.

No wonder the idea of being with Ivy made him panic.

Logan let out a sigh, the tension loosening from his body. "But time does heal. Dad and I have never been closer. And he's even got a girlfriend now," he said, pinching the bridge of his nose. "He's sixty-three and sending me pictures of outfit options before dates," he grumbled.

Logan's dad sounded delightful.

"Is that weird for you? Seeing him with someone else?" I asked. "I know James was a bit of a basket case when his mom started dating. But he gets on fine with her partner now."

"At first but I'm happy for him. If anyone deserves it, it's Dad."

Logan's respect for his father was crystal clear. Perhaps seeing him prioritize love made Logan realize he could do the same. I could certainly already see the big alpha thawing out since we'd started our courtship of Ivy.

"What do you have planned for your date tomorrow?"

Logan settled back against the couch. "Reservations at Chez Lumiere."

I whistled. "Sounds fancy."

"It's the only Michelin starred restaurant for miles." He scrubbed a large hand across his beard. "I promise I'll do my best with her, Rome."

I was slightly taken aback by that. "You don't . . . have to promise me anything. I already know you will." Logan seemed surprised, like he had been expecting me to hold him to his vow instead of just trusting him.

This was what he needed. People with faith in him. And an omega he could take his time with. One who would love him exactly as he was.

I was pretty sure Ivy was up to the task.

"Should we try the level with all the pitfalls again?" I suggested, shunting whatever James was doing into a far corner of my mind.

"Yeah, let's do it."

IT DIDN'T FEEL RIGHT leaving Logan behind as I went home to James and Ivy a few hours later. He should've been there with us. Even if we had to sleep with our limbs half off the bed. My alpha was disgruntled about treating our packmate this way.

I told myself it was early days. Courtship took time and there would be many nights to come with all of us together in Ivy's nest.

I quietly let myself in the front door. James had texted that Ivy didn't mind me coming home and joining them. I took off my shoes, hung up my coat and made my way through the kitchen. There was a sweet smell lingering in the air from whatever they'd cooked together.

The bedroom door was slightly ajar and I could already detect their combined scents. *Fuck.* They were utterly perfect together.

James' softer chocolate and marshmallow offset the myriad of spices from Ivy's more potent gingerbread. My dick jerked and I mentally told it to back the fuck down as I opened the door.

It was a futile task, because the picture they made together was a revelation. James' hair was a rumpled mess, his nose resting lightly on Ivy's bared shoulder as they lay spooned together. She was in one of his shirts, the fit oversized on her smaller frame. James' arm was curled protectively around her, their fingers lightly intertwined, having loosened in their sleep. I could see his dimple and the ghost of a smile on his lips.

Ivy was angelic. Her expression was so unguarded and relaxed. I never realized there had been a weight to her features at the school, even somewhat when she was out and about in town. There was no trace of it here and the difference staggered me.

It was almost painful to turn off the hallway light and bathe the room in darkness again.

I didn't know if they had done it on purpose but Ivy was in the exact center of the bed, leaving enough room for me. I undressed down to my boxers but left my t-shirt on, erring on the side of caution instead of sliding into bed naked like I normally would.

I cursed internally when Ivy stirred.

"Rome?" she mumbled.

"Go back to sleep, baby," I whispered, reaching out until I found her cheek.

Ivy shifted closer to me but James remained asleep. But that didn't surprise me. James could sleep through a fire drill. In fact, he did so—not once, but twice—when we lived in our first crappy apartment together in the East Village.

"How are you?" she asked. Her fingers meandered lightly across my chest and up to my face.

"Good. I see you tired James out," I teased.

She made a cute little noise, a mix between a scoff and a nervous laugh. I knew if the lights were on I would've seen her blush all the way up into her hairline.

"Did you have fun with Logan?"

"Yes." I smiled. "I think you're going to have a great time with him tomorrow."

"I think so too." Ivy went quiet but she continued to trace my features lightly. She found the edge of my bandage and paused. "How are your stitches?" she asked gingerly.

I let out a self-conscious chuckle. "They're fine. I just . . . feel a bit silly, that's all."

Recalling my *poetry* was an excruciating experience. I was no stranger to performance art or musical theater thanks to my job but that had been a horror unto itself.

"We all enjoyed it, Rome."

"Don't lie to me." I found the sweet little dip of her waist and gave her a light poke, eliciting a breathy giggle. Since my hands were already there, I took the chance to wrap myself around her a little more. "I hope I'll get the chance to redo our date."

"Of course you will. But honestly Rome, I loved it so much even though it was cut short."

She sounded completely sincere, further proof she was too good for me.

"Can I tell you something?" she said tentatively.

"Anything, Ivy."

"Before the date," she began slowly, "part of me was worried Starlight Grove was going to be too small for you and James. That you would get bored of it eventually."

And bored of her, was the unspoken implication.

"But I don't feel that way anymore."

I released a slow, relieved breath. "What changed?"

"Seeing you genuinely excited for our tiny run-down rink, just like I was. It made me realize that in the short time you've been in town and worked at the school, you never made us feel like we didn't measure up."

I thought back to the way I felt when I had first seen that job listing. When I had first googled Starlight Grove and seen the outdated website showing Stanley standing proudly in front of the welcome sign. It was so old his hair was a bright orange instead of the gray he sported today.

"There's not really much to measure up to, Ivy," I admitted to her quietly.

I could almost hear the audible click as something fell into place for Ivy. "You weren't happy in New York or anywhere you lived?"

She gasped a little as I buried my nose into her neck. I wanted her scent on my skin as a comfort. A moment transported to happy childhood memories, slathering icing on still-too-hot cookies before gorging ourselves on the sticky mess.

My words came out stilted, each syllable feeling heavy. "I grew up in a small town a lot like this one, actually. But when I was thirteen, we started moving every couple of years. Two of my dads made ridiculous money in oil and gas."

Ivy mulled over this. "Thirteen . . . so all through middle and high school?"

"Yep."

"Hard time to be starting over again and again," she said softly.

Of course as a teacher she would understand how cruel teenagers could be to those they perceived as different. I didn't answer but my silence did it for me. Those years were veiled in a kind of humiliation that I still didn't fully understand. It didn't matter how much adult logic I applied to it.

Ivy rubbed gentle circles into my back. "Is that why you go by Rome and Mr. C?"

Always so perceptive.

"I stopped introducing myself as Romesh a long time ago. I made the choice to go by Mr. C on my first day of teaching because it was easier for me. And truth be told, as a defense mechanism too."

I'd had enough assumptions made about me based on my name and the color of my skin to last several lifetimes.

"You could be Romesh here. If you wanted," Ivy said tentatively.

I shrugged. "I'm used to Rome now. It feels more like me."

"As long as that's the reason. But even if it's not . . . well, I don't want to say I get it because I don't and never will. But I understand why you would choose that." She hugged me tight. "We do what we can in an unfair world."

I tilted her chin up and kissed her. Timid and slow as we learned each other.

I was glad she didn't tell me that I had nothing to worry about, push me to use my full name or tell me everything would be fine.

Maybe what I was about to say next would scare her but I couldn't hold it back any longer.

"I need you to know, Ivy. This pack of ours. You, me, James and Logan. Nothing in my life has ever felt like this."

Ivy seemed lost for words.

"You don't have to say anything," I continued. "I just wanted you to know."

She kissed me hard, my face clasped in her small hands, pulling me down to her greedily.

"I'm really glad you're here," she said fiercely.

"Oh." I was dumbfounded. "Good."

We kissed a few more times, but it remained light and careful. Eventually we broke apart and she snuggled close. Her leg tangled with mine and I threw my arm over both her and James.

Once Ivy's cheek was against my chest, she sighed happily and her breathing evened out into sleep. It was impossible not to join her, sinking slowly into the velvet night.

Chapter 16

ROME

"Let's never leave this bed."

That was James. I would recognize his sultry, ready-to-play voice anywhere.

"We have to . . . at some point."

I felt the mattress shift and Ivy was rudely yanked out of my arms. I made a low noise of displeasure but they were far too busy to hear me.

"Why?"

"To eat. Shower. Work our jobs so we don't get evicted and actually still be allowed to use our beds."

"Mm, those things are all overrated."

A light kissing sound followed by a stifled moan.

"Shh, you'll wake him."

"He's almost there anyway."

More kissing. Ivy's scent was making my morning wood grow into a morning tree.

"How can you tell?"

"Because of the bond," I said out loud.

Ivy shrieked. I found it cute that she scared so easily. I opened my eyes to Ivy squirming in James' arms while he did his best work along her exposed neck.

"That was rude of you to take her," I chided him. "I was sleeping so well holding her."

"You're right. I'm very, very sorry," James said, not sounding sorry at all. "I'll make it up to you."

James had always been good at an innuendo-laced invitation. A skill that was not lost on Ivy either as her perfume sweetened noticeably.

"Will you do that . . . right now?" she asked breathlessly.

I caught James' eye over her shoulder. Our girl liked the idea of us together. Triumph and lust surged through our bond, fueling the growing need in my bloodstream. It all went south, directly to my throbbing cock.

James kissed Ivy right behind her ear. "Will you help me, sweetheart? He's aching right now. I can teach you how to make him feel better."

I was too afraid to even breathe. Everything hinged on Ivy's next words.

She bit down on her lower lip and I swallowed a groan.

"Ok." She nodded. "Show me what he likes."

I almost came right there and then and ruined everything before it even began.

James threw back the duvet, happy to take the lead and shuffling the three of us around. I ended up in the middle of the bed, naked except for my tented boxers. Ivy's delicate fingers traced the large tattoo on my upper thigh while I jerked beneath her touch.

"This is pretty," she said, running her fingertip along the rose petals.

"It's . . . for my family pack," I explained with some difficulty. "A rose for my mom and four thorns for my dads. Leaves for . . . all the rest of us, I guess."

She followed the line of a spiked branch up, drifting closer and closer to my crotch.

I really, *really* did not want to think about anyone related to me right now.

James removed my last item of clothing. My cock sprang back against my stomach with a hefty smack.

"Is that all for us?" he asked mildly.

"You know it is," I shot back.

The hunger in their eyes made it so much worse. My muscles were coiled tight, the strain of holding myself back from taking what I wanted verging on pain.

Let them have their way. For now.

"He's really sensitive here," James murmured, taking me in his hand. He licked the spot beneath my crown and my hips kicked. James could put on a poker face all he wanted but his satisfaction was satiny sweet in our bond.

"See? You try."

Ivy leaned over and took her first taste of me. A quick swirl tracing along the ridge of my cockhead.

Fuck me.

There were two tongues now. Licking. Exploring. James was encouraging Ivy the entire time and making *suggestions*. I felt them kiss around the head of my cock before lapping up the precum that dribbled uncontrollably from my tip.

"God fucking dammit, just end me," I snarled.

"Babe," James said, feigning surprise. "We've only just started."

I was going to fucking murder him.

James instructed Ivy to take my thick, swollen shaft in her fist.

"Spit on it."

Saliva slid slowly down my length.

"Bit more."

Fuck fuck fuck. The wet glide of her hand squeezing me was heaven.

"Now suck on the tip. Like this."

James bobbed a few times over my cock before offering it to Ivy. Her pace was slower as she tried to figure out the rhythm of her mouth with her stroking fist.

"I know he's big but you can take a bit more."

I grasped the headboard as she filled her throat with my cock. Her hand wrapped around my knot, massaging the growing swell with a little twisting motion.

"You're a natural, gorgeous," James praised her. "Keep going. It's good that there's two of us because—"

All I could see was the top of James' head as he ducked down. Ivy took me even deeper into her mouth with a happy little moan just as James sucked lightly on my sac.

"Fuck, I'm close," I gritted out. "I don't know where you want my cum but figure it out quick."

Ivy didn't pull back. Instead she let my aching head hit the back of her throat, tracing my shaft with her tongue and squeezing my knot in her palm. At the same time, James pressed a saliva-coated finger against my ass.

Holy fuck.

I came hard. Hot, surging contractions took over as I released ribbons of cum onto Ivy's tongue. I couldn't stop myself from thrusting up into her mouth and she took everything I gave her like she was made for me.

There were white spots dancing in my vision, a dizzying kaleidoscope every time I blinked. James' stern voice broke through the fog as I lay there catching my breath.

"Don't swallow yet. I want to see how well you did."

I sat up just in time to see him kiss her passionately, sharing my release between them. My cock, against all odds, twitched against my thigh.

"Did I do all right?" Ivy asked shyly.

"Did you—" The words could barely scrape their way out of my throat.

I needed to reward her. Spoil her. I could smell her sweet, needy pussy from here, dripping with slick from sucking my cock.

"James," I growled, my urgency and demand lashing at him in the bond. He was amused, but had the self-preservation to know my alpha needed to take charge.

"You did perfect, sweetheart." James kissed her one more time. "Now let us take care of you."

"Wha? *Oof—*"

Ivy fell backward onto the pillows. James tore his shirt off her and exposed her bouncing tits. Perfectly rounded, with tight nipples and the cutest smattering of freckles across her chest.

God, I needed the rest of our lives to do all the filthy, depraved things I had in mind for her.

I got rid of her panties, almost see through because they were so fucking wet, and pushed her thighs open.

"Wider, baby," I demanded. "You need to fit both of us between here."

Ivy's mouth dropped open. "What do you mean?"

James wriggled down, our shoulders bumping before we both dove in for our feast.

"Oh my *god*." Ivy's scream cut off into a shaky moan.

James went for her clit, laving that hot little button with his tongue. I was greedy and wanted to drink down all that slick straight from her pussy. I threw her leg over my shoulder and pressed my face deep into her pretty cunt. The longer we worked on her, the more her legs fell open, her hips lifting and chasing our touch.

Ivy's telltale little twitches began and I licked her pulsing entrance until I was rewarded with her release down my chin. Seeing her pussy contracting around nothing inflamed my alpha instincts. I wanted to shove my cock deep and feel her milk my knot.

Instead, I yanked James to me by the back of his neck and kissed him. We were all tongues and teeth, letting Ivy's addictive spiced taste fill our mouths.

"Another one?" I prompted.

"Yep."

We fucked her with our fingers this time too. Two each deep inside her, our tongues running over her clit. Kissing her addictive pussy, each other, having the goddamn time of our lives. It was almost a disappointment when she came, bucking against our mouths.

Ivy had the heel of her palms pressed against her eyes, possibly muttering some kind of prayer. She jolted when we both slid up and sandwiched her between us.

"Pretty gorgeous girl, coming so hard for us," I purred. I kissed her neck and James did the same. Ivy looked like she was barely able to compute what language I was speaking. "You have your date with Logan tonight. I'm going to be respectful and not knot you because of that. Maybe in the future we can send you off to each other dripping with cum. But it's still early days so I won't be doing that."

"Rome," she whimpered, even as she curled her fingers in our hair. "S-stop saying those things."

I raised an eyebrow. "Because you don't want it or because you do?"

Ivy clamped her mouth shut but couldn't stop a small whine escaping.

"You're so fucking cute." I kissed her nose and up along her cheek. "Soon. I promise. Right now, let's see how many times James can make you come while I fuck him."

Her pupils grew so wide the blue of her iris was only a thin ring.

I caressed her throat, the hold just dominant enough that I could feel her omega melt under my touch. "Do you like the sound of that, baby? Watching us?" I murmured.

"Yes, I . . ." Ivy took a deep but shaky breath. "I w-wondered what it would look like . . . even before my heat."

She wanted us all the way back then. I was equally exhilarated and frustrated. All that time wasted. We could've started courting her earlier, spent every night just like this, fucking until we were completely worn out and—

"Ow," I grumbled as James gave my nose a flick. He chuckled, rolling over and grabbing the lube from the bedside table.

James seemed to think I wanted to take him from behind while he got to be face-first between Ivy's legs. Definitely something I wanted to do in the future but not today.

"No," I growled.

James cast a surprised glance over his shoulder. "No?"

I flipped him over with a rough push and he landed hard on his back.

"Sit on his face, Ivy," I said, holding my hand out and guiding her to her new throne. "Other way. Facing me."

James wasted no time tugging her down to his mouth. Her hands flew backward to the headboard to balance herself.

"That's it," I whispered. My thumb flicked open the lube and I began to work it into his tight hole. His abdomen clenched but he was a good boy and didn't stop whatever was making Ivy shudder above him.

Another squirt, slicked all over my length and rubbed over my cock head.

She let out a small, almost feral noise and I realized it was because she was glued to the sight of me teasing my tip against his entrance.

My girl wanted a show.

I couldn't disappoint her, could I?

"Does he look like a good cockslut for me?" I asked her.

Ivy panted faster, squirming over James' tongue and lips.

"Do you think he deserves my cock?"

"Yes!" she gasped. I wasn't sure how much of that was her agreeing with me and how much was because of whatever James was doing between her legs.

I could feel my alpha rising as I pressed my cock into his slickened hole. James twitched, his groans muffled by Ivy's pussy as I pushed past his ring of muscle.

"Doing so well, love," I said, running a soothing hand along his thigh. I hooked his leg over the crook of my elbow so I could slide even deeper.

James' poor neglected cock jerked as I took him into my fist, smearing the leaking precum all over him. I slammed into him all the way up to my knot, mimicking my thrusts with a reckless stroke of my hand. His harsh cries only drove me to fuck him harder.

"What do you think, baby?" I asked Ivy wickedly, my fist pumping James' cock. "Should I let him come like this? Or should I see if I can get him to finish all over himself just from taking my dick?"

Sweet, never-cursed-in-her-life Ivy, surprised me by picking neither.

"Let me have it," she said, her eyes burning.

God, she was perfect.

Ivy mistook my silence for hesitance.

"Please, alpha," she begged.

The urge to sink my teeth into her neck and claim her right there and then was immense.

"Take it," I snarled instead. "He's yours."

We both are.

Ivy bent down and his entire length disappeared between her pretty lips. James came hard down her throat, the intense spike of his pleasure a lightning storm in our bond. Our perfect omega, swallowing down a load from each of us. I couldn't hold back the tide and a moment later I burst, squeezing my knot tightly in my fist as I flooded him with cum.

"Don't move," I ordered both of them, stroking their sweat-damp hair as they lay collapsed on the bed.

I returned with warm towels for them both, and left again to fetch water for everyone. I wiped Ivy's slick-soaked thighs and James' spent cock between kisses.

"How are you feeling?" I asked Ivy. I couldn't stop caressing her bare, flushed skin.

"I don't even know how many orgasms I had," she wheezed.

That sounded like the right amount. "Good," I said, satisfied.

"But there's a part of me that still wants a knot. Is that crazy?" Ivy shook her head in disbelief. "I've never been this horny in my life."

James brought her knuckles up to his lips. "I think it's the scents," he suggested. "Scent compatible alphas making you crave them."

"Not just alphas," Ivy corrected him fiercely.

Even more reason she was ours. She was forming and shaping our pack right before our eyes and she didn't even know it. I curled up against her, each thump of my heart ringing my truth in my ears.

Mine.

Chapter 17

LOGAN

I couldn't breathe.

There was a great weight on my face. Each time I inhaled I drew in a lungful of . . . fur?

I spasmed, clawing at whatever was suffocating me and *it fucking clawed me back.*

"Felix, get the fuck off me!" I roared.

The gigantic orange menace skittered down my bed as I sat up. He had the audacity to hiss at me like *I* was the one who had inconvenienced him with my almost-death.

"How did you get in here, anyway?" I grumbled. I hadn't remembered Felix choosing my house after Rome left the night before.

Felix turned around and showed me his butthole instead of answering.

I threw off my covers and got up. No chance of going back to sleep after that. My heart began racing as I realized today was my date with Ivy. *Finally.*

Strange how I could've gone so long without something and now it couldn't have come fast enough. Despite knowing that I hadn't been brave enough to court Ivy until now, I still felt like an idiot for never trying.

No wonder I felt like I had to make up for lost time.

I trudged over to my wardrobe and threw it open. A furry blur shot past me like a torpedo and launched itself among my clothes.

"You fucking—" I tried to catch him but Felix was as slippery and nimble as ever. Carefully folded shirts flew off my shelves, guided by quick little paws. He was shedding like crazy, leaving orange, black and white hairs all over my pants. Finally, he went full acrobat and latched onto my hung up clothes with his sharp claws.

Once he had sufficiently decimated my wardrobe of wearable clothing, Felix scampered out of the bedroom like his tail was on fire.

"Yeah, you better run!" I yelled at him. What the fuck had gotten into him? "Jesus," I muttered, picking up what had fallen to the floor. I paused in horror when I realized what Felix had managed to get his claws into.

My nice jacket. The only one I owned that would've been suitable for Chez Lumiere tonight. I had no idea how Felix managed to shred such long tears in it so quickly.

I didn't even think. Opened my group chat with Rome and James and shot off a text.

> Felix fucking tore my jacket

ROME
> I'm sure Ivy will like whatever you wear, Logan

> No you don't understand

> Felix tore my ONLY jacket

JAMES
> One jacket!

> Are you on a strict jacket budget?

> I have no use for jackets and
> this was my nice one

ROME

> How long have you had it?

That was a good question. How old was it? I'd gotten it to attend my cousin's wedding.

Who now had a daughter about to go into third grade.

> I dunno, a while?

I winced. Neither of them responded. Eventually, I threw my phone onto the bed and returned to fixing Felix's treachery.

A playful series of knocks sounded on my door. It was odd that my first thought was that the rhythm sounded *exactly* like James. Sure enough, I opened it to find him and Rome standing there.

"Come on. Let's go shopping," James said, pointing toward town with his thumb.

It was a mystery to me how they always managed to look good even in casual clothes. "Were you up and dressed already?" I asked, feeling like a slob for sleeping in. Probably would still be asleep if Felix hadn't asphyxiated me.

They exchanged a glance. "We've been, er, up for a while," Rome said, clearing his throat.

"Ivy stayed over and we took her home," James added.

Of course. James' date *went well* last night. And if Rome's averted gaze was any indication . . . that extended to this morning too.

I forced out a dry laugh. "I'm surprised she's not courted out."

"She's not," James said mysteriously, adjusting the lens of his glasses.

"How do you know?" I frowned.

All I got in return was an infuriating shrug. Great.

"Don't think about our dates," Rome said, combing his fingers through his hair repeatedly. "I mean, both of ours went wrong so whatever you planned is going to be incredible in comparison."

I still couldn't believe their luck. An ice skating accident and James managing to mess up dinner and a movie.

After I got dressed, the three of us made our way to Star Styles, Starlight Grove's main clothing store. As a result, there was a chaotic range of stock as they tried to cater to every single person possible. Ordinarily, something like that would've overwhelmed me but I already knew where I'd be making a beeline for.

I strode to the big and tall rack, tucked in a corner of the men's section. "Well, this is it," I said, giving it a familiar pat.

Rome and James blinked at it, taking in the sparse selection.

"We can make this work, right?" Rome turned to James.

"Yeah," James said slowly. "Absolutely."

The two of them began to comb through the rack. I noticed they did not limit themselves to jacket options and I had the faint suspicion some sort of makeover was in my future.

"I don't really get . . . all of this," I admitted gruffly. "I put on what keeps me covered and that's it."

"Rome just fakes it anyway," James said offhandedly as he continued to sweep through.

Rome looked affronted. "Hi, just standing here?"

I must have looked confused because James leaned over. "Rome wears all black so he automatically looks put together," he explained. Rome scoffed but he was also unfortunately dressed entirely in black today.

"Well, it works," I said diplomatically. "You seem to know what you're doing too, James."

Rome nudged me with his elbow. "Don't say anything else, his head is already big enough," he said baldly, clearly not trying to hide it from James. "That's why he has to wear beanies all the time."

"Your insult would have worked better if I was actually wearing a beanie," James said, not missing a beat.

Rome waved a hand at him. "You know what I meant."

"I did. Takes a *big head* to make sense of the stuff you say sometimes. You're very lucky to have me."

"Excuse me?"

There was something comforting about their bickering. Seeing them with their guard down being less than perfect versions of themselves.

A jacket and pair of pants was pressed into my hands by James. "Here."

"With this," Rome added, laying a patterned shirt on top of the small pile.

"Oh, that's great."

"Isn't it?"

I realized they reminded me a lot of the way my parents were with each other before my mom passed. Mom could be smacking Dad's hand away from taste testing her bolognese one second and then slow dancing with him the next.

The idea of building that same unconditional kind of love around Ivy with our pack made a scratchy kind of heat build behind my eyes.

"I'm gonna . . ." I said gruffly, indicating to the change rooms.

I spent far too long turning this way and that in front of the mirror. Everything had buttoned up easily and I wasn't in danger of exploding out of it. But something didn't look right and I wasn't sure if I was supposed to pretend I loved what they chose for me.

A neutral sort of smiled grimace was the best I could come up with as I stepped out.

Rome and James glanced at each other. "The colors are right, aren't they?" Rome asked.

"Yeah, pretty much perfect. Good job," James said as they bumped their knuckles together.

I must have been more clueless than I thought.

"Now all we need is for Lucy to tailor it. I called ahead and she can squeeze you in if you head over in the next fifteen minutes," Rome said, checking his watch with a deft flick of his wrist.

Tailoring. It all made sense now. I could feel a flush creeping up my neck from my own idiocy. "Is that why I feel like it's so . . ."

James pushed off from where he had been leaning against the wall. "There's no shape to it right now," he explained. He stood behind me and gave the fabric a few strategic pinches and I could instantly see the difference in the mirror. "It needs to be fitted properly."

No wonder sometimes I wasn't sure if I was wearing a shirt or a camping tent. "That makes a lot of sense," I mumbled. "Thanks."

Rome and James browsed the regular men's section of the store while I got changed and went to pay. As I got closer to the counter, I noticed a bored-looking man stuck to the wall like a gecko. He glanced at the women's department where his wife was presumably shopping, sighed heavily, and returned to scrolling on his phone.

My steps slowed as I drew closer and realized who it was. Sean Prior.

Ivy's ex.

I was the last person to pick up on town rumors (guess I didn't have a face that invited gossiping) but even *I* knew that their breakup had been years ago. Yet he would turn up in Starlight Grove every winter break and Ivy would do her best to stay out of his way.

It never sat right with me.

I was content to ignore him but he did a double take when he saw me.

"Logan."

I gave him a curt nod.

Sean peered over to the other end of the store where Rome and James were. I turned to see Rome chasing a laughing James with a beanie. The scorn on his face incensed me when I turned back.

"So. The three of you are courting Ivy, huh?"

I hated her name in his mouth.

"Yes," I gritted out. "Problem?"

"No problem," Sean said a little too quickly. He held his hands up, flashing his wedding ring like it was the Holy Grail that absolved him of the bullshit that was about to come out of his mouth. "*Good luck*, is all I'm saying."

"Is that *all* you're saying, Sean?" I asked dangerously.

"What?" His face contorted into an over-the-top attempt at confusion. "I said good luck, didn't I?"

My eye twitched to the rack of belts and I wondered how he would look strung up to the rafters.

"Aren't you supposed to be going back to Briar's Landing soon?" I snapped.

He smirked knowing that he got to me. *Fuck*. Rookie move.

"Oh my gosh, I'm so sorry!" The flustered shop assistant came rushing over. "I didn't realize Emma went on her break."

"It's fine," I grunted. I deliberately turned my back on Sean, purchased my clothes and met Rome and James on the way out.

"You all right, man?" James asked. Half his hair was sticking up at a crazy angle.

"Yep," I said shortly. The encounter with Sean left a bitter taste in my mouth and I wasn't in the mood to explain.

Felix was sitting by the lamppost right outside the store. Waiting for me like the furry little villain he was. His whiskers flicked as he glanced at the bag in my hand.

"*You*," I said accusingly.

He ignored me—of course—and yawned, baring his wickedly

sharp teeth. He rose onto all fours preparing to leave, his big bushy tail swishing dismissively.

"I wonder if he's chipped," James pondered. "Imagine if he's belonged to someone this whole time." He reached for Felix and the cat yowled and darted off. "Ah well. Next time I guess."

Rome stuffed his hands in his pockets. "We're gonna head off. James has work soon and I'm due for a video chat with my family. Are you good to head to Lucy's yourself?"

"Yes, I'll be fine," I said, before thanking them again for their help.

I waved good-bye and wondered why it already felt odd that we would be returning to separate houses.

Chapter 18

IVY

Lucy had texted "you're welcome" to me right before my date. I didn't understand until I saw Logan.

Good lord.

The fit of his clothes was impeccable thanks to Lucy's handiwork. The navy jacket framed his broad shoulders perfectly. He'd gotten his hair and beard trimmed and there was an extra shine in the ocean blue of his eyes. Logan looked good and he *felt* it too.

It was completely wasted when we turned up to Chez Lumiere. They caught us off guard with a surprise degustation menu that promised an enhanced tasting experience.

With blindfolds.

Chez Lumiere de Nocturne they called it.

"Isn't this a wonderful surprise?" the waitress gushed as she handed me a silken eye mask. "Chef Gerard has been feeling particularly inspired the past twenty-four hours."

"I don't know if wonderful is the right word," Logan muttered, staring at the eye mask he'd been given.

"Oh, it *is*, believe me," she continued, oblivious to our unease. "The wait staff have been lucky enough to sample some of the dishes. Trust me, you are in for a *treat*." She grew more impassioned, speaking faster and faster until I was worried smoke would pour from her ears. "And the blindfolds only elevate the experience. The choices he's made knowing one of your senses is veiled, gah! You will truly understand why Chef Gerard is a trailblazer unlike any other!"

She flittered off, ready to proselytize the gospel of Chef Gerard to the next table of victims.

Logan was clearly frazzled but was valiantly trying to make the best of it.

"I'm so sorry, Ivy. I had no idea they were going to do this." The previously perfect sweep of his hair did not hold up to his nervous tugs. "I'm sure the food will still be delicious."

It *was* delicious.

Shame there was so little of it.

We were three courses in and I had eaten an odd garlicky foam, three paper-thin slices of beef and a single mushroom.

"Lucky there's still more courses, right?" Logan said for the fourth time from across the table.

I couldn't see him but I could sense his anxious energy. The way he kept adjusting his position, his leg bumping mine each time he did so. Every second sentence was laced with an apology and his ordinarily comforting scent was harsh from his unease.

"Logan." I stretched my hand out trying to find him and he grasped it immediately. "This sounds crazy but all these starters have made me really crave one of Char's burgers," I said casually.

The tension ran out of him in an instant. A rush of water cascading down jagged mountains.

"Yeah?" I could hear the way he was fighting to sound neutral when relief made his voice lift. "Me too, actually."

I whispered conspiratorially across the table like we were two prisoners planning a daring escape.

"Should we get out of here?"

The next moment I was being lifted out of my chair, a strong arm wound around my waist and the blindfold ripped off me. "Come on," Logan urged, as I blinked away the prickling light. "Before they make us drink soup from a seashell."

I huffed with laughter, as we wove our way through the tables of other blindfolded guests. Maybe it was just me but I thought they all looked extremely hungry.

A fresh wave of waiters made their way out of the kitchen. We quickened our steps to avoid being caught in a swarm of black and white.

"Logan, look," I said, trying to discreetly point with my chin.

The next course was a single scallop shell filled with a mystery grayish broth.

"You're psychic," I told him delightedly.

Logan recoiled. "I'm *not*. I had no idea."

Maybe the mushroom I'd eaten had special properties because I was positively giddy.

"Then this must be your secret venture," I gasped. "Eccentric restaurateur masquerading as an electrician. No wonder you knew what was coming next on the menu."

Logan had a pained expression on his face. "Ivy, don't insult me."

"Chef Gerard who? I bet this was *your* idea." I waved my hand around me with a flourish. "All this belongs to you," I giggled harder.

"Ivy, I swear to god . . ." he growled. But Logan couldn't hide the corner of his lips twitching as he hauled me the rest of the way to the hostess table.

I didn't even want to think about how much Logan paid for us to have one quarter of a terrible dining experience but he didn't seem to care. He was much more focused on getting me into his truck and racing full throttle back to Starlight Grove.

"Should we stop at a drive through instead?" Logan asked, his eyes a little crazed as he gripped the steering wheel tighter.

"No!" I gave his knee a squeeze. "Char's burgers. Eyes on the prize!"

Logan drove for approximately twenty seconds before wanting to negotiate again. "Maybe one nugget?" he suggested.

He was behaving like one of my students trying to get his way. "They won't sell you just one," I reasoned.

"Then I better buy ten."

"Logan!"

His whole body drooped. "I'm starving, Ivy. I barely ate anything today." He sounded almost delirious.

"You were really looking forward to this dinner, weren't you?"

He nodded glumly.

"Well, it's not over yet." I smiled.

Logan was a little lost in my eyes. At least we were stopped at a red light. I turned his chin forward so he was back to facing the road.

"Come on, Logan," I encouraged him. "We're almost there."

Logan and I crashed into Rosie's Diner like pirates dying for their first drink after months at sea.

"Burgers," Logan croaked.

"With extra fries," I added.

He groaned appreciatively. "You're so smart, Ivy."

Char looked us up and down, taking in our dressy outfits. "Are you sure you're in the right place?" she asked with a raised brow.

"YES," we practically shouted in unison.

Logan and I collapsed in a corner booth, both sighing with undisguised pleasure. I could actually see the pressure seep out of him as he removed his jacket and rolled up his sleeves. His forearms were thick and covered in fine, dark hair. *Perfect arms for such a big alpha, making it easy for him to lift you up and—*

I managed to tear my eyes away before he noticed me staring.

Gosh, my omega is such a trollop for man arms.

Who was I kidding? We were one and the same.

I settled into the familiar cushion of the booth. I didn't care if this was the millionth time I'd been to Rosie's, I was so glad our date ended up here.

"Logan."

"Yes, Ivy."

"I appreciate the thought. Always. But don't ever make me eat mystery substances blindfolded again," I teased him.

Logan palmed his face. "Deal. If I do then you'll know I've been body snatched."

"Like . . . aliens?" I asked curiously.

He tilted his hand in a so-so motion. "I was thinking more of an evil twin scenario."

"More realistic."

"Exactly."

I was learning new things about Logan every day. Who knew he was hiding an adorably dry sense of humor. And apparently had another version of him running around.

"What's his name? In case I meet him and he pretends to be you."

Logan scratched his beard pensively. "Schmogan Schmennett," he finally said.

"All right," I hummed. "I'll make sure to remember that."

Char arrived soon after with our burgers and we fell on them like rabid animals.

"Gave you pickle fiends extras. Enjoy!" She winked before gliding away.

I took a huge bite of my burger. It wasn't enough. I picked up several fries and stuffed them in my mouth too. Out of the corner of my eye I noticed Logan staring at me.

"What are you looking at?" I said without thinking, my words muffled around my food. Oh, that was not an attractive move. I was pretty sure there was a fry pointing directly out of my mouth *at* him.

Logan went pink. "I don't know," he said, averting his eyes and mumbling so low I barely heard him. "Felt like a moment I'd tell the grandkids about."

I had never wanted to do so many conflicting things at once. Laugh. Cry. Finish my gigantic bite so I could hug and kiss him without being gross.

Of course I ended up doing none of those things and chose to make a garbled, bubbly sort of noise instead. *Real smooth, Ivy.*

"You, uh, want kids?" I asked quietly once I had swallowed.

"Yeah." Logan remained an interesting shade of fuchsia. "Only child here so I always wanted my kids to have a ton of siblings." Panic dawned on him as he realized the implication of what he said. "Not a ton! A normal amount of siblings," he said in a rush. "Whatever number you would be comfortable with having, really. Not like *you* as in you have to be the one to have them. But not anyone else, Ivy, I swear to god you're the only one that I'm, *we're* courting right now and—"

"Shhh." I shushed him by putting a fry in his open mouth and forcing him to chew. He looked extremely relieved I'd dug him out of his grave. It was sweet and the last thing I wanted was for him to feel like he'd said the wrong thing. "I want kids too," I said shyly. "A normal amount of siblings sounds wonderful."

If Logan went any redder, Char could slice him up and serve him up between bacon and lettuce to the lunch crowd.

We ate quietly for a while, starting to feel halfway human again with each bite. I did a double take at his plate and then mine, realizing something crucial.

"Wait, Char gave you extra pickles too?" I pointed at the dwindling pile next to his fries. "But the other day . . . you gave me your pickles because you said you hated them."

"Oh that." Logan ate a few more fries, chewing thoughtfully. "I lied," he said frankly.

I'd eaten *all* of them that day. "You gave them to me because you knew I liked them? Even though you like them too?" I said in a small voice.

"Yep. Get used to it."

"I will *not*."

"Then I will only eat whatever you can't finish."

My eyes narrowed. "I might lie too," I said with a defiant lift of my chin.

He seemed shocked by this. "Why?" he demanded.

"For the same reason as you, silly."

Logan couldn't tear his eyes off me. His gaze traveled down to my lips. Then back up to my eyes, burning hotter than ever. He was a magnetic force and I felt myself lean forward.

"Damn, you two made quick work of that."

We leaped apart as Char refilled our drinks. "Can I tempt you with dessert?" she asked.

"Sure," Logan rasped. "Just . . . give us a minute."

Char eyed us knowingly and left.

"I think I owe you pie," I said, giving him a light nudge with my elbow.

He gave me a blank look.

"Because of the bet we made?" Still nothing. "Hank's hip. Marisol's knee . . ."

"Oh god." Logan palmed his face. "That is the last thing I remember about that night, Ivy."

Surprise classroom heat *was* probably more memorable than trivial townie arguments.

"But this is our first date. So my treat," Logan insisted.

"I'll get you pie on the next one," I offered shyly.

His eyes widened and his chest rose with a big shaky breath.

Did he really think he wasn't going to get a second date with me? My hand crept across the leather booth and found his.

Logan entwined his fingers with mine. He remained very still, like he was worried one wrong movement might scare me off.

I don't think he realized it was only making me like him more.

It was snowing very lightly when we left Rosie's. I followed the tiny individual flakes and their spiraling journey downward. Little flowers of ice dotted along my coat and settled in my hair. They were especially radiant when they caught the light from the nearby streetlamp. I couldn't resist opening my hand and seeing them land in my palm.

"I feel like we fucked up, Ivy."

I turned around in surprise. Logan had his hands in his pockets, shoulders slumped in defeat.

"None of our dates worked out the way they were supposed to. This wasn't what we wanted when we said we wanted to court you," he said heavily.

I couldn't go another second without touching him. I strode over and cradled his bearded chin in my hand. "Don't." He sank slightly into my palm as I stroked his cheek with my thumb. "I've loved the last few days."

"Ivy, you don't have to—"

"Life isn't going to go our way all the time," I said firmly. "I feel closer to you all *because* it hasn't gone our way." I wrapped my other arm around his neck, rising onto my tiptoes to reach. Logan groaned and hauled me tight against him.

"You're not just saying that?" he asked. Our foreheads pressed together and I could see the fog from our breaths mingling.

"I think if it was perfect, it wouldn't feel real," I whispered. "And I really want it to be real."

Logan closed the last bit of distance between us. He brushed his lips over mine once, our noses bumping lightly, before capturing my mouth fully. Even knowing it was coming and craving it didn't stop it from stealing my breath entirely. Blood rushed instantly to my head as a freefalling sensation swooped low through my belly. Logan kissed me and kissed me, holding me safe in his embrace.

We eventually surfaced but he kept his forehead against mine. "I can take you home now," he said tentatively.

I hated that idea.

"Or . . ."

Everything went still as he left the possibility hanging in the air. It felt golden, a newly lit path waiting for us.

"Take me to yours, Logan."

Chapter 19

LOGAN

It wasn't a long drive from Rosie's Diner to my place but it sure as hell felt like one.

I couldn't stop glancing over at Ivy, sitting in the passenger seat of my work truck that had seen better days. By all accounts she did not belong there. She'd done something to her short brown hair and made it wavy, framing her beautiful face like the work of art she was. Her black dress was simple but something about the way it clung to her body was driving me mad. Enough of a sweep to the neckline to draw my eyes to her breasts, a tied knot at her waist making her curve and dip. I'd been half hard all night because of that damn dress.

She belonged in a limo or at the very least something with four doors. But she was a saint and was completely unfazed when I pulled up at the start of the night.

Now here she was, filling it with her sweet omega scent.

My hand was on her thigh, the tease of bare skin just out of reach beneath her tights. I traced circles as I drove and she squirmed under my touch. It took everything—*everything*—not to pull over, flip her skirt up and rut her hard against a fogged up window.

Get her in your bed.

Get her home at the very least, Logan.

My alpha prowled impatiently inside me, rising to her needy pheromones.

I screeched into my driveway, uncaring that I'd parked askew. In one smooth movement, I shut off my engine and unbuckled my seat belt. Ivy's hair was tangled in my fingers and my mouth covered hers, swallowing down her whine. Her lips were almost frantic as they moved against mine, my shirt in her clenched fist pulling me closer.

"Logan, please."

Fuck, that unraveled me. Two words and I would do anything for her.

"Inside, princess." It was agonizing to pull myself away. I tore out of the truck with a low growl, and wrenched open her door. She was in my arms before I could even think, chest to my chest and legs wrapped around me. I fumbled with my key, letting loose every curse word I knew as she nestled her nose into my neck.

We crashed inside and I pressed Ivy up against the wall. I bent down to reach beneath her skirt and hooked my fingers over the waistband of her tights. Ivy gave a little shimmy to help me and I unwrapped her like the gift she was.

"Now, princess," I murmured, sinking lower so I could help her one foot at a time, "I know you had a good time with James last night. And based on how content Rome seemed, I can only assume that extended to this morning as well."

My rough palms ran over her smooth thighs and she shuddered, her legs already falling open for me. I buried my face into the junction of her thighs and caught the fabric of her dress between my teeth.

"Which begs the question," I began, my voice rough from the scent haze of her slickened pussy, "why are you a needy mess for me right now?"

Ivy seized my hair and her hips jerked against my face. "He didn't knot me," she said, her voice tight.

"What?" I said hoarsely. I was certain I'd misheard her.

"Rome didn't knot me," she repeated. "Or anything else. Only James, um, *you know*. Last night. But neither of them did this morning," Ivy continued, blithely unaware my entire body was going up in a flame of alpha urges.

Rut your omega. Sate her.

And mark that pretty fucking neck with your teeth.

"Why didn't they?" I ran my nose up her stomach, between her breasts and caged her with my body.

"Rome said . . ." Ivy swallowed and started again. "He said it would be rude to send me off to you dripping with . . . um . . ."

I began to loosen the knot at the waist of her dress. "So what did they do instead?"

Ivy squeezed her eyes tight. "Went down on me . . . and used their fingers."

"Did you come?"

"Yes . . . a lot."

They got her ready for me.

My pack got her ready to take my knot.

One deft pull and her dress fell open, revealing her tits sitting pretty in a lace bra and her pussy covered by a barely there thong. I stared hungrily, drinking in the sight of her.

It took her gentle hand on my cheek to bring me back. "I want to see you too, please," she whispered.

My jacket had already been left in my truck. But the rest?

"Come on," I said evasively, hauling her back into my arms. Her dress fluttered to the floor as I carried her deeper into my home.

"Logan, are you—"

I kissed her hard next to a framed picture of a mountain that was my dismal attempt at decor.

There wasn't really a plan once I got her into my bedroom but at least it was as close to pitch black as I could get in there. A tiny sliver of moonlight sliced through a gap in the curtains, dividing my bed in two. It seemed ominous somehow.

Ivy reached for my shirt button and I flinched. Curses imploded in my head hoping she didn't notice.

But of course she did. She released my button and laid her hand flat against me. "You're worried about what I'll think of you?" she asked. Her slow movement down my chest and belly filled the gaps of unspoken words.

"I don't . . ." God, I knew exactly what I needed to say but insecurity wrapped my tongue in barbed wire. "I don't look like *they* do, Ivy."

Younger. Fitter. A hell of a lot slimmer.

"Scent me."

Confusion flickered across my features. "What?"

Ivy took control, bringing my head down into the crook of her neck.

"What does my scent tell you?" she whispered.

I inhaled and let it fill my head with dreams. Of a million homecomings to her smile. Nights of companionship, drowsy never-ending conversations with all of us in her nest. Secret gingerbread cookies that would find their way into my bag, my pockets and the kisses I would thank her with.

"Keep breathing." Her voice felt far away yet rooted in my soul, a command I couldn't fight.

I felt her unbutton my shirt. Her fingers ran through my chest hair and I sensed the change. Arousal, sweet and delicate, as simple as a caught eye from across the room.

Ivy ventured lower, exploring my thick waist and the full curve of my stomach. Cloves and cinnamon burst free, an edge of desperation and need taking over.

"Fuck," I swore. I couldn't deny what every sign from her body was screaming at me. "You love this?"

"*Yes.* I told you." Ivy pushed my shirt off my shoulders and fumbled with my belt buckle. "Please." A metallic clank and pull as she tried to loosen it. "Help me, I—"

Suddenly clothes seemed stupid. Why did I still have them on? Every layer that fell to the floor only made her perfume thicken. We collapsed on the bed, her eager hands tugging down my boxers while I tried to decipher her bra clasp.

"Holy shit, Logan."

I had never heard her swear before.

Hearing her do so at her first glimpse of my cock made me feel invincible.

"You've seen it before," I grunted. She took me in both hands, one stacked on top of the other like she was measuring me. I got impossibly harder, the thick vein down my shaft pounding.

"I don't remember too much from the heat, Logan," she confessed. "And you didn't . . . you know."

Cute that she blushed because she couldn't say *fuck me* while double fisting my dick.

"Lie down," I told her gently. I braced myself on my elbow, looming over her. Anticipation glimmered bright in her expression as she subconsciously began to stroke me.

My fingers dipped between her thighs, finding her soaked. I groaned, kissing her as she spread herself wider for me. Her clit felt swollen and slippery with slick. I drank in her reactions as I circled it, her mouth falling open and her nipples tightening to hard points.

I didn't have a lot of experience with women. But I only needed to figure out what *this* woman needed and tattoo it into my brain forever.

Neither of us wanted to look away as we learned each other's bodies. I loved the flicker of triumph when a twist of her wrist made me stifle a moan. The way she whispered my name when I filled her with two fingers. I found the sweet spot inside her that drew a strangled scream from her lungs.

"I need a little"—She mimed a small circular motion—"to get me there."

My thumb immediately began to swipe across her clit. She was so beautiful like this, on the verge of falling apart for me. Hair messed from my pillows, pink spreading beneath her freckled skin. I felt her squeeze my shaft and wetness shone from my tip.

Her breathing quickened, the sucking sound of my fingers thrusting in and out of her pussy filling the room.

"I'm really close," Ivy breathed. She released my cock and grabbed my wrist. *Yes.* I wanted her to be greedy, only focusing on her pleasure right now.

"When you come, princess, you can have my cock," I said, leaning down to scent-mark her.

A shiver rippled through her. "Yes. Please."

"Is that what you want? For me to fill this greedy little pussy of yours?" I added a third finger and she cried out. "It's going to be a much bigger stretch than this."

Her hips were moving harder and faster against my hand. I covered her mouth with mine, savoring her little pants as she came. Once the tense arch of her back relaxed, I lifted my slick-covered fingers to my lips.

There it was. That fucking taste that had decimated me last time. I gripped myself tight to the point of pain to force the building pressure in my cock to subside. Ivy's glistening pussy was inches from me and I couldn't resist tapping the tip against her clit.

"Logan, I'm—"

"Still a bit sensitive?" I asked. I traced her entrance over and over, letting the head dip inside every now and then. She had to be begging. Desperate. So slick the stretch would feel good.

Ivy gasped as I pushed in until a third of my cock was buried inside her.

"God, that's . . ." she panted. "You feel even bigger than I thought you would."

I fucked her slowly, not plunging any deeper and letting her acclimatize to my size. "You can take me," I murmured, smoothing back her hair and kissing her. I watched as a few more inches of my shaft disappeared inside her.

"Are you all the way in?"

"Almost." I guided her hand down to her clit and she began to touch herself slowly. The rest of my cock sank easily into her slick hole. "There we go," I breathed, feeling her pussy choke me in her perfect grip.

She traced where we were joined, her fingers feeling the swell at the base of my cock nestled against her stretched lips. "How is your knot supposed to fit after all that," she whined.

I slid almost all the way out before thrusting my entire length back in with a loud wet smack. She had already adjusted so easily, I had no doubt she would take my knot beautifully too. "It'll fit, princess," I assured her.

Determination and instinct drove each rock of my hips against hers. In and out, the slickness coating my shaft unmistakable even in the dim glow of the moonlight. Ivy clung to my shoulders, the nape of my neck, my hair, losing herself in the sensation of my cock moving inside her.

I could see her clit, peeking desperately out from beneath its hood, humming for some attention. A light caress and she bucked, my knot partially pushing into her.

"Do you want it?" I demanded.

"God, yes. More than anything. Please, Logan, knot me, I—"

I pushed and kept pushing. One hand splayed on her ass, spreading her open, the other working her clit. I held on through the tight squeeze of her fluttering cunt, the gush of slick down my cock. A noise I couldn't even describe tore from somewhere deep as I locked fully inside her.

Release. It was a tidal wave, the break of foam after the longest, highest crest. I didn't know how long I hung here, filling her with spurt after spurt of my cum. My alpha was fiercely triumphant, marking her this way the next best thing after teeth on her skin. He wanted to keep her permanently sated, snug around my knot or with my cum leaking from her.

I only just managed to stop myself from collapsing on top of her and crushing her. Ivy was trying to catch her breath too, her eyes rolled to the back of her head. I could still feel the last few convulsions of her orgasm around my knot.

Words were too difficult. Instead, I held her tightly to me and rolled, settling on my back with her draped over me. I wished I was a little less sweaty but she didn't seem to mind.

Ivy laid her head on my chest and her hand came to rest on my stomach. I automatically let out a self-conscious sort of grunt.

"I like it," she said, firmly. She bent down and managed to nuzzle the top of my belly despite the fact that we were locked together. "I love how cuddly you are. I feel like I'm in my nest right now."

"Fuck," I breathed. "Sleep on me any day, princess."

I held her in the gentle quiet until the soft caress of her hand over my body felt like love.

Chapter 20

IVY

"Thanks so much for coming with me." I flicked a grateful smile at Olive and Lucy's reflection in my rearview mirror. Summer ran point in the passenger seat, commandeering the map and playlist.

"Of course," Olive said immediately. "Thanks for driving, Ivy."

"Road trip!" Lucy threw her hands up with a loud whoop. "Sort of. Does an hour and a half drive count?"

Summer unearthed a giant bag of M&M's and cradled it lovingly like some sort of prize fish. "We have snacks and tunes. It counts," she insisted.

The four of us were on our way to Nest Wonderland, which as the name suggested, was a nirvana for blanket-burrowing omegas. It spiked my anxiety though. It had been years since I'd set foot in the store because I found it so overwhelming.

Lucy and Summer were chatting excitedly about finally being able to feel the fabrics and test-squish products and how much better this was going to be compared to online shopping. Olive's eyes were bright, probably thinking about what she could find to make her pack nest even more perfect.

I could see my friends flitting through the store, responding to some well-honed signal in their brains telling them which items belonged in their nests. Mine was defunct or at the very least, running on some cheap batteries. I barely kept up with what was in fashion clothing-wise, let alone what the latest must-have nest additions were.

But I wanted to try today. I had three very good-looking reasons for wanting to improve my nest.

Lucy mimicked an angelic heavenly choir the moment the big box store came into view on the highway.

"Maybe it was a mistake only coming in one car," Summer said, chewing on her fingernail. "How am I supposed to fit everything I need?"

"What else do you need in your nest, Summer?" Olive asked curiously.

"Ok, let me rephrase. How am I supposed to buy everything I think is cute?"

"Stick with what you can carry, maybe?" Olive suggested.

Summer sighed. "That won't work, I have noodles for arms."

Hopefully some of their enthusiasm would rub off on me.

As we stepped through the automatic double doors, the girls linked their elbows with mine so running away was not an option. Why was it so freaking big? So many different departments and an infinite amount of products all stacked sky high. I had visions of myself trapped beneath a fallen avalanche of sheet sets.

"It's going to be fine, Ivy," Lucy said quickly, tightening her grip on me. "Let's just look first. No pressure."

They stuck with me as we wandered and slowly but surely their excitement began to feel infectious.

"Ooh, these chunky knit throws are cute."

"Shut up, a croissant pillow! Who needs a pack when I can hug a giant pastry."

"Gosh, every time I come here I'm *convinced* I need a canopy."

We ended up in the pack section of the store and Summer darted toward one of the displays. She picked up a large wedge-shaped pillow and spun around to face us with a flourish.

"Olive, do you want some intimacy positioning cushions for you and your pack? They now come in a plush water-resistant fabric!" Summer said, showing it off at all different angles like a game show hostess.

"Intimacy . . . what are those?" Olive's nose crinkled as she picked one up herself. "And why does it need to be water resistant?"

Lucy leaned in. "They're sex pillows," she said out of the corner of her mouth.

Olive let out a small screech and dropped it. She eyed it calculatingly and after a brief moment of contemplation, picked it back up again. "Maybe just one," she said sheepishly.

Summer was trying to foist two more on her. "Three, Olive, you have three alphas!"

"What about you, Ivy?" Lucy asked, waving one enticingly in front of me.

I evaded the question with another question. "How would you even use this?" I said, holding up a pillow with a ski ramp sort of design.

Lucy shrugged. "I don't know. But I think most of these you can just bend over like—" She proceeded to demonstrate with zero concern about who might walk by and see her in such a compromising position.

Summer lay back on one with a particularly steep curve. "You could also spread yourself out and—*ahh!*"

She screamed, rolled backward off it and landed headfirst in a tub of even more sex pillows. It was too much and we all lost it. Giggling uncontrollably, clutching our sides. A funny-sounding wheeze from one person would set off another. Once our laughter finally subsided and tears were wiped away, I was struck by how lucky I was to have these girls.

Maybe that's why I decided to blurt out what had been plaguing me from the moment we had left Starlight Grove.

"I want to ask my pack to celebrate New Year's Eve with me tomorrow night. And possibly invite them into my nest," I said in a jumbled rush.

They gaped goldfish-like at me.

Lucy was first to recover. "We are going to circle back and scream about the fact that you called them 'my pack' in a second but oh my *god*, inviting them into your nest? This is big," she murmured in awe.

A nest was an omega's most sacred space. It's where we felt most comfortable and for most, every detail down to the textures and scents was important. Even *I* felt territorial over mine. To invite someone else into it was a big deal.

"Ivy, I knew you were being courted but I had no idea it was so serious already," Summer said in a hushed tone. "When did they ask you out, right before Christmas, wasn't it?"

That was true. How long ago was that . . . a week?

What was I thinking?

"You're right." I nodded soberly. "It's too soon."

Panic crossed Summer's face. "No, I didn't . . . I'm not trying to talk you out of it!"

"But you made a good point. Maybe I should wait until next New Year's," I said thoughtfully.

"*Next* . . . as in a year from now?" Lucy said, bewildered.

Olive patted the empty spot next to her. I sat down automatically and she gave me a friendly nudge with her shoulder. "Inviting your pack into your nest is a big deal," she began kindly. "But it also . . . isn't. It's not a bond or a visible bite on your neck. It's wanting to sleep next to the ones who make you happy and have their scents in your safe place."

Ok, that did sound good.

"There's no timeline of when it should happen. It's whatever feels right for you."

Summer crouched down so we were eye level. "Olive is right, Ivy. What do your instincts say?"

I knew the answer. Of course I knew. Even the thought of sleeping alone in my nest tonight already felt wrong.

"They belong there," I admitted quietly.

Lucy gave my hand a reassuring rub. "Then you should invite them in."

I fiddled nervously with my sleeve, folding it and unfolding it between my fingers. "I need to make plans with them for New Year's Eve first. What should I say? What if they're busy?"

The deafening silence from the girls was pierced by an announcement requesting more staff at the front registers.

"Ivy, do you *really* think this pack will want to spend New Year's Eve with anyone else?" Lucy raised a brow at me.

No, probably not.

Summer held out her hand. "Give me your phone, we can ask them now."

"Yeah, we'll help you with what to say," Olive perked up.

The three girls huddled close, treating their task with the seriousness of a diplomacy letter. Summer's fingers flew as Olive and Lucy whispered suggestions.

Finally, Summer cleared her throat and announced what they had come up with. "'Ring in the New Year with me tomorrow? I would love to have you all over at my place. Bring something to cheers with and lips for kissing.'"

"Summer!" I cried out. "Not the last bit!"

"Why not? It's cute, is it not cute?"

I winced. "Is it too forward?"

"*Too forward*. The alphas have knotted you, babe."

"Shhhhh!" I tried to grab my phone back.

Lucy put her hands on her hips exasperatedly. "What did you want to say instead? *Bring something to cheers with and hands for holding*?"

"Maybe I do want to say that," I said defiantly.

Olive rubbed her forehead. "Send it and save this poor girl from herself."

Summer was poised like she was going to press send. "We think they'll love it but you don't have to if you don't want to," she conceded.

"Yeah, only consensual meddling here." Lucy's voice dropped to a furtive whisper. "But you should really send it."

I shut my eyes tight. "Ok. Do it," I finally said.

"Attagirl."

Summer deposited my phone back into my hands right as it started buzzing. "Here, you can look at the replies in case they send nude things."

"Then update us on the nice stuff, we don't need to know about the dicks," Lucy said with a wave of her hand.

I hugged my phone protectively. "They won't send any dicks," I retorted. I quickly checked my notifications in case someone—let's face it, James—made me a liar. "They *didn't* send any dicks," I said with extra confidence.

"Bummer."

It was going to take a special kind of pack to handle Summer, that's for sure.

I peeked at the messages from the guys.

ROME
Of course we want to spend New Years with you

JAMES
Yeah otherwise who's Logan gonna kiss

LOGAN
I would've just gone to bed early

JAMES

Don't say that

I could've tracked down Felix for you

LOGAN

I'm not kissing Felix, he destroyed my wardrobe

JAMES

But you look so good now

ROME

What they are trying to say is thank you for inviting us to your home, we can't wait to see you Idiots

I couldn't wipe the grin off my face. "We're really happy for you, Ivy." Olive smiled knowingly. "Let's make sure your nest is exactly the way you want it."

Maybe Nest Wonderland wasn't that bad, after all.

I WOULDN'T BE SURPRISED if my car was sagging slightly as we puttered back to Starlight Grove. Spirits were high despite an atrocious lack of snacks—four omegas couldn't ration chocolate, *shocker*. I dropped each of the girls off at their homes, thanking them profusely for their help. They wished me luck while assuring me I didn't need it in the same breath.

I sat in my car, a little sniffly, wondering what I did to deserve friends like them.

My good mood and rumbling tummy was the perfect storm that had me pulling over at Mariposa Market. I couldn't stop thinking about everything I could serve tomorrow. A huge charcuterie board was a must, as were more of the gingerbread cookies that I'd made them for Christmas. I'd left all my shopping totes at home but I had several gigantic bags on hand thanks to Nest Wonderland. I emptied my new pillows out of one of them and headed inside.

I made a beeline for the cheese fridge. Carmen and Marisol had excellent taste in cheese and that only made my job more difficult. How many cheeses would be too many cheeses? Was such a thing possible?

"Hi Ivy."

I'd know that scent anywhere. Soapy and a little powdery. Inoffensive if not a little boring. I'd thought I liked it once upon a time, but now it had the appeal of tepid bath water.

I made sure my polite smile was firmly pasted on before turning around to face Sean. He was allowed to return to Starlight Grove whenever he wanted, I reminded myself. I did not own the entire town, nor was I allowed to ask Stanley to install some sort of barricade coded only to his DNA.

My omega, however, wanted to hiss and scratch him a little.

"You look well." Sean's gaze was just a little too intense for a supermarket encounter. The man used his alpha energy like a mallet. Fitting because his head shape was also rather cylindrical and stout, the effect exacerbated by his blond buzz of hair.

What on earth did I used to see in him?

Thankfully, he did not make a motion to hug me. And I should hope not, considering his wife stood beside him, a chubby toddler glued to her hip. We were all on a first name basis and civil until our molars ached.

"Hi Sean. Hi Laura," I said perfunctorily. "Gosh, Tyson is getting big."

Laura proudly smoothed down his drool-soaked bib. "He is. Got his dad's genes. He's going to be an alpha, I know it."

I always found it weird when parents imposed designations on their children but it wasn't an uncommon sentiment.

Just as I wondered where their other son was, there was a loud crash followed by a giggle in the next aisle. Laura's eyes popped out of her head. "Oh lord, what is that demon up to now?" she cried, running off.

Sean didn't follow.

"Been doing some nest shopping?" he asked, pointing at my bag.

I bristled at his interest. *My space, not yours.*

Suddenly I regretted my environmentally conscious decision.

"Just wanted to reuse the bag, you know," I said tightly.

"Oh Ivy, you were always such a stickler for the environment."

Not wanting to live on a ball of fire and trash made me a stickler, I guess.

Sean clicked his fingers. "Wait, I thought you were being courted. Why are you nest shopping?"

Alphas loved to spoil their omegas with new items for their nest. I knew it, Sean knew it. Heck, I'd seen several packs at Nest Wonderland today.

I paled at the implication that I hadn't been worth the same consideration.

"Omegas buy things for their nest all the time, Sean."

Terse. Too terse. He was going to know.

"I know, Ivy. I didn't mean anything by it."

There was nothing in his expression except a sympathetic sort of calm. I jerked when he palmed his face and laughed. "God, remember that blue cushion I got you? You loved that thing."

Loved was rather inaccurate.

I hadn't given it a second thought since I got rid of it, the same day he broke up with me.

Laura returned, hauling a sullen five year old. She wordlessly dumped the toddler into Sean's arms and he looked surprised she wanted him to parent his own child.

He recovered quickly and gave her what I supposed was an affectionate look. "Honey, Ivy just reminded me of when I got you that massive body pillow."

What?

Laura brightened slightly. "God, that body pillow. I'm not even an omega and it's the best thing ever."

"Th-that's wonderful," I stammered.

There was a sick, burrowing sensation in my stomach. My innards cannibalizing themselves. I was not blind to what Sean was doing by bringing up that he bought nesting materials for his beta wife. But instinct did not respond to intellect, my reaction visceral and emotional. All the feelings I'd felt when he left me years ago came rushing back.

It wasn't even about *him*; it was the rejection that stung. The reminder of my failure as an omega. Was I an idiot for shopping for my own nest? It didn't feel like that when I was with the girls and we'd all made purchases today.

So why was I feeling like this now?

All the bags and boxes sitting in my car suddenly felt like a burden.

"I, um, better go," I mumbled, turning away. "Have a good New Year's," I threw over my shoulder quickly.

I wasn't hungry at all anymore and left Mariposa Market empty handed. I very nearly tripped over Felix in my rush to get back to my car. His big golden eyes shone like medallions as he looked me over.

"I'll be fine," I sniffed.

He meowed and curled around my legs. I stroked his fluffy back a few times before retreating to my car, just wanting to be home. Felix sat sentinel-like on the sidewalk, watching me until I had turned out of view.

Chapter 21

ROME

Ivy wasn't ok.

And I had no idea why.

Logan, James and I had been embarrassingly happy when we got her text. There may have been some celebrating on our front stoop. High fives exchanged across property lines. We coordinated what we would bring—drinks and kissing lips were a given—plus a plate each and a gift from all of us.

I should've known something was up when Felix scratched at the door and made dramatic dying noises until we let him in. He behaved nothing like the overgrown slug I was familiar with, meowing urgently as he nipped at our ankles. By the time James and I made it out the front door, Logan was already waiting for us outside. He glanced down at Felix and then back up at us looking resigned.

"Yeah, he bit me until I hurried up too."

James knelt down, scratching beneath Felix's chin. "We're heading over to Ivy's now, ok?"

Felix slumped with relief. *Finally*, the determined swing of his tail seemed to say. He was eerily still as we piled into my car, watching us from the top of the steps one minute and then vanishing from my rearview mirror in the next.

Ivy lived in a quaint blue townhouse, the greenery lining the steps a little too overgrown and one of the stone pavers wobbling on our way up. I could already see Logan making mental notes to return another day to fix it. There was a clay sign hanging next to her door—*Winter* carved with a steady hand and a myriad of messy little thumbprints surrounding it.

She was a vision when she opened the door. Lifted straight out of my dreams. Her velvet blue dress sparkled when it caught the light, like a night sky spilled out across her body.

"Ivy. Wow."

I would've said something more eloquent but my tongue had decided to stop working.

"It's old," she immediately countered, adjusting her hair and smoothing out her hemline even though both were perfect. "I know I'm a bit too dressed up considering we're only going to be home but—"

James stepped over the threshold and kissed her. I didn't think I would ever tire of seeing them together. The soft gray of his loose button-up shirt matched her perfectly. "You look gorgeous," he said, giving her cheek a reassuring stroke of his thumb.

"Oh, you brought food too, you didn't have to do that. I went to the market this morning," Ivy babbled as she stepped aside. Her eyes widened when she noticed the giant bow-adorned present Logan was carrying. "What's in there?"

The present looked tiny in Logan's hands but was giant in hers. "Another courting gift. It seemed like time for another one," Logan said, bending down to press his lips to hers as well.

Each kiss seemed to fluster her more. Not in an elegant, *may require a fainting couch* way. She was so jittery I was concerned she was breaking out into hives.

I laid my hand on the small of her back, hoping to steady her as I followed her inside. Her entryway opened up into her living room and we sat down while she opened our gift. She gasped as she held up the cashmere wool blanket in a soothing cream color. It had been exorbitantly expensive and completely worth it, simply for the tiny squeal she let out when she rubbed it against her cheek.

"Is it for my nest?" Ivy asked hesitantly. Shades of emotion flickered so quickly across the fragile blue of her eyes I couldn't read them.

Shit. Had we fucked up? Was she feeling pressured to invite us into her nest because of the gift? That was the last thing I wanted.

"It's for whatever you want it for," I said quickly.

Her features went tight and I immediately knew I'd said the wrong thing.

"Of course," she said woodenly. "I love it." She sort of lay it over her couch, adjusting and patting it until she was satisfied. "Are you hungry?" she asked, standing up and motioning for us to follow her to the kitchen.

Ivy's home was lovely if a little sparse. There were only a few personal touches here and there—a framed photo with her friends, a glitter snow globe, an overstuffed bookshelf. I thought of her classroom in comparison. Brimming with life and color, decorated so thoughtfully with personalized touches for her students everywhere. There was barely a fraction of the same care expended here.

"We need to buy her more homewares and decorations," I hissed low at James. "Maybe some plants too. Really sturdy ones that won't ever die."

"What?" I could feel him prodding at the bond, confusion on his end. "Are you having an alpha moment?" he said suspiciously.

Maybe I was but that didn't make me *wrong*.

Ivy had a beautiful grazing spread laid out on the kitchen table for us. Cured meats draped artfully, fat wedges of cheese, dollops of jam and fruit pastes. Bread and crackers fanned on the edges with fruit and nuts sprinkled all over. There were pastries laid out on a tray ready to go in the oven too.

James whistled appreciatively. "Ivy, you didn't have to go to all this trouble." With our addition of curry puffs, skewers and some homemade dips we were going to be rolling into the new year.

She glanced at the pastries and whispered behind her hand. "Those are store-bought. Technically everything is."

"Good." I grinned.

Ivy fetched a bottle of champagne from the fridge. "Anyone? I mean, it's New Year's, right?"

I caught the longing glance Logan gave the six pack of beer he'd brought, right before giving her an enthusiastic yes. I'd never seen more dumb in love behavior.

We cheersed her and gave her the kisses she had asked for in her text. While she was giggly afterward, I still couldn't shake the feeling she wasn't all right.

I wrapped my arm around her waist and pulled her against my hip, head tucked perfectly beneath my chin. I kissed her temple lightly as I breathed her scent in. There was the slightest burned edge to it. Subtle but definitely present. I scent-marked her and she let out a small sigh and leaned into my touch. That was a good sign. "Is everything ok, Ivy?" I asked quietly.

She looked caught for a moment. It disappeared quickly, smoothed over like a clean sheet of ice. "Yes. I'm really glad you're all here."

The scent of charred sugar did not wane.

It went downhill from there. Ivy started drinking more and eating even less.

Logan kept trying to feed her but it seemed like for every bite he managed to get her to take, she offset it with two mouthfuls of champagne. There was always an excuse—she was refining the playlist, she swore she had sparklers tucked away somewhere that she had to find and did we want to play some cards or board games?

"What's wrong with her?" Logan said, pulling me aside. "Why is she not eating? Have we done something?" He'd worked his hair into quite a state from all the stress.

"I asked and she said she was fine."

"So she was lying."

"Yes."

"Fuck, this is going to drive me crazy."

At least I wasn't alone in feeling this way.

James took a pack of cards from Ivy. "Want to play? I can teach you Big Two," he suggested, shuffling them easily.

Yes. Good. Something to keep her hands busy and distract her so we could slip her some more food.

"I'm worried about her too, you know," he murmured privately to me before helping Ivy clear some space on her coffee table.

James and I took a few minutes to explain the rules to Logan and Ivy and soon we were embroiled in a practice round.

"Should I put this down now?" Logan asked, holding up a three of spades next to the three of diamonds in the middle. "Since it's low?"

James peered at his cards. "You should save it because you can . . ." He pointed out several cards in Logan's hand.

"I didn't know that was—"

"Yeah, all spades. A flush. It'll also get rid of—" More pointing. "And it means you can keep *this* as a potential move."

Logan settled back into his cushion looking smug and then threw out a Jack of diamonds.

"Jesus." I stared down at all my single cards. I couldn't put down any of them anymore.

"Oh no." Ivy trembled. "It's too high."

Logan panicked. "I'll take it back."

James stopped him with a laugh. "There'll be other chances to get rid of cards," he assured Ivy. His cheeks were glowing red from only half a glass of champagne and I found him moderately adorable.

Ivy picked up the game quickly and was soon trouncing us even without help from James. Which was an issue because she celebrated every hand she won with a deep drink from her glass.

After I managed to eke out a win, Ivy fell back against the couch. "Gosh, my hand was terrible that time." She stretched her arms to the ceiling and let out a huge yawn. "I really do love this blanket," she sighed, snuggling up against it. I only just managed to catch the last thing she mumbled. "It would've been so perfect in my nest."

Her eyes fluttered closed and a soft snore began to emanate from her.

It was 10:00 p.m.

"I guess she's a sleepy drunk who's good at cards." James shrugged. "Probably the most ideal situation, really."

"How can you joke about this?" Logan bristled.

James gathered up the cards carefully, turning them all one way and letting them fall into his palm neatly. "Look, something was clearly bothering her tonight and she wasn't ready to tell us. We've only been courting her for a week, we can't expect her to spill out everything she's feeling to us yet. You forget that just as we're worried about doing the wrong thing, she's probably feeling the same. And she probably feels it threefold."

Shit, he was clever. I did not manage to hide that emotion in the bond fast enough and James shot me an exasperated look.

"So what do we do then?" Logan asked, massaging the back of his neck.

I thought for a moment. "I think if we leave she will feel awful when she wakes up," I said quietly. "But we haven't been invited into her nest so that's not an option for us."

"Let's put her in her nest, clean up and sleep over where we can out here," James suggested. "Nurse her through the wicked hangover she's going to have tomorrow and hopefully she will feel like she can talk to us then."

Logan wrapped her in the blanket carefully and carried her easily through the house. "Do you think it's ok if we step into her nest so we can put her in it?" he asked anxiously.

"It can't be helped," I reassured him. "There's not much of a chance of you getting your scent on her things but even if you did . . . we know she likes it. She'll understand."

Considering how practical the rest of her house was, Ivy's nest surprised me. It was luxurious and overflowing with soft textures. There was a squeeze of satisfaction as I realized our blanket matched perfectly with the warm neutral shades already there. Like most omegas, her nest mattress took up the majority of the floor in the small room. She had built a protective little circle using cushions and duvets with a giant mountain of pillows on one side where she presumably lay her head.

It felt wrong to be staring at it without her permission. I turned my head away as Logan laid her in the middle.

Once she was settled, we left immediately, closing the door tightly behind us.

Chapter 22

IVY

SOMETHING FURRY HAD CRAWLED INTO MY MOUTH AND DIED.

I got flashbacks of many gulps of champagne. Well, that would certainly explain it. My skin felt like it was stretched too thin and there was someone playing drums on my forehead. The echo in my ears rang faintly of . . . card suits?

Right, I learned how to play Big Two last night. *Diamonds, clubs, hearts, spades.* From James who—

I sat up sharply and almost threw up from the sensation that my head did not follow at the same time as my body.

Oh no.

You invited your pack over for New Year's Eve and instead of ringing in the New Year in your nest, you got drunk and fell asleep before midnight.

I mashed a pillow over my face and let out a silent scream.

Where were they now? Probably at home rethinking this courtship. Omegas were meant to bring packs together, not implode them. I couldn't believe I'd let Sean set up rent free in my head and ruin everything.

I stood up gingerly and wobbled my way down the hallway. Water.

Two giant aspirins. Maybe then the marching band would vacate my skull.

A startled scream trapped in my throat as I nearly stumbled over a dead body. Two feet stuck out lifelessly between my couch and coffee table.

"Oh my god, I'm never drinking again," I wheezed.

I inched forward slowly, wincing at what I was about to find when I entered my living room. What I saw made me feel even worse and made me wish it *had* been a misplaced corpse instead.

Logan, Rome and James were asleep in uncomfortable piles. James was curled up in my armchair, Rome on the couch and Logan was the aforementioned dead body on the floor with a single cushion. They'd given him one of my throws at least.

They slept out here because you never invited them into your nest.

So thoughtful to the point of martyrdom. I could scream from the frustration of putting them in this situation. I tiptoed to the kitchen and found it sparkling. They must have cleaned up last night after I passed out.

"Ivy, you are the absolute worst," I berated myself.

Should I wake them? Invite them into my nest now? I caught a glimpse of myself in a mirror and flinched. Maybe I should look less like I had been mauled by a raccoon first so they wouldn't say no.

I threw back some aspirin along with about a gallon of water before making my way quietly to the bathroom. I stared at my closet as I brushed my teeth, trying to decide what to wear. What would say *I am not in fact a hot mess express, please come into my nest?*

A quiet knock rapped on the door.

They're up. Instant panic.

I threw on a t-shirt, rinsed my mouth furiously and opened the door to a rumpled, slightly worse-for-wear James. Who was still so damn cute even after a terrible night's sleep.

"Are you spiraling in here?" he said with a knowing smile.

"How did you—"

"I was semi-awake and heard you insulting yourself."

Great.

"The others are still out cold though," he said, throwing a look over his shoulder. "Can I come in?"

He asked it so casually, like it wasn't a big deal that he would be entering my nest for the first time.

"Yes." I swallowed and stepped aside for him. Something about seeing him in the space I had worked so hard to make perfect for them cracked something inside me. I gave a low sob and threw my arms around him. He held me tightly, rubbing soothing strokes up and down my back and assuring me it was ok.

"Can you," I stammered into his neck. "I need, um, I want you to—"

"Lie down?"

"Y-yeah."

I started to feel much better when he was propped up against all my pillows. I rubbed my nose impulsively against his shoulder and wondered if it was too soon to ask him to let me have his shirt. His beta scent was fainter compared to the alphas, but after sleeping in it all night, his shirt was creamy, sugary sweet. My fingers fiddled with the buttons, wanting to slide them free and slowly reveal more of his golden skin and feel the toned muscles of his chest.

"Do you want to tell me what was bothering you last night?"

Well, that yanked me firmly back from my fantasy.

I did owe him an explanation. I owed all of them, but it was certainly easier to start with one person.

"Um, this is not my first time being courted." I stole a glance and found him waiting patiently for me to continue. Suddenly, I was grateful that it was James here with me. No chance of triggering some sort of alpha outburst. It made my next words flow easier. "After I graduated college, I started seeing an alpha I'd sort of grown up with. Sean. He asked me to be his omega after a couple of months and I said yes." I let out a resigned breath. "We never even made it close to the bonding stage though. It didn't work out because I should've prioritized him better."

James didn't counter what I'd said but the hard line of his jaw tensed visibly.

It was good that he didn't waste his breath because Sean had been right. Memories of fights rushed by me like passing trains. Our past voices snatched by the wind until only the most devastating words lingered. That time I canceled a date because I had to revise a whole stack of planning documents after a last-minute curriculum change. When I'd promised to cook dinner the same day there had been a terrible bullying incident and I stayed back to mediate. And of course, why I was never ready to go off suppressants so we could spend a heat together.

"When we broke up, he said he was disappointed in me. That I was barely an omega." I forced each painful syllable out. "That got to me harder than losing him, to be honest. I accepted that we weren't compatible but that comment . . . I think I . . . closed off that part of myself for a long time."

I could feel how angry James was on my behalf. There was a stiffness to the way he kissed my forehead and tightened his hold on me.

"Sean comes into town every winter break to visit his parents," I sighed. "I bumped into him at Mariposa's yesterday after I'd gone nest shopping with the girls. H-he made a comment about shopping for my own nest. Reminding me that packs are meant to provide and even though I was being courted, I *still* had to—" I snapped my lips shut and shook my head.

"Ivy."

"It's stupid. But it made me feel so unworthy all over again."

James picked up the blanket they had given me last night and draped it over my shoulders. "This was for your nest, Ivy. It always was." His deep voice was laced with both tenderness and regret.

"It was? But Rome said—"

"He was afraid of scaring you off, Ivy. We're trying to figure this out just as much as you are."

Gosh, we'd all made a mess of things. James played with the ends of my hair, curling and uncurling it around his fingers. "Is it all right if I get the alphas?" he asked me hesitantly.

My reply blossomed warm and ready at the base of my throat. I wanted my nest to feel complete. I had wanted it since last night. Or if I was being entirely truthful with myself, probably since that first morning when I woke up between James and Rome.

"Yes," I whispered.

I wondered if James would tell them what I'd shared with him, but it felt like they were at my door within seconds. Logan was still blearily rubbing sleep out of his eyes but Rome had a little glint of crazy in his. What did it say about me that I *really* liked it?

"Ivy." His roughened tone made something primal inside me sit up. "Can we—"

"*Yes.*"

I practically dragged them in there. The twist of fabric in my fist called to me and I instinctively lowered my nose to Rome's shirt. *Alpha, alpha, alpha.*

"Off," I demanded.

There was something else driving me, my body on auto-pilot. My pack hurriedly shed their slept-in clothes and I hugged them covetously. *This* is what I still needed in my nest. Every item I wove among the lush new bedding sparked a satisfying kind of bliss inside me. The final touches that made a house a home. Once I was done, I settled back onto my pillows with a contented sigh and motioned for them to join me.

Our limbs were tangled, over and under, arms overlapping until the space between us vanished. The heat of their skin on mine, their perfect combined scents. My nest had never felt like this before. I let out a small whimper and buried my nose into Logan's chest.

A gentle purr began to thrum immediately from him. Right beneath his breastbone, the vibration traveling all the way down my spine. The sensation was like a pleasurable head scratch amplified several times over. Behind me, Rome pressed closer, his own purr rumbling against my back.

"You have such a pretty nest, baby," Rome said, burrowing against my neck and leaving his aromatic scent on my skin.

I arched into his touch. "Is it really ok?"

I honestly had no idea.

"I never want to leave," Logan groaned against my hair. "How have you . . . it's just . . . it makes me feel so safe and hidden in a good way."

Despite how tightly the alphas had me sandwiched between them, James still managed to have a leg hooked with mine, our fingers interlaced. "Do you want to tell them what you told me?" he prompted me carefully.

I should. They deserved to know.

It was probably a good thing I'd gotten the story out first with James. I was able to retell it feeling much more detached. Even so, by the time I was done, the alpha purrs were long gone and it felt like I was holding the leashes on two rampaging bloodhounds.

"He's fucking dead," Logan growled.

"Logan," I gasped.

"We'll murder him so quietly for you, baby." Rome's purr was different now, like the rev of a car engine presumably getting ready to run Sean over.

James yanked him back by his hair. "You are a *music* teacher," he scolded his alpha.

"Princess, I'll find out where he lives." Logan was undeterred. "A few little snips and his house will be back in stone ages. Maybe he'll go into debt trying to fix it. Maybe it'll be the first of many terrible incidents that eventually results in him living in a cardboard box somewhere."

"Logan, sometimes your inside thoughts should stay that way," James said after a beat.

I really didn't understand their vehemence. "It was a cruel thing to say but he was right, too. I didn't know how to be a good omega for him," I confessed.

James squeezed my hand. "Ivy, why don't you think you're a good omega?"

"I researched it," I said matter-of-factly. "After we broke up."

"You . . ."

I began to recite my findings, ticking them off on my fingers. "Omegas are able to balance the needs of several alphas. I wasn't able to manage even one. Many omegas find their packs by the age of twenty-four because alphas are driven to want to care for them. I'm thirty-one." I tapped my chin, trying to remember the rest. "I'm also nowhere near the ideal omega's waist-to-hip ratio. Omegas have the highest sex drive of all designations and I have trouble, um, *finishing* sometimes. So even physically I fall outside what's normal."

They gaped at me with horrified expressions.

"All the evidence supports that I am not what is expected of an omega," I said, waving my fingers to emphasize all the points I laid out. "I accepted it a long time ago."

Logan smashed his head into the pillow. "God, I don't even know where to start."

The crazy glint in Rome's eye was back and dare I say it, more insane than ever. "*You* are not supposed to be a one-size-fits-all omega designed to be matched with any alpha." He pressed my fingers down one by one as he countered each argument. "A pack is a living, breathing relationship where all parties contribute to make it work. Does age really matter when it gave us time to become our own people first?"

"I-I don't, um—"

Rome skimmed the shape of my waist, the slow glide worshipful and loving. "I couldn't give a shit what's *normal*, Ivy. You fucking drove me crazy from the day I met you, wondering what was hidden under those sweaters of yours. And now that I know, I'm only more addicted. Addicted to everything that makes you who you are." He kissed me right over my pounding pulse point in my neck. "*Especially* how long we get to enjoy earning every single one of those orgasms of yours."

I had no words. He'd ruined me, broken me down brick by brick.

Logan gently nudged my chin, turning me to face him. "I wish I'd been brave enough to court you earlier," he confessed. "But I don't think either of us were ready."

Years of polite smiles exchanged seemed silly now.

"There's nothing to regret, though. I think you were meant to bring us together." He swallowed thickly. "I think you were meant to make us a pack."

Me? But I'd barely done anything.

"Pack Winter has a nice ring to it, doesn't it?"

I stared at James, propped up on his elbow and casually tossing a proverbial stick of dynamite into the already volatile chaos of emotions.

"You can't," I protested.

"Why not?"

"It's meant to be one of yours," I said, looking between Rome and Logan.

James tilted his head. "Is it? This pack is whatever we want it to be."

All those years of wondering what the intimacy of pack life looked like. Trying to figure out what an omega was supposed to *do*. I looked around at my nest, imbued with scents I'd come to crave and the men I cared for.

Was it really that simple?

I was intimately aware of all the ways we were touching. How easy it would be to close the distance between us all. Guide a grasping palm to the aching parts of me and stroke the hardening flesh against my thigh until it—

My stomach growled loudly, a rude and uncouth intruder smashing the dreamy atmosphere of my nest.

"Oh no." It happened again and I shrank, hugging my traitorous tummy. My night of drinking on an empty stomach was catching up on me at the worst possible time. I couldn't believe we'd just become a pack with a *name*. There was a brief pang of disappointment, worried I'd ruined the moment somehow.

But Rome just kissed my nose. "I think we can all do with some food," he chuckled. "And if you're willing to let one of us have at least a pair of pants back, we can grab some fresh clothes too."

As much as I didn't want to pillage my perfect nest, I was not about to feed the town's rumor mill for a month by having a naked alpha leave my house.

"No need to rush this," James reassured me. "Whatever we want it to be, ok?"

"Whatever we want it to be," I repeated, feeling hopeful in a way I hadn't felt in a very, very long time.

Chapter 23

IVY

I STARED AT MY CALENDAR, WILLING IT TO FLIP BACKWARD and tell me that school was *not* in fact returning in two days. It remained stubbornly static, as did the mountain of prep work I still had left to do.

Logan was doing some maintenance upgrades for Stanley at the town hall. I had already received several texts outlining ways the mayor's demise could be disguised as an accident.

But nothing was as rude as James sending me a *single* photograph of a kitten in his scrubs pocket and then presumably getting too caught up in work to respond.

I was working from home, papers fanned across my dining room table and giving myself future back problems in my unergonomic chair. At least, I was *trying* to work. As was Rome, who was seated on my couch in plain view.

We both knew inviting him over to work was a thinly veiled excuse to spend the day together. And by spend the day together, we meant attempting to steal glances from across my living room.

I didn't know why he was sitting like that. Knees wide open, sleeves rolled up. Flashing those exposed forearms every time he scraped a runaway lock of hair back. He stuck his pen into the corner of his mouth and I chewed on my lip. My thoughts were consumed with crawling into laps. Touching, exploring. With tentative fingers to whole palms then hungry mouths.

It was pornographic and I wasn't sure how I was supposed to work under such conditions.

"You're perfuming, Ivy," Rome stated easily, not looking up from his work.

I forced myself to tear my eyes away. "I need to switch seats," I mumbled.

"If you think that will help."

I plonked myself down on the opposite side of the table, reshuffling my laptop and papers to face me. *Focus*, I told myself. Lesson plans first. Then your classroom setup to-do list. That was the bare minimum of what I had to accomplish today. I'd never left things this last minute before.

Not looking at Rome did nothing to alleviate all the *other* ways his presence was affecting me. The letters on my page danced as his spiced wine scent filled me with a heated ache. I pulled my collar away from my neck as I inevitably slid into a daydream again.

We went on a pack date yesterday. There was a poetic brilliance to what they'd planned—making up for (almost) all the ways their individual dates had gone wrong. We skated without incident on the last day the rink was open. Gorged ourselves silly on everything Rome picked for us at Elephant Corridor. The banana leaf–wrapped lamprais were a hit but to no one's surprise, the spicy pickle dish achcharu was my favorite. Was I an independent woman? Maybe not anymore because I *really* liked sitting down, making no decisions and having delicious food appear for me. Finally, we stopped in at La Dolce Vita for Antonio's famous tiramisu before heading back to my place clutching our middles.

Chez Lumiere, we all agreed, was an experience that did not need reliving.

They were a bit too ambitious with their plans in the end. Logan put on a film that had lots of explosions and not a single succulent plant in sight. I fell asleep before the heist team had even formed. I got carried to my nest—again—but this time, they knew to snuggle in with me.

After a full night exposed to the delirious cocktail of scents it was no wonder I had this . . . *need* building inside me. What had been done about it? Absolutely nothing. All I got were very thorough good-bye kisses from Logan and James this morning which made things worse. No wonder I'd practically begged Rome to bring his work over and spend the day with me.

I crossed and uncrossed my legs uncomfortably.

"How is your lesson plan coming along, Ivy?"

My blinking cursor mocked me from a blank page.

"Great," I lied.

"Are you having trouble focusing?"

Rome's tone was so *mild* it made me crazier. How was he so calm when I was sitting here roasting alive?

"Nope." I couldn't hide the grit this time.

"Good." A beat passed. "I'm glad you suggested working together, I'm making excellent progress."

I spun around to face him. "I'm sorry, but *how*?" I flung at him accusingly. If I was perfuming then his alpha scent was certainly responding to it. The air was thick with citrus and spice swimming in dark wine. Drunk, hazy. Clouding my judgment with every breath.

No wonder it took me longer to notice the long, hard shape against his thigh.

"You *liar*." I marched furiously. "Show me how much you've done."

He snapped his laptop closed with a hard click. "That's confidential."

"We work at the same school!" I snapped, reaching for his stack of papers. He dodged me easily and I scrambled over him, trying to snatch them from his grasp. *Stupid tall alpha with long arms to match.* "I want to see what you've done so far!"

Rome held them high over his head, a smirk fighting to escape those full lips of his. I couldn't get ahold of them despite my best efforts. But I could see there was no writing anywhere matching the blue pen he'd been practically making out with earlier.

"You haven't written anything on them!"

"They were simply for reference."

"Sorry, since when is blank sheet music for reference?"

Rome tossed them aside and they scattered haphazardly across my living room floor. His hands bracketed my waist and he yanked me down hard, setting me firmly in place in his lap.

"Do you have a problem with how I plan my lessons, Ms. Winter?"

Holy hell. I'd been called "Ms. Winter" for the better part of the last decade but it had *never* sounded like that. I squirmed and his hard bulge settled deeper against my core.

What was the question again?

"Do you know what *I* have a problem with?"

"What's that?" I asked thinly.

His hands were sliding up my thighs and spanning wide over my ass, his grip possessive.

"You thinking you're not a good omega." He leaned close, his breath fluttering against my bare neck. "While you're sitting there all pretty and perfuming, filling the room with the scent of your slick."

I choked back an indignant gasp. "You're lying. You can't detect that."

Rome hummed. "It's so much more than that, Ivy." His throat bobbed simply from the graze of his nose against my skin. "It's everything your body is telling me just from how sweet you smell. It feels like . . . matchsticks. Striking me all over. My instincts want me to tend to you and give you what you need."

He combed his fingers through my hair. "You know it's a two-way street, right?"

"What do you mean?"

He placed a firm hand on the back of my neck. That alone made a very innate part of me go *weak*. My nose slid against his warm brown skin.

"Don't think. Read what my scent is telling you and do what feels right."

There was a flash of a familiar scene—Logan and I, except I was guiding *his* head to my neck.

Scent me.

I'd done it in the heat of the moment, without thinking. Being governed by our designations didn't have to be a curse. Not when we could understand each other this way, speak without words this way.

I let Rome's alluring scent fill my lungs. Limbs loosened and the edges of my world softened.

My hand snaked beneath his clothes. I relished the catch of his breath at the first electric touch of skin. His scent subtly changed. More of that alpha need, calling to me and drawing me in.

I unbuttoned and pushed aside his shirt slowly, admiring how the sunlight drew golden shapes across the contours of his chest. The intricate patterns of ink sprawled over his shoulder were beautiful. I ran the pad of my thumb along the strong line of his neck, leaning down to press a kiss where his pulse thudded. His scent flooded my senses harder as my tongue darted out to mark him with my own, blurring the line between us further.

"I told you . . . your instincts were perfect."

So much held back behind those clenched teeth.

I continued to dot kisses around the base of his groaning throat as I slid the zip of his pants down. Fabric pooled at his feet, his thick cock laying hard and ready against his abs. His alpha rose closer to the surface, wanting to take over. Dissatisfied with my slow exploration.

I undressed carefully and the light shifted in his pupils as Rome's ironclad will faltered. "Such a good omega for me," he said, a hint of a purr rolling across his words. The cool air hit the slick coating my inner thighs as I spread myself over his lap again. I let my weight relax, my pussy settling right on top of his partially swollen knot.

"Fuck." He shuddered. "Are you trying to make me break, Ivy?"

I leaned close, my hair falling to one side like a curtain. "I want my alpha," I whispered softly into the shell of his ear.

Then I bared my teeth and—without breaking skin—bit deliberately into the strained muscle between his neck and shoulder.

The snap of his control felt so incredibly *loud*. An unstoppable, primal force. Fueled with the same energy that drove a guitarist to shatter their instrument against a sweat-soaked stage.

Rome sheathed himself deep inside with me with a single, powerful stroke. My teeth lost their grip as I cried out into his shoulder. The stretch was more than I expected but *god*, I loved it. I could barely remember what it had felt like to have him during my heat and I didn't know how badly my body had been craving him until now.

"God, baby. You feel—" I didn't catch the rest, his lips muffled by my cheek and hair.

Even if I wanted to ride him, I couldn't. He was holding my hips, fucking up into me relentlessly. I wrapped my arms around his neck, every pounding thrust creating a hurtling friction between our bodies. My pebbled nipples across his hard chest. His knot rocking against my clit.

"So fucking wet and made for me. Dripping all over my cock." My fingers seized in his hair at his filthy words. "Are you close already, baby?"

He already knew I was. It was written all over me, in the shake of my thighs, the clench of my pussy. That mind-numbing *spot* he was hitting over and over.

"Rome, *god*," I begged.

Maybe it was how his pace stuttered for one brief moment before he surged up into me even harder than before. Or maybe it was the punch of dominant alpha pheromones straight into my hindbrain. Or his consuming, hungry kiss, holding me by the nape of my neck. Probably all of it at once, really. I came with a thin scream, riding out each powerful convulsion to the sound of his praise.

"Look at you, baby." Another rough kiss. "Coming so pretty for your alpha."

I collapsed against him, breathing hard. "Nest," I managed to get out. "Want you in my nest."

Rome lifted me easily and I whined as soon as he slid out of me.

"God, soon. I promise, you can have it back soon."

I bit him again in the hallway and he swore, crashing us against the wall and fucking back into me.

He groaned. "Shit, I—"

Another ragged thrust.

"We're . . . almost at your nest."

I gave the tiniest shake of my head against his shoulder and he cursed again. Rome adjusted his hold on me, my legs hooked firmly over his arms, spreading me wide as he watched his cock disappear inside me. I rolled my hips against him, my slick letting me rub my clit easily against his hard knot.

"I want to come like this, alpha."

"*Fuck*."

I decided then and there that I had to be an omega through and through because I *loved* his knot. If I wasn't riding it then I wanted it inside me. I imagined palming it in my hands as I sucked his cock. Finding all the ways I could grind against it no matter what position he was taking me in. And finally having it lock tight inside me. The slight sting. The *stretch*. *God*. He would let me have it soon, right?

My head fell back, baring the column of my neck to him. He scraped his teeth along it and I felt myself rushing toward release.

"You're going to make me lose control," he snarled. "Bond you right here and now."

Too soon, rang a warning bell somewhere in the foggy recesses of my mind.

"Mark me, instead," I said desperately. "Suck on my neck and give me a—"

My last word disappeared in a choked inhale as he latched onto me furiously. I was going to bruise in the perfect shape of his mouth.

"I'm going to do this for real one day."

A soft, drawn out lick over sensitive flesh.

"You're mine, omega."

The orgasm that seized me certainly felt like it belonged to him.

We were moving again. Rome threw open the door to my nest. We dropped onto the mattress and he pulled away, leaving me sprawled and panting on my back.

"Rome, what are you . . ."

I stared up at the black, possessive gaze of an alpha teetering on the edge of rut. Without heat pheromones, the likelihood of him tipping over the line was slim. But his alpha was the one in control here and there was only one thing he wanted right now.

I swallowed, knowing it was *me*.

"Present for your alpha," Rome demanded. A trace of his alpha bark filtered through. Command and dominance laced through every word. Assuring my omega that I was safe. Cherished. The most overwhelming urge to get on my hands and knees consumed me. I flipped onto my front, my ass rising into the air and exposing *everything* to him.

Waiting for him to touch me was achingly slow. I jerked as he cupped my pussy firmly in his large hand.

"This is mine." I could hear the *predator* rippling in his voice. His other palm was heavy on the small of my back. I bent lower, my cheek against the sheets. "I won't be satisfied until I've fucked you full of my cum."

I whimpered when I felt the rounded head of his cock nudge against me.

"Yes," I whispered, pushing back against him and letting my pussy sink a little over his tip. "I want it. *Please.*"

He drove back inside me to the hilt. It was madness. Wild. As close to a claiming as it could be without my blood on his tongue. My body was driven by pure, lust-soaked *need* like a heat. Yet my mind was present, writing the feel of him into my DNA. Long powerful strokes, the sound filthy and wet as my pussy clung to him greedily.

"Finish inside me." My throat was hoarse from crying out each time his knot thudded against me. It already felt huge and I didn't know how it was going to fit let alone expand even further inside me.

Rome snarled and fisted my hair. "You feel what you've done to me, baby? Can you take all of it?"

"Yes," I begged.

His chest curved over my back, sweat mingling with mine. Cinnamon. Cloves. We matched so perfectly. He palmed my breast and roamed down my stomach. Clever fingers swirled slick over my clit until my pussy clenched hard around his shaft. Only then did he grunt and push his knot deep, slurring my name as he came. He swelled and locked easily, *perfectly*, right against my G-spot. I felt the heat of him spill and spill inside me, each convulsion of my pussy coaxing more cum out of him.

"You wrecked me, baby." I wasn't sure if Rome was even aware he was talking, eyes half-lidded and mumbling against my skin.

I wanted to wear it like a badge of pride. *I did that to him.*

He let our joined bodies fall gently into the nest and pulled me against him possessively. I went slack against him. Safe. Warm. Sated. My world slowly faded down to the caress of his hand along my body. Along the top of my breast, sneaking down to trace the curved underside. Following my sternum and splaying wide fingers across my stomach. I traced up and down his forearm, our own language without words.

His knot remained inflated for a lot longer than I expected. Half an hour at least, if not more. When he finally loosened and slid out of me, he pushed my thighs back together immediately.

"Don't lose it. I want you to keep my cum inside you."

Possessive, feral beast.

It was almost frightening how much I loved it.

Rome rolled onto his back, his tattoo warping as he stretched his long body out. His half-hard cock was covered in slick and cum, listing to one side against his belly. Despite three orgasms and being fucked senseless all over my house . . . I wanted a taste.

"Alpha," I whispered.

His eyebrow rose as he followed my line of vision. He fisted the base, fingers wrapping around his deflated knot. "You want more?"

I averted my eyes and nodded. He nudged my chin, forcing me to face him as he rose onto his knees. "Never be ashamed of needing anything from your pack."

I couldn't hold back a moan as I sucked his cock between my lips. My tongue explored along his crown, sliding down to lick his shaft too. I cleaned him thoroughly, streaks of white disappearing and leaving his length glistening. His grunts were dim and far away as I focused on my task. I was doing it for *me*, because I couldn't get enough of the taste of us. Feeling him grow heavy on my tongue as I bobbed and stroked him back to hardness.

Rome let me play for as long as he could hold out before he was between my thighs, easing his way back into me again.

I sighed with satisfaction. His cock had barely left me all morning yet it was somehow not enough.

"Such a greedy little pussy." He swiped my clit and I bucked against him. "So full of your alpha's cum."

The wet sound as he pushed deeper into me was unmistakable.

"Tell me, Ivy. Do you like taking your alpha's cock and coming all over it?"

Every rational thought scattered when he spoke like that. "Rome, please."

He kissed me, my top lip caught gently between his, one hand cradling my cheek. All while he *held* himself inside me without thrusting, working my clit and teasing the most slow-building, melting orgasm out of me.

I clung to him even as the aftershocks dissipated. My abdomen ached from clenching so hard, a thin layer of sweat beading my brow. He was still hard inside me, the heft and feeling of fullness so satisfying. There was such a quiet intimacy being with him like this, his kisses close by and the way he stroked my hair back from my damp forehead.

"Rome." My voice came out shaky. Vulnerable.

"I know, baby."

Time? Responsibilities? What were those? I didn't care about anything except my alpha right now. I wrapped my arms and legs around him possessively. Needing more of this. More of *him*.

"I can do this for as long as you want me." He was dotting little kisses all over my cheek and jaw. "I'll be so good for you, Ivy, I promise. Tell me what you need."

I shuddered. "I want to stay in my nest all day and keep you inside me," I managed to rasp.

"Why?"

"Because you're mine." My throat tightened. "And good omegas take care of what's theirs."

Rome groaned and scent-marked me. His hand woven in my hair, tongue and teeth and lips against the sensitive spot right behind my ear. It was pointless, we were so intertwined yet I still chased his scent like it was the first time.

"You're perfect." He began to rock against me. "Now come for me again."

Chapter 24

IVY

I CHECKED THE CLOCK ON THE WALL OF MY CLASSROOM FOR
the third time in ... how had it been twenty minutes already? If time
was a standardized unit of measurement, why was it moving so fast?
Served me right. I'd never left things so last minute before and I was
being thoroughly punished for it. My head was in shambles, and I
had an odd feeling there was something I had forgotten. The big
hour hand crept closer to 8:00 a.m. and the mandatory morning
briefing with the entire faculty.

For a brief, mad moment I considered skipping it so I could finish
setting up my classroom but promptly chased that thought away.
No, Jeff would kill me or at the very least berate me within earshot of
a colleague who would give me superior looks about it afterward. I
stuffed Christmas decorations away in a storage tub while I tried to
figure out my learning theme for the next couple of weeks. At least
my new seating plan was done and I had a barely passable lesson plan
meted out for the first day back.

In the final dying seconds before 8:00 a.m., I hurriedly stuck a
solar system poster on the wall—unlaminated! So unlike me—and
rushed to the teachers' lounge. I squeezed into the already packed
room, offering quick greetings to the other teachers.

"Ivy, I thought you'd be front and center as per usual," chortled Tom, our PE teacher who lived in shorts all year round.

"Not today, I guess," I replied, frazzled.

One of the other elementary teachers accosted me. "Want us to shuffle along so you can head over in *that* direction?" Francine tittered behind her hand.

"Nope, I'm perfect right here," I said firmly.

It was important that I nipped that in the bud immediately. Rome was already here, leaning against the far wall and I stayed exactly where I was near the door. We had both agreed to keep our interactions at school professional even though I knew word of our courtship had spread.

There was no need to feed the gossip mill, so I pointedly ignored him. I did not need to be thinking about what we had been doing two days ago. Especially not the way he had handed me over to Logan that evening before heading home. How I had been too wrung out to do anything but sleep but was more than willing to let my big alpha do some territory marking the next morning.

I recognized Rome's not-so-subtle cough from across the room. I'd slathered myself in No-NonScent Deodorant as a preemptive measure so he must have read it all over my face. Embarrassed, I dropped my head, giving the worn patch of multi-colored carpet between my shoes a very thorough examination.

Think about seating charts. Fractions. The effects of La Niña and El Niño on global weather patterns.

Much better.

"Gooooood morning, everyone!" Jeff called out, clearly angling for a new job as an announcer. Too bad he had the gravitas—and physique too if I squinted a little—of a lemur. "Are we pumped for the second half of the year?"

I cringed internally at the silence that followed. Not sure what Jeff was expecting; our brains were still asleep.

"Now as you know, we had a power outage over winter break," Jeff continued undeterred. "Rest assured maintenance has confirmed everything is back up and running smoothly. If you run into any issues, let Bruce know."

Thank god all evidence of our *activities* during that power outage had long been scrubbed clean, our scents dissipating to nothing in the chilly winter air.

Jeff began to drone on about our academic goals for the semester and upcoming curriculum changes to expect. I could see everyone's attention wandering, filtering out what wasn't relevant to them. But it only stressed me out more, my to-do list growing longer by the minute.

"And most exciting of all, I've gotten word that Preston Eberhart himself wants to stop by to make an *important announcement*." Jeff emphasized the last two words with a clap of his hands. "So, we'll be having a special assembly at the end of the week. I've got a good feeling about this, folks. I think one of us has won that grant money."

I perked up. The Preston Eberhart Educator Empowerment and Excellence Grant. I hadn't expected a result so soon. But it couldn't have come at a better time. I crossed everything that my application had been enough.

"Rome, I'd like you to prepare a performance for the occasion."

"Sure," he said easily. "The choir and I will put something together."

Jeff beamed. "Wonderful. Don't forget your team meetings after school this Wednesday."

Gosh, like I already didn't have enough to do.

"Let's have a great first day back, everyone!" Jeff pumped his fist in the air and held it, living out his freeze frame movie dreams. I died a little inside from the secondhand embarrassment.

I wondered if I could sneak a quick hello to Rome—nothing salacious, a squeeze of his hand and maybe an eyelash flutter too while I was at it—when Robyn grabbed me.

"Ow." Her nails pinched into my arm.

"Oops, sorry about that Ivy! You looked like you were in such a rush, I didn't want you to get away."

Her wide frog-like smile filled my vision. Over her shoulder, Rome met my eyes for the briefest moment before disappearing out the door. I sighed internally. Maybe I could say hi during recess instead.

"Hello, did you hear me?"

"Hmm?"

"I *said*, did you get the IEP done?"

I stared at her blankly. "What IEP?"

Robyn huffed. "You said you'd do the IEP for me for my incoming student."

Did I?

She was extremely unimpressed by my silence. "Remember? Because you did Tanner's already," she said slowly, enunciating each word carefully like I was an idiot.

I got a flash of a distant memory from last semester. Robyn had asked me . . . *something* about her IEP. She had a huge bow around her neck. I didn't remember Robyn needing me to write the whole thing but by the way she was tap-tap-tapping her shoe impatiently on the floor, I must have forgotten.

"I can't believe this, Ivy," she said, frustrated. "He starts *today*."

This was Robyn's first time having an autistic student in her class. I felt awful that I'd let him down. His first day would set the tone for how he felt about the class and the last thing I wanted was for him to struggle from the outset.

"I'm so sorry," I apologized, distressed. "I'll do it during recess. You can handle the morning at least, right?"

"I'm going to have to, I guess," Robyn said sullenly.

"If he has comfort items, make sure to explain to the class that it's part of helping him learn," I rifled off desperately, hoping Robyn would not lose any tenuous trust the new student might place in her within those first few hours. "Assure him he can take a quiet break if he feels overwhelmed at any point."

"Yeah ok, Ivy." Robyn walked off, waving a hand dismissively behind her.

I trudged through the long halls back to my classroom, feeling like a leaden weight was on my back. My students were lined up outside waiting for me, and I squared my shoulders with a deep breath and put on my game face.

"Hi Ms. Winter!"

"Happy New Year!"

"Ms. Winter, did you hear the news about Robbie?"

The familiar warmth rushed back in. I'd missed them. And this was where I was supposed to be.

So you had a bit of a shaky start to the semester. It happens. You'll get back into the swing of things soon.

"So lovely seeing your faces again." I smiled broadly, opening the door. "Come in, everyone!"

My students poured inside, many of them racing to the thriving fish tank. I heard a couple of them say *Hi, Fish James* and tucked away my grin. After what had happened at the start of the break, James installed an automatic feeder for me. Still, I made the effort to check in during the break when I could and there had luckily been no more power outages. Everyone found their new seats, chattering away excitedly.

"Did you hear about Robbie, Ms. Winter?" Riley asked again eagerly.

I shook my head as I leaned against my desk, wondering what news Riley O'Hara had about her brother in tenth grade.

"He went *viral*," Riley said in an awed tone, her eyes saucer-wide. "His piano cover of *Fever Love* got over a *million* views. Blissa Nova even commented and reposted it!"

I only understood half of those words.

The rest of the class, however, burst into noise, either to add that they had seen it too or asking for more details.

"That's amazing," I gushed anyway. "How is he feeling?"

"Already practicing his next cover like *crazy* and planning on posting it tonight." Riley glowed, clearly so excited for her big brother.

I wondered if Rome had heard about this yet. I made a mental note to ask him later.

"All right, class." I clapped my hands to get their attention. "Let's kick off the new semester with a quick writing exercise—I want to hear how your winter break was." I smiled at the satisfying sound of twenty-five exercise books being opened.

Chapter 25

IVY

I WAS A HAMSTER ON A WHEEL. RUNNING AND RUNNING and staying in the exact same place.

Robyn got the bare bones of an IEP I threw together during recess and I promised to walk her through the rest tomorrow. I was on cafeteria duty for lunch and then when I finally thought I could get back to my own work after school, Jeff stuck his head into my classroom.

"Fundraising initiatives. Can you get the ball rolling on that? You've done a lot of that sort of thing for the town, haven't you?"

I think he was referring to all the festival participation Stanley had unwillingly roped me into.

"S-sure."

He clicked his fingers appreciatively. "Knew I could count on you."

My to-do list resembled a CVS receipt at this point.

Rome came by at 5:00 p.m., made sure the corridors, classroom and outside the window were all clear before kissing me stupid.

"Missed you."

I sighed, feeling warm for the first time all day.

"Ready to head off?" he said, lightly massaging the nape of my neck and turning me into a happy little puddle.

My incomplete planning documents mocked me from my desk.

"I've still got a lot to do." I rubbed his stubbled cheek affectionately. "You go though."

"Not without you," he said stubbornly.

"I won't be long. Promise."

He gave me a piercing look, kissed me again and grudgingly left.

My solar system lesson plans consumed the rest of my evening. I tapped my pen on my chin, wondering how I could get a scale model exercise going. Maybe using buttons and string for each student? I made a mental note to talk to Lucy and see if she had any spare buttons I could steal. My supply closet had been limping along on hopes and dreams since last semester, my roll of brown kraft paper a sad little tube and rationing Post-it notes like they were made of gold. I wondered if I'd be able to get one last big wall project out of it.

It only served as a reminder that the grant was being announced in a matter of days. But just in case, I'd better think of some ideas that did not require me dipping into supplies.

Kids, close your eyes and imagine you're an astronaut!

It was almost 8:30 p.m. when I looked at the time again. Where had my evening gone? I hadn't even started thinking about fundraising ideas for Jeff. I rubbed my eyes, wincing when I saw a barrage of texts from my pack.

5:17PM

JAMES

Hope you had a good day! I had TWO anxious poopers today

LOGAN

Why would you share this

JAMES

For anyone out there listening so they feel less alone

6:33PM
ROME
Have you left yet, baby?

JAMES
I'm in the kitchen

ROME
I am CLEARLY not talking to you

LOGAN
Are you inviting me over Rome?
Because I think of you as a pack brother
nothing more

JAMES
Hahahaha

6:35PM
ROME
Did James just run next door?

LOGAN
Yes. To high five me

ROME
This chat is dumb whose idea
was it

7:02PM
ROME
Baby please tell me you're leaving soon.
You have to be getting hungry, right?

JAMES
Ivy, come by for dinner if you want.
I'm making chicken and rice.

He'd added the cutest photo of himself grinning at the stove in front of a huge stockpot.

7:13PM
LOGAN
Princess, do you normally work this late?

I don't know what James has done to this chicken but it's so good if you don't get here I'm going to eat it all

JAMES
He's lying, he already put aside a plate for you

7:45PM
ROME
We're getting worried baby

Text us when you see this

8:19PM
LOGAN UNSENT A MESSAGE.

ROME UNSENT A MESSAGE.

ROME UNSENT A MESSAGE.

LOGAN UNSENT A MESSAGE.

JAMES

> Ignore the alphas being . . . alphas. Sweetheart, I know you probably just got caught up in your work. But please let us know when you're leaving.

They were adorable and hilarious and I'd missed all of it.

> I'm so sorry, I lost track of time!

> I'm leaving now, I promise!

Before I got in the car, I sent them a tired selfie, both as proof of life and showing that I was actually on my way home.

ROME

> Thank god

LOGAN

> Next time ask one of us to come walk you to your car, it's too dark

I glanced up at the bright glare of the streetlamps. Stanley could be a bit much but he was fanatical about making sure safety standards were exceeded in our town.

> But then I would have to wait around longer.

I added the emoji with the biggest sad face.

> **LOGAN**
> Ok fuck don't do that
>
> Drive safe
>
> **JAMES**
> I'll cook for you again another night

It started to rain as I pulled out of SGS, hammering noisily on my windshield. The miserable weather sapped any remaining energy I might have had left as I ran up my front steps, feeling like a drowned rat by the time I made it inside.

I definitely wished I hadn't missed out on dinner with the others now. I grabbed myself some crackers, cheese and made a cup-a-soup (did that count as a hot dinner?) and sank into the couch in front of an old episode of *The Grand Sugar Rush Showdown*.

> I'm really tired so will probably have an early night
>
> Good night

I added three kissy faces (one for each of them obviously), and fell asleep as the judges were fighting over meringue. The entire rest of the season had happily finished streaming in the background by the time I jerked awake at 11:00 p.m. I pointedly ignored the drool puddle I had created on my cushion, dragged myself to my nest and passed out again.

The rest of the week didn't improve very much. Rome made a habit of stopping by at the end of the day, urging me to leave when he did. It became easier to not argue and take the work home with me instead. But the things I couldn't do from home—like laminating cards and printing handouts—I left for when I snuck in earlier in the morning. It was rough trying to whip my body back to its previous efficiency after it had been lounging in holiday mode for two weeks.

But despite my late nights and early mornings, something still managed to fall through the cracks. I had completely forgotten I needed math blocks for my morning lesson and another teacher had already reserved them. I pivoted to the best of my ability but I could've done better. *Should've* done better. Inside I was berating myself, upset that I'd let something like this happen.

It just wasn't like me.

My Thursday evening was spent pretending I knew a lick of graphic design, making flyers for an art auction and read-a-thon. I was extra mad as I clicked through cartoon stock photos of books because I had sent Jeff a bunch of fundraising ideas yesterday and all he replied with was "yes."

I was more than happy to abandon it when there was a knock on my door.

"Surprise!"

Rome, James and Logan. My heart gave a little pitter patter seeing them all together after a long week.

But the true object of my affection was the bag of Chinese takeout James was holding.

"Did you get new jobs as delivery boys at Red Lantern without telling me?" I said with an arch of my brow.

Before Rome and Logan could answer, James jumped in. "Maybe. Would you still date us?"

I pretended to consider it. "Only if you brought orange chicken."

James pumped his fist. "You two can wait outside, that was my pick," he said, before trying to close the door on two outraged alphas.

"Ivy, we've missed you," Logan grunted, shoving his way past James. "And you weren't answering."

I wasn't answering? I winced as I finally noticed the flood of missed texts. *Again.*

"I didn't even realize it was so late," I said feebly. Their timing was perfect as I had drunk my last cup-a-soup yesterday. I was keeping that fact to myself as I didn't think they would approve of my dietary habits.

They made themselves at home easily, fishing plates and cutlery from my cupboards. It only made me feel worse that I had seen so little of them.

"First week back is always manic," I said quietly, wanting to explain myself. "Especially since I didn't do any of my usual prep work leading up to the first day." I stroked Logan's arm reassuringly and he wrapped me tightly against him. "I'm still adjusting to pack life as well. Bear with me, please?"

Rome lifted the back of my hand to his lips. "You know we're always here to help," he offered.

I knew he meant well but it didn't seem feasible. I wasn't about to put Logan and James to work cutting out flash cards after they'd already worked all day. Plus, it wasn't like I could hand my reports and assessments over to Rome.

Nevertheless, I gave them a smile. "Stay in my nest tonight?" I asked. That should help the undercurrent of tension I was feeling and slight bitter edge of their scents.

The effect was immediate, their shoulders loosening as they reached out to touch me. Reconnecting in my nest was what we needed, even if it was just for sleep. Simple. Doable. Right?

I was sure I could manage everything.

Chapter 26

IVY

PRESTON EBERHART LOOKED EXACTLY LIKE HIS NAME sounded. He wore a pinstripe suit, had a mustache big enough to twirl and his blood was bluer than the paint I had spilled this morning trying to draw Uranus. He stood out among the sea of students and occasional bored staff members in the assembly crowd.

I bored my eyes into the back of that perfectly coiffed head, willing him to stand up and give the grant to me.

Annoyingly, he leaned over to whisper something to Jeff and then laughed uproariously at his own joke.

The choir had shuffled their way to the front of the stage, made up of a mix of students from middle and high school. Rome's expression was calm as he murmured a quick word of encouragement before he turned his back to the audience, preparing to lead.

I didn't get to see him in his element nearly often enough, I decided.

The performance was lovely, but knowing he had arranged it and rehearsed it with them in such a short time made me admire him even more. I hadn't been the only one sacrificing my lunch times this week to work.

"God, that's a good view, isn't it?"

I bristled, my head swinging sharply in the direction of the voices, immediately going on high alert. *My alpha.* My vision went red, infuriated that the whole assembly could see what was mine.

Robyn was being elbowed hard by Francine. A lot of furious whispers were exchanged before both their gazes caught on mine for a brief second and skittered away immediately.

I overheard Robyn's indignant hiss. "Why did no one tell me? How was I supposed to know? I've been out of town the entire winter break!"

What would she have done if she did know?

I conjured a million terrible scenarios all at once. And a million more equal and justifiable retaliations for each.

The sound of applause cut through my thoughts of eyeball scooping. I couldn't believe I'd zoned out for nearly the entire performance. I felt terrible watching the children file back to their seats.

I caught Rome's eye from across the hall.

Need you.

We didn't have a bond, yet I felt the tether between us light up. My anxiety zigzagged to him, all my insecurities crackling in the air between us.

Rome strode purposefully toward me, down the narrow gap next to rows of seated students. I didn't even notice Jeff going on stage. Barely heard him introduce Preston. All I could focus on was my alpha.

It took everything not to leap into his arms and bite down on that hard muscle between his neck and shoulder in front of everyone.

He knew just the right thing to do though. Rome slipped behind me and wound his arm around my waist, his palm flat against my stomach.

"Are you all right?" he said it so quietly I could barely hear him.

"I heard . . ." Saying it out loud felt stupid. "Robyn said you looked good."

He didn't laugh. He could have and I would have wholly agreed with him. Instead he used his nose to push the round neck of my sweater to the side so he could place a kiss directly on my skin.

Oh. That was wonderful.

"Settle, baby. I'm yours." His scent enveloped me, the warm reassurance detaching me from all my problems. My racing heart slowed. The sound of blood in my ears quieted.

I couldn't believe such a tiny thing had set me off.

It's because you didn't get enough time with your pack this week.
Fix that and things will be better.

I turned my attention back to the stage where Preston had taken over the mic to the sound of polite applause.

"Guess we're going to find out who gets the PEEEEG. Oink."

"*Shh.*"

Preston grasped the lectern and squared his shoulders. "I have made my fortune in the big wide world. But let me tell you . . . I am a Starlight Grove boy at heart."

Oh boy. I didn't realize we were here for Preston Eberhart's life story.

"And all I want is for people to recognize the greatness"—He gestured grandly—"that lies hidden here. We are sleeping giants and our future is bright."

I had no idea what Preston was talking about. I glanced around and found a mixture of confusion and boredom among the students.

Preston was undeterred and continued orating like an emperor addressing his subjects.

"Some may ask why the Preston Eberhart Educator Empowerment

and Excellence Grant only gets awarded to one teacher. Why just one, Preston? Surely everyone deserves it? They sure do. That's why I also fund grants specifically for STEM. Literacy. Even professional development if your superstar teachers wish to pursue that!" He placed his hand on his chest magnanimously. "But this one, this one's special."

Special how?

"Because I am the sole decider of the recipient of this grant, and I choose the ones who wake the sleeping giant."

Maybe I shouldn't have bothered outlining my specific plans for the grant money in my application. Needn't have researched and provided the far reaching educational impacts of each initiative. Maybe I should've drawn a picture of a giant bell if Preston was going to ride this stupid metaphor to the bitter end.

"This grant is for someone who has brought more eyes to this school and what we are capable of. I cannot even tell you how thrilled I was to see Starlight Grove's own Robbie O'Hara make the news for his wonderful piano covers. Such talent! I couldn't believe it."

Wait, what? Surely the basis of Preston's grant rewarding wasn't hinging on Robbie's lightning in a bottle fame.

"As soon as I saw that, I knew. I said to myself . . . what better use of the money than to make sure our future Robbie O'Haras have the chance to shine? Ladies and gentlemen, it is my pleasure, *nay*, my honor! To award the Preston Eberhart Educator Empowerment and Excellence Grant to Rome Chandrasinghe, your wonderful music teacher. Rome, where are you?" he called out, scanning the crowd.

My heart plummeted to the floor.

"What?" Rome sounded dumbfounded. "But I had nothing to do with Robbie going viral."

I barely heard him.

I didn't get the grant.

I had been so desperate to get Rome close to me earlier. Yet I let my hand slip out of his easily as he was pushed forward to the waiting stage.

I wasn't good enough.

Chapter 27

ROME

I WANTED HER TO BE MAD AT ME.

It would have been better if she was mad at me.

Anything would've been preferable to the way she iced over, blankness behind her eyes as she regarded me.

"I can't this weekend, Rome. I have so much I need to get done before Monday."

"Will you stay home at least?" I asked desperately. Maybe we could bring her food again. Coax her away from her laptop.

"I'll probably be at school so I can focus."

Great.

I was standing at her door. I couldn't even get past her threshold anymore. She had been numb to me ever since the assembly, numb to everyone really. I'd seen Francine ask her something in the corridor and Ivy had walked away mid-sentence, completely unaware.

James had warned me to give her at least twenty-four hours of space when she asked for some alone time. But my alpha couldn't bear it after one night. I needed to know where we stood, when I was going to see her again.

So here I was on a Saturday morning. Pining.

I leaned my forearms against the frame, my hair a mess over half my face. "Ivy, if you're mad at me, be mad," I said heavily.

I was ready to present her my still-beating bloody heart in my fist if I thought it would help.

"Rome."

She laid a hand on my chest. Hope bloomed like nothing I had ever felt before. She carefully tucked my hair behind my ear before leaning in to kiss me.

Hope. So much fucking hope.

"I'm not mad," she promised me softly. "You are a *wonderful* teacher. You are so deserving and I think you are going to do amazing things with the money. SGS's music department is incredibly lucky to have you."

Sincerity shone through every word.

So why did it feel like she was carving me open?

"Ivy," I choked out. "I-I'll talk to Preston. See if it can be divided, or even transferred—"

"Why would you do that?" She shook her head. "The arts rarely get an opportunity like this. No, Rome. You *have* to make the most of it," she said adamantly.

God, she was killing me.

"I have to get back to work."

"What are you working on?" I asked, searching for a chance, a window of opportunity, *anything* to spend a little longer in her presence.

"Fundraising initiatives."

She may as well have sunk a dagger directly into my heart.

"Congratulations, Rome. I mean it." Ivy kissed my cold, dead lips. "I better get back to it."

She closed the door carefully in my face.

I drove home but knocked on Logan's door instead.

"I need you to try too," I said without even greeting him.

Logan clicked his tongue. Odd to think that we were strangers mere weeks ago and now he was *pack*. "I don't know if it'll help," he said warningly, running his hand over his beard.

"Anything is better than this."

I tried to distract myself and give Logan time to work his magic. Moving knickknacks around the room, deciding it would be a good time to rearrange the fridge. James extricated the milk I was trying to squash horizontally on the top shelf, *lovingly* told me I was being a pest and ordered me to go jam on my guitar instead.

Logan's familiar knock sounded a mere fifteen minutes later and I nearly ripped the door off the hinges. I was, however, disappointed he hadn't made his way into Ivy's nest and had her happily knotted on his anaconda of a dick.

"Well?"

"Terrible."

I squashed my face into the wall and let it muffle my pathetic throat noise.

Logan gave me a concerned look. "I told her that we understood how important her job was. And all we wanted was to be there for her through whatever she was feeling—good or bad."

"Really? You said all of that?"

"That's what you told me to say!"

That was true.

James came over. "What did she say?" he asked Logan.

"She repeated that she wasn't mad at you," Logan recounted. "But it was really important that she get back to work." He stared down at his hands. "I . . . told her that I missed her and we'd be here whenever she was ready."

Off script but I approved.

"She told me she wasn't going anywhere and invited me to stay in her nest tonight." It should've been a cause for celebration but Logan sighed heavily instead. "I don't know. I think she doesn't even realize she's—" He made a wall-like motion with his hand in front of his face.

James was silent for a while, processing our predicament. He shrugged, shaking the tension loose from his body. "All right. Get dressed both of you. Warmly," he instructed us decisively. He noted Logan's jacket and boots. "Or rather Rome and I, I should say."

"What? Why?" I asked.

"Seems like a good day to try out the 1000 steps."

Starlight Grove sat in the shadow of Solstice Mountain. One of my first thoughts when I first arrived was how beautifully the town was hugged by sea and earth. A sanctuary.

I'd heard of the 1000 steps walk. A steep winding trail to a look-out point partway up the mountain. It was very well-maintained and safe regardless of the season and the views out to the shining ocean were supposedly spectacular.

Even so, I never had the urge to climb the damn thing.

"1000 steps on Solstice Mountain?" I said skeptically. "Why does it sound like there's a witchy ritual waiting for us at the end?"

James was already partway down the hall. "Well, there *are* three of us."

"James!"

"Bring something you want to burn in a cauldron!" he called over his shoulder.

I sighed. He was silly but he was still mine.

Logan pursed his lips. "Is he serious?"

James was an exercise-gives-me-endorphins deviant and *very* happy in the bond.

"Yes," I said, resigned to my fate. "I better get ready before he threatens me with a broomstick."

"I HATE YOU."

"Save the foreplay for later, Rome."

I was leaning on my thighs, panting as I mentally prepared for the next set of steps. Picking up heavy stuff and putting it back down again—fine. I did that with (semi) regularity at the gym. But this burning in my lungs, calves, ribs, every-fucking-where was the worst. Even breathing hurt, every inhale made of needles.

I was the only one suffering. Logan must have been part bear. Maybe portions of his DNA were finding their home again among the snow-capped conifers. His strides had been long and easy, and he was currently waiting an entire flight of stairs ahead of us.

"Come on, this sign says we're nearly there!" he called down.

He probably sensed a salmon stream nearby and wanted to catch some in that big mouth of his.

I spotted a thin stream of smoke on the horizon, a gray thread unspooling into the sky.

"Do people live out here?" I huffed. "Who would do that to themselves?"

James snorted and loped ahead like a deer.

The three of us did eventually make it to the end of the 1000 steps. I lay on a bench wheezing, unable to even enjoy the view. James and Logan were leaning against the wooden railing, pointing out landmarks they could see. A fat little bird landed near them— more feathered chest than anything else—and James oohed, immediately pulling out his phone to try and figure out the species. Logan attempted to coax it closer with nothing more than clicking sounds and it flew away haughtily, unimpressed by the big alpha's offering.

"This was a good idea. Thanks, man," Logan said, unfazed that he was not a Disney princess.

"Good to get out in nature, isn't it?" James replied.

"Yeah, really puts things in perspective."

I was glad my arm was back across my forehead so they couldn't see me roll my eyes.

"Stop being a baby and get up here with us," James scolded.

I hauled myself onto my jelly legs and collapsed against the railing next to the rest of my pack. Starlight Grove looked like a miniature toy town beneath us and the ocean glittered beneath the winter sun.

Ok, maybe this was kind of nice.

"What we're doing with Ivy is long game," James said quietly. "I don't get the feeling she's being malicious, do you?"

I shook my head.

Nothing about the way she spoke to me today was cruel. Even though it hurt like hell. Plus, if she had been trying to push us away purposefully she wouldn't have invited Logan into her nest.

"I think Ivy has been cautious all her life," James reasoned. "And she's gotten used to being independent. We can't expect her to know how to be a pack omega straight away."

Doing so would make us no better than her ex, I realized.

"Slow and steady." An incorrigible smile began to spread across the beta's face. "One step at a—"

"If you turn this hike into a metaphor, James, I swear to god I will—"

Logan clapped a large hand on James' shoulder. "We should do this again sometime. Bring Ivy here too."

I didn't like this new alliance. Especially when I said words and they ignored me.

"I'll bring cards."

"A picnic basket."

"Yes! Make a day of it."

My eyes darted between the two of them, resentment bubbling.

"You're in, aren't you, babe?"

James' smile was infuriating and dazzling.

"Yeah," I said grudgingly. "And you're right, by the way. About Ivy."

His face grew serious. "I know your alphas probably want to keep her permanently fed and happy in her nest but that's not who she is." James gave me a wry look. "Ok, sometimes it is."

That was a good fucking day.

"But I wanted to court her because she's Ivy. Not because she's an omega."

Logan agreed immediately. "Same."

"This is going to be an adjustment for all of us. But especially for her." He straightened his glasses across his nose.

I exhaled in one long breath, anxiety quieting, heartbeat slowing. "So we give her time."

"And show her we can fit into her world," Logan finished.

An actionable plan. Maybe things were looking up after all.

I stared at the stairs heading back down and felt queasy.

James slipped his hand in mine. "Let's enjoy the view a little longer."

"Ok," I said, relieved.

"You just let us know when you don't feel like a freshly born foal anymore."

I glared at him to the sound of Logan's laughter.

Chapter 28

IVY

THIS WAS NOT GOING TO BE AN ORDINARY GIRLS' CATCH-UP.

Summer, Lucy and Olive were *all* seated across from me at Beans 'n Bliss. It was an odd and . . . deliberate choice. They had been trying almost too hard to get me to meet up.

LUCY

Who's free for Beans 'n Bliss tomorrow?

SUMMER

ME!

OLIVE

I am! Ivy, what about you?

I'm working but you all have fun!

SUMMER

Oh no! When are you next free?

LUCY
Yeah we'll make it work!

I'm not sure

OLIVE
Check your calendar!

And so on and so forth until they had locked in a time with me. I almost drowned in exclamation points and sparkle heart emojis.

Summer pushed a hot chocolate toward me, prepared exactly the way I liked it with extra marshmallows. Their smiles were so broad I felt like I was facing a dentist commercial. If you minused the tremulous apprehension behind all their eyes.

"Olive, what are you planning to get Lars for his birthday coming up?" Lucy nudged her lightly.

That wasn't suspicious. Lars *was* Lucy's brother.

"Gosh, I'm not sure. It's my first time celebrating my alpha's birthday."

Summer scoffed. "Oh please. You could wake up the day of, slap a bow on your chest and call it a day."

They tittered and it felt scripted. Every line polished until it gleamed.

I was the only one left without pages.

"Ivy."

Here it was. Whatever bombshell they wanted to drop on me. Tied with as neat a bow as they could possibly manage.

"How are you and *your* pack doing?" The emphasis on "your" was so heavy I was surprised Summer didn't injure her back.

"Fine," I answered shortly.

But my mouth went dry as I thought about the real answer. How long had it been since I last saw them? Rome just yesterday at school, obviously. Logan a couple of days before that. He'd brought me coffee. James . . . I was blanking on.

No, wait. I'd seen him earlier in the week. I actually remembered to reply to a text between grading tests and stressing about upcoming mandated assessments. He came by with takeout and I was too brain dead to hold a conversation.

I'd just been so busy since the grant announcement a couple of weeks ago. That first-week stress only snowballed. I didn't know how to keep up with their texts. I didn't know what to do when they tried to make plans with me. Eventually I stopped responding because I could only explain so many times that I didn't have time. Most days I was too tired to do anything when I got home except eat something quick and pass out in my nest.

It barely smells like them anymore.

I wedged the betraying thought deep down, tucking it away where the light wouldn't reach.

Lucy leaned forward, hugging her mug so tightly her knuckles whitened. "That's wonderful to hear, Ivy."

Her smile was tight. Lie.

"When was the last time you saw them?"

"What is this?" I said accusingly.

Their gazes swung between each other. Panic and recalibration.

Summer tried this time. "We're concerned, that's all. Things seem different compared to when you were on winter break," she finished tactfully.

Well, of course it was. I wasn't in some la-la land with no responsibilities anymore, was I?

Olive's turn. Passing the baton between them like relay runners. "I don't mean to speak for all omegas, obviously," she began hastily, already sounding apologetic. "But when my alphas started courting me, well"—Pink dappled across her cheeks—"I couldn't spend *enough* time with them."

I rubbed my temples. "Not everyone has the luxury of their pack *literally* setting up their workplace in their h—"

"Just the ladies I wanted to see!"

Summer smacked her forehead loudly, not even attempting to hide her frustration over the mayor's inconvenient appearance. "Bit busy, Stanley!"

Ever oblivious, he waved her concern away like a gnat. "Oh, this will only take a minute," he said, waggling his beloved clipboard. "Valentine's Day Festival is coming up!"

"It's a month away, Stanley," Lucy retorted.

"Good heavens, I wish! Twenty-five days to be exact, Miss Lucy." Stanley pointed his pen at her, the way all grown women liked to be spoken to. "Planning takes time, people, and we have *got* to be on it! Vendors to hire. Booths to map out. Decorations to source. It's pandemonium if we don't do it right!"

We stared blankly at him, our attention spans frittering away with each passing second.

Stanley heaved a huge sigh, clearly unimpressed we hadn't been whipped into an inspired frenzy by his speech. "I need you to tell me what booths you will be manning," he said, all business.

"Why do we have to man booths?" Summer countered. "Does the term *man* not disqualify all of us immediately?"

"Summer, I cannot have this argument with you every time."

"I'll do the Love Letter station," I said shortly. I did it every year so I don't know why he bothered to ask. Cute stationery, deploying my wax seal and suggesting words that rhymed with "heart." It really wasn't that complicated.

"Fantastic." The scribble of his pen was irritatingly loud. "And can I count on you and your pack to do a shift in the Cupid's Counsel tent this year? Olive, you too? The people *do* love to chat with packs."

An icy knot of dread twisted in my chest. The Cupid's Counsel

tent was silly but also something I'd secretly wished I could partici-
pate in for years. Happy packs and couples set up on ornate (hired)
velvet chairs and dispensed love and relationship advice to anyone
who needed it.

The timing felt like a cruel prank from the universe.

"I'll put you down for . . . 12:00," Stanley prattled on. "And Olive, you and your alphas can go right after at 12:30." He peered at the
other two girls. "Lucy. Summer. I hope you will do your neighborly
duty and step up for our great town." He gestured at Lucy. "Corsage
making?" Then at Summer. "Themed baked goods?"

His proposition was met with a cold silence.

"I'll come back later," he grumbled. "When you ladies are more
amenable, perhaps."

Summer called after his retreating back. "Good-bye forever then,
Stanley!"

I sipped slowly at my drink, not wanting to return to our previous conversation. The melted marshmallow I normally loved was
sickly sweet on my tongue.

"It's ok to say no sometimes, Ivy," Lucy said quietly.

My defenses immediately went up. Prickles deployed like a cor-
nered animal.

"What do you mean?" I'd *never* in my life snapped at my friends
before, yet it rose out of me, wolf-like.

Summer flinched but her jaw remained set. "You don't have to do
the booth if you don't want to."

"Well someone has to. It really doesn't cost very much."

"I don't know if that's true, Ivy." Olive wouldn't look at me, her
voice barely audible.

They weren't talking about the booths anymore.

They were talking about—

Shard-like pain invaded as my mind stumbled on a truth I was
not willing to hear.

I stood up sharply, the screech of my chair unbearably loud.

"It was good to see you all," I said woodenly. "But I have to go."

"Ivy, come on. We're only looking out for—"

"See you," I cut Summer off abruptly, turning so I didn't have to look at their disappointed faces anymore. "I've got a lot to get done before dinner at my parents' tonight."

I tried to work when I got home. Then I blamed my friends when I couldn't focus. By the time I had to leave again, my mood was muddy black misery sticking to everything. I drove to my parents' house and slammed the car door hard enough a rustle of birds flew away in a panic overhead.

Mom and Dad exchanged a glance and steered clear of me when I stormed in. Even Teddy slunk away, choosing to watch me warily from the safety of his dog bed.

"Ives, frowning like that will give you wrinkles."

Caitlin thought it would be a good idea to pinch me between my brows. *After* she had squashed herself into the *single-person* armchair I was already ensconced in.

But Caitlin's ability to read the room had never properly manifested.

"Good," I said curtly, making sure to scowl even harder.

"Hey."

My pupils listed sideways, giving her the barest minimum of attention.

"I remembered wine tonight," Caitlin sang, producing a bottle and waving it in front of my face.

I rolled my eyes. Of course Caitlin wanted a parade for doing the absolute minimum.

"Jeez Ivy. I don't know whether to offer you the whole bottle or keep you away from it."

"Do whatever you want," I muttered. I elbowed her until she finally got the hint and slid out of the chair. I resettled back into the cushion, making sure there was no space for her to ever think about trying that again.

Caitlin was unbothered, flipping her hair over her shoulder as she sat down on the couch. "Sean came into the restaurant for dinner and asked me about you. He pretended he was making small talk but I *knew*." She tapped her temple shrewdly. "He was trying to find out how your courtship was going."

"What?"

"Yeah. All backhanded like, wondering if you'd gone back to your old ways now that school has started."

My ears filled with a roar of noise, blinding white crowding the edges of my vision.

"Why would you tell me this?" I ripped the accusation clean out of my throat.

"I dunno." She shrugged. How could she be so incredibly dense? "I thought you'd want to know that your ex was talking shit about you. I defended you, by the way. Told him you were officially Pack Winter and delirious with happiness. *You're welcome.*"

She thought this knowledge was a *gift*?

Suddenly, I had worse than no appetite. I wanted to retch the few measly bites I had managed to consume that day. I could only stomach three bites of Dad's roast chicken and a single buttery carrot before I was done.

I offered to wash up by myself for the perverse pleasure of scrubbing violently on the stained pans.

Mom slid an empty salad bowl my way and I took it from her wordlessly. She gave me a cautious look before finally deciding to place a tentative hand on my back.

"Relationships are hard work, Ivy," Mom said quietly. "Three at once must be especially so."

I worked the scourer sponge even harder against a stubborn discolored spot.

"Whatever it is . . . never forget that you're on the same team. It's not *me* versus *you*, but *us* against the problem."

I squeezed my fist and felt the drip of escaping water running over the dish glove.

That doesn't work when I'm the problem.

"Mom, I love you. But please stop."

I hated the way her mouth pressed into a thin line. The sympathetic rub I wanted to shake off.

I don't deserve it, I don't deserve it, I don't deserve it.

My behavior hit me like a tidal wave as Mom and Dad saw me to the front door. Choking and spluttering on what a colossal bitch I'd been. "I'm sorry. I didn't mean—"

Dad hugged me. There were very few things in my life as unconditionally loving as one of his hugs. It had felt that way ever since I was little.

There was a Tupperware of leftovers in my hands when we parted. "In case you get hungry later."

He was smiling despite everything. Was there no bottom to this hole I was falling down?

"Sorry I, um," Caitlin trailed off, staring at the floor. "I won't mention Sean again. I always thought you were way too good for him. I realize I've been going the wrong way about reminding you of that."

God, I was such a mess that even Caitlin felt sorry for me.

Numbness overtook me as I drove home. I saw a familiar figure sitting on my front step and the pressure crushing my ribs became unbearable. Tears rushed up immediately, hot and stinging. I dabbed my fingertip hurriedly on my inner corners, trying to get my breathing under control. Inhale. Exhale. It came out stuttered and weak.

I can't do this now. Not after today.

But James was waiting for me and I had to face him.

The closer I got to him the worse I felt. He looked like he'd come straight from work, his lanyard still around his neck. Weariness etched lines framing his eyes and folded his posture inward. His faint scent was dull, devoid of its usual sweetness and warmth.

"You shouldn't have waited for me, James."

He stood slowly, pushing his hands deeper into his coat pockets. "You seem to have a very clear idea of what we can and cannot do," he sighed.

The defeat in his voice made me recoil.

"But I have to be honest with you, Ivy. This distance . . . you're hurting us."

Us. All of them.

I was a poison. Decay. Eating them alive.

"I'm always on your side and I've done my best to give you time." His voice faded, mired with regret.

He'd held back the alphas, I realized. Held them back from saying things, doing things that might push me too far. Overwhelm me. Scar the tenuous links between us irreparably.

It was pointless. I'd already done that all on my own.

"But I'm starting to wonder if that was the wrong thing to do."

He was questioning himself but he shouldn't have. I realized there was nothing they could've done differently. All roads led here. My guilt grew claws, sinking deep.

It was difficult to look at him. There was no trace of his flirtatiousness. None. He was all hard angles, granite in his jaw and immovable obsidian black eyes.

I did this to him. Turned him into a version of James I didn't recognize.

Push him away.

You've dragged them down enough.

"I warned you," I said, my voice low and dangerous.

James looked both surprised and heartbroken. "What?"

"I warned you that I didn't know how to do this," I repeated, sharper this time. Slicing away at him so the blood would drain faster. "Don't act surprised all of a sudden."

The way he crumpled absolutely shattered me. I stared at the ground, knowing I would fall apart if I looked him in the eye.

You're a coward.

I didn't move the entire time his footsteps faded away. A car door opening and closing. Finally the rumble of an engine driving off.

A soft rustle came from the bushes nearby. Two yellow orbs glimmered in the shadows. A round feline face emerged, silent paws taking tentative steps toward me.

I shook my head. "Not tonight, Felix."

I'd never turned down Felix before.

But tonight, I shut the door on him and everyone else who had ever cared.

Chapter 29

JAMES

"Do you really think this is going to work?"

"It has to."

Rome took up the entire length of the couch, laid out on his back like he was ready for mourners. Logan was hunched over in our armchair, fingers steepled and his leg bouncing restlessly.

Neither of the alphas had taken the news of my encounter with Ivy well.

"When did he say he'll post it?" Logan asked Rome.

Rome rubbed his eyes with the heels of his hands. "He's doing it tonight." He was always stressed these days. Stretched far too thin, dark shadows a constant beneath his eyes. It wasn't like I was much better. But at least I didn't have to endure the pain of seeing Ivy day to day, feeling like I could never reach her.

"Have you heard back from the organizations you contacted?" I asked, leaning my hip against the couch. I threaded my fingers through Rome's hair and watched his eyelids flutter.

"No, but I gave Robbie their handles too so he'll tag them," Rome said tonelessly.

It hurt to see my alpha like this. I couldn't lie either and say that Ivy hadn't devastated me yesterday. But the pain I saw beneath the icy surface of her eyes was more for herself than for me.

I don't know. That was a heavy thing to glean for someone I hadn't known for long. Maybe we were being idiots.

But something in my gut told me not to give up on her. Not to give up on us.

"There's no guarantee this will work, anyway. People expect piano covers from him, not this," Rome sighed. Pessimism ran heavy cracks through his resolve.

Robbie O'Hara had blown up far beyond his original *Fever Love* cover. He had a knack for covering songs before they went big. With it came sponsorship deals—both legitimate and predatory—along with local news reporters. He was bewildered by it all and just wanted to make music.

Rome encouraged him to let his parents help him navigate his newfound fame and approached all three with his idea—asking if Robbie would be willing to utilize his platform to draw attention to resources SGS was sorely lacking.

"You said so yourself that Robbie wanted to help," I reminded him. "That he knows there's no pressure and we're grateful regardless of what happens."

Rome massaged his forehead worriedly. "I don't like that I might have put him in a position to blame himself if it doesn't work."

I loved that Rome was more concerned with the impact it would have on Robbie instead of what we were hoping to get out of it. It was times like this that made me feel like he was too fucking good for this world.

Logan leaped up, his hand shaking slightly as he stared down at his phone. "Shit. I think he's done it. Posted ten minutes ago."

We crowded around him and watched Robbie's video play out.

"Hey guys!" Robbie's youthful smile filled the screen as he brushed his mop of blond hair out of his eyes. "I've got something a bit different for you today. Here's a day in my life as a tenth grader at Starlight Grove School."

I recognized the hallway on the edges of the frame. Robbie was filming close so no other students could be seen. He remained positive and upbeat as he went from class to class, undeterred by minor setbacks. Robbie rifled through a ball rack to find the least worn down basketball possible during PE. He had to share a scientific calculator with a classmate in math. His study session at the library was cut short when he realized there wasn't a copy of a reference text he needed. His little sister had scraped her knee and he couldn't find a band-aid that was the right size.

The video ended with him jogging down the familiar school steps. "I'm a bit embarrassed because I know it's not as fancy as some of the schools you guys go to. But the teachers really do their best here." Robbie held up a math test with a red A circled on top. "If you have some ideas for how I can show them some love, let me know," he said before waving good-bye.

Logan looked lost. "Was he . . . supposed to tag people?"

"This can't be right," Rome muttered. He rewatched the video, the line between his brows deepening. "Fuck. What do I do now? I don't want to tell him off."

"Wait." I clicked on the comments that had already begun to pop up. "People are tagging brands themselves," I said in awe as I scrolled. Stationery, sporting goods, health, tech. "If this gets traction—"

"It'll probably get more attention because *everyone* is asking for supplies, not just Robbie," Rome finished. He shook his head. "Man. Kids these days. They're really in a league of their own."

It was hard not to feel hopeful. The feeling was so unfamiliar after the last few weeks it lurched almost painfully beneath my sternum. "What about the organizations you had in mind for the second part of your plan?" I asked.

Rome scratched his stubbled jaw. "I'll talk to Robbie tomorrow. But somehow I feel like he knows what he's doing more than we do though."

"How will we know these companies have even seen it?" Logan asked, clearly feeling out of sorts as he looked over the comments.

"We don't. We just have to—"

"Don't say wait."

I gave him a helpless shrug.

Logan grumbled impatiently, clearly ready to get back to never letting Ivy out of his sight again.

"Do you want to feel even more stressed by playing Overcooked?" I offered.

His lips flattened into a resigned grimace. ". . . Yeah."

A side effect of Ivy's distance was that Logan spent almost every night at ours now. We ate together, wound down from our work days together. One time I got home and did a double take at Logan chopping onions in the kitchen. "Did Rome not tell you he gave me a spare key?" he said offhandedly before asking me if bolognese was ok for dinner.

It was odd, Rome and I never felt like he was a third wheel and I didn't think he did either. It was like we all wanted to forge a different kind of connection while things felt so in limbo with our omega.

Sometimes Logan stayed so late he was half asleep when he trudged back to his home next door. Tonight felt like it would end up being one of those nights, seeing as he was still glued to the TV with Rome at 10:00 p.m.

Rome's phone buzzed on the table and he swore. "James, can you grab that? We're literally—"

Logan was practically levitating off the edge of the couch he was so tense. "Take the burgers, take the burgers, take the—YES!"

I bit back a laugh and grabbed the phone. I frowned at the caller ID—why was Marisol calling us at this time of night?

"Hi, it's James. Rome's a bit busy," I answered quickly, backing away from the alphas howling about lettuce.

"Oh hello dear. Glad I caught at least one of you." Marisol's usual chipperness faded into concern. "Look, I'm not trying to be a busybody . . ."

A loud snort almost slipped out. Being a busybody was Marisol's default state.

". . . but I couldn't help but notice that Ivy's car was still parked at the school."

Dread chilled me to the bone. "What?"

"Felix chose my place tonight and he was kicking up *such* a fuss over not having his treats. Wailing at the empty box I usually keep them. Lord, it was like he was holding a funeral in my kitchen. I finally told him I'd head back to the Market to fetch him some. That's when I noticed Ivy's car. It's the only one still in the lot," Marisol said pensively. "She's not still working, is she?"

The thought of Ivy working alone in that big school was heart-wrenching. "We'll take care of it. Thanks for the call, Marisol," I said quietly before hanging up.

The alphas swore when I told them where Ivy was.

"We have to go check in on her."

"Obviously."

We piled into my car and drove in a stilted silence. I didn't even care if we were overstepping after how we'd left things with her. I needed to know she was ok.

Ivy's little blue car sat in the parking lot of SGS like an abandoned toy. How many nights had she walked to it alone in the bitter cold after a grueling day?

"Is this how it's going to be from now on? Because if I have to sit by and watch her self-destruct, I don't know if . . ." Rome looked utterly defeated, unable to finish his sentence.

I hated that it had come to this. The best I could hope for was that this would be the wake up call Ivy needed.

The entrance to the elementary wing was unlocked.

"I don't believe this," Logan said furiously, pushing the door open easily.

"Fucking Bruce," Rome cursed low and angry. I'd heard enough stories about SGS's custodian but this was beyond the pale. How could he leave Ivy alone in a building where anyone could get in?

There was a sense of déjà vu as I strode down those darkened halls. The familiar hum of the heat on low. That creeping sensation that someone or something would suddenly appear like a wraith. The last time I was in the school after-hours was because of Ivy. Her recklessness. Her heat spike.

We had no idea what we were stepping into last time but tonight we were single-minded.

Her classroom was the only one with a soft orange glow filtering out beneath the door. My steps quickened and I ripped the door open, needing to see that she was all right.

My heart plummeted at the still form of my omega draped over her desk.

"Ivy!"

I was by her side in an instant, the alphas not far behind. She began to stir from the sudden noise of all of us rushing over. I pulled her into my arms, tucking her under my chin protectively.

"J-James?"

Her words were groggy but the tight vise of trepidation in my chest loosened slightly. She blinked hard several times, taking us in.

"I fell asleep?" She sounded too tired to even be surprised that we were all there. She could barely keep her eyelids open as she drooped against me.

Rome tapped her laptop and the screen lit up. "You were applying for grants?" he asked. He sounded so broken. "Ivy, I haven't even heard of half of these."

"Just . . . trying to do my best," Ivy said faintly.

The need to care for her absolutely overwhelmed me. This was what I was meant for, why I was part of this pack.

Logan tucked his face into the crook of her neck, taking in her scent. I could barely detect it, but I knew he was reading more into that faint gingerbread than I ever could. "We're going to take you home now, all right?" he said carefully.

"You two go," Rome ordered us.

My brow furrowed. "What are you—"

He opened and closed the drawers on her desk, his mind calculating and taking stock. His finger ran along a shelf and came away dusty. "I need to show her that she doesn't have to do this all on her own anymore," he insisted.

His determination in the bond was impenetrable. Nothing I said right now would change his mind.

I felt around until I found Ivy's bag and fished out her car keys. I tossed them to Rome and he caught it, eyes blazing. "We'll take care of her. See you when you're done," I said simply.

He took a stricken Ivy from me and held her close, assuring her he wanted to help and was happy to. She kept shaking her head, not understanding.

I hated that she thought we were inconvenienced by this. My girl needed to know that this was what we were here for. The physical care was obvious—making sure she'd eaten, working that tight tension out of her muscles she didn't even realize had built up, letting her rest. But more importantly, I wanted to get to the bottom of why she felt compelled to push herself this way.

I glanced at Logan, unsure if his alpha was going to let me lead.

"Logan. When we get home, I want to take over. Be in control," I said slowly. "Is your alpha ok with that?"

He shot me a surprised look. Assessing me. "I want my scent on her," he admitted.

"That's fine."

"Is this . . . you're not into pain, are you?" he asked me warily.

I don't know why he thought I was going to solve Ivy's problems with my penis.

Although to be fair, I couldn't conclusively say that it wasn't going to end up in that direction.

"No. Definitely not. Quite the opposite."

A touch of curiosity bled in. "Yeah, James. Whatever you need."

Rome handed Ivy back to us and we left him behind in her classroom. Logan held her in the backseat the entire drive home, her head tucked perfectly beneath his bearded chin.

"I didn't mean to worry you guys," Ivy said in a small voice. She kept looking between us, growing nervous at our silence. "James, I want to apologize for the other night. I shouldn't have—"

"It's ok, Ivy," I said gently. "Let's just get home first and we can talk."

"Right," she said softly. I could already see the detachment in her eyes. She probably thought this was one last favor we were doing for her before leaving her forever.

No wonder she was surprised when I pulled up in front of my place. "Not mine?" she asked hesitantly.

Logan thumbed her chin tenderly. "No, princess."

It did make more sense to take her home to her nest. But reconnecting as a pack came first. Showing her we hadn't given up on her came first. I knew we'd made the right choice when she sucked in a big, shaky breath as soon as the door opened. She hadn't even realized how much she'd been missing our scents.

Ivy was nervous as I sat her down on the couch between us. I tucked a stray lock of hair behind her ear before leaning in for a kiss. She started, eyes widening as my lips lingered over hers. She kissed me back tentatively and I could sense her confusion.

"I'm really glad you're here, Ivy."

Her eyes brimmed with tears. "How can you . . . after everything

I said. I was awful to you." She didn't know who to look at and settled on the floor. "I don't know how to fix this," she whispered.

"It's not something you're meant to fix on your own," I told her gently. "We're a pack."

A flicker of understanding crossed her face. "Us against the problem," she said quietly to herself.

"Hmm?"

"Nothing . . . it's something my mom said."

I phrased my next words carefully. "Sweetheart, I want to understand why you think your needs are supposed to come last."

She looked caught. Her mouth opened soundlessly, ready to say *I don't*, but she closed it after a beat, really thinking about it.

"I can't pinpoint it exactly. But probably for a lot of different reasons," she finally admitted. "Making sure I didn't cause trouble for my parents when they were dealing with whatever predicament my sister got herself in that week. Wanting to be the best teacher I could be. Feeling like it was easier to do everything myself so it was to my standard. Not wanting to disappoint people when my help would make a difference. A lot of small things that just . . ."

"Snowballed."

"Yeah. Until it cost me—"

A shaky hiccup swallowed her last word.

You.

"It hasn't, Ivy."

Logan spoke at the same time. "Never," he said fiercely.

I could see the steel melt from her spine. The veil between who she thought she had to be and who she wanted to be faltered.

"But there is something I need." I tested the waters cautiously.

"Anything," Ivy said immediately.

The last few weeks had been difficult in many ways. But the unsettled feeling was the worst part of it. It was a simpler fix for the alphas—keep their omega close, marked with their scent until she perfumed sweetly for them.

It was a little different for me though. Seeing her spiral and pull away tapped into my caretaking instincts hard.

I always did have trouble resisting a wounded bird.

The Rome I first met was beautiful and a little lost and the Ivy in front of me had an inexplicable need to burn the candle at both ends. Both woke up a different side of me. In day to day life, that usually manifested in trying to lighten their hearts, finding happiness in the little things.

But that wasn't what would satisfy me right now.

"I'm going to need you to let me take care of you," I said, my voice quiet but firm.

Ivy's eyebrows knitted together in confusion. "What? That doesn't seem fair."

"You would have to let go, Ivy." My hand moved up and down her arm, repetitive and steadying. "Let me give you what you need."

She swallowed visibly. "Is this a sex thing?"

"It might lead there," I admitted. "But it really isn't the core of what I want."

"You're serious."

"Yes."

There was no playfulness in my tone. I felt myself sink deeper into this side of myself, hungry to see her surrender to me.

"Let you take care of me," she echoed. "That's it? You don't need some sort of grand gesture? For me to quit my job and build my nest in your home?"

"If those were not things you wanted for yourself, giving them to us would be meaningless."

I could see the weight of my words settle, the blue in her eyes deepening as she understood what I was saying.

I want you for you.

Logan was watching us, letting me lead like we agreed. But he was part of this too and Ivy brought him in so perfectly on her own.

"I'm sorry." She traced the wrinkles around his eyes before raking her fingers through his hair. "I'm sorry for pushing you away."

"These last few weeks sucked, Ivy," he said bluntly.

"I-I know."

"I'm ready to move on. Not to how we were. Something better."

Her eyes welled up. "I want that too."

He was tender with his kiss but she seemed to want to be consumed by him. Grasping his collar, bending herself back so he would loom and overwhelm her with his size. A throaty purr thrummed from his chest, his hand splayed across the small of her back as he pulled her hard against him. He broke away, only so he could brace her exposed throat and trail a dozen heated kisses down her skin, marking her with his scent. Crisp, like a freshly cut tree in the frosty mountain air. Ivy whimpered, melting into him and letting his alpha have his way with her.

Logan didn't take it further, swapping kisses for a careful perusal, smoothing her hair back from her face.

"When did you last eat, princess?" he asked.

Ivy lowered her eyes. "Lunch," she confessed.

"I'll make you something," he said firmly, standing up. "You go with James."

Ivy's gaze lingered around the room. "Is Rome going to come home soon?" she asked, clearly having felt his absence and finally gathering the courage to ask.

"He's taking care of you too. In his own way."

I could still feel his focus in the bond, reverberating in the background like a steady bassline.

I knelt so our faces were level and slid my hands up her thighs toward her waist.

"You ready?"

She had to make the choice to close the final gap between us.

"James."

We were in the eye of a hurricane. Me, her and the way she said my name.

"Right here, gorgeous."

"I'm yours," she promised, right before her lips found mine.

Chapter 30

JAMES

Kissing Ivy was always addictive. Kissing a gradually submitting Ivy going all loose and docile in my arms? Fucking live wire of electricity splintering my brain.

Again.

I slid my tongue against hers and earned every little whine I drew out of her.

More.

My fingers raked through her hair, close to her scalp, and gave it a light tug. Not for pain.

As a reminder of who she belonged to right now.

Ivy only sank further into me.

Good.

"Come on," I said, massaging a firm line from her hairline down her neck. Up and down as her lashes fluttered.

I took her hand and led her to the bathroom. Kissed her and told her to wait as I dimmed the lights and ran a bath. I pulled out a few large candles and lit them, the golden glow illuminating the rising steam. Finally, I selected a bath bomb that would turn the water silky soft and set it to one side.

"I didn't realize you were such a bath person." There was curiosity without judgment in her voice.

"I do this for Rome sometimes," I admitted.

The idea that alphas didn't need to be cared for was silly. After the grant announcement, he had been a ball of stress. More than that, he was on the verge of acting rashly. Wanting to practically set up on Ivy's doorstep and in her classroom every day. It would've overwhelmed her, caused her to lash out harder than she already did.

The hike had taken the edge off somewhat but his mind still churned with what-if scenarios.

So I ran him a bath just like this one and fucked him into a moaning puddle on our bed.

I began to lift the hem of her sweater up. Ivy instinctively reached to help me and I stopped her.

"Let me," I insisted.

Her lips parted, a flush spreading across her cheeks as she raised her arms obediently so I could pull it over her head.

I knelt down, unbuttoning her pants and sliding the zipper down. It fell to the ground, exposing her thighs and simple black cotton thong. I couldn't resist leaving a light kiss right below her navel, but nothing more.

Ivy stayed still as I carefully worked the small neckline of her turtleneck over her head. I smoothed the wildness of her hair back down. There was a mark on her skin from where her bra strap had been sitting. I kissed that too as I unclasped her bra. More marks, faint but slightly pink, curving beneath her breasts. I ran my fingertips over them until they faded and softened. More kisses as her breathing grew uneven.

Her scent was sweetening, buttery and spiced and sugared. As I hooked my fingers over her waistband, I didn't miss the damp spot darkening the fabric nor the glisten of wetness over her short curls. But all I did was let the panties fall to the ground, letting her step out of them.

I turned my attention to the bath, shutting off the water and dropping in the bath bomb. We watched the water bubble and froth, settling into an opaque milky color. I took her hand, guiding her to step inside.

"Oh. It's really just a bath, isn't it?"

I gave her a wry smile. "Just a bath, Ivy."

I was honest when I said this wasn't about sex. I wasn't trying to rile her up, even though I could see her blown pupils and hardened nipples. This was going to be all about her, as slowly and indulgently as possible.

Something about seeing the curve of her breasts rising out of the silky water while everything else was hidden beneath the foam almost made me scrap my whole plan.

"Perfect timing," I said, relieved at Logan's appearance with a late dinner for Ivy. The two of us flanked the rounded, free-standing bath.

"The three of us went on a hike, you know," Logan said, as he hand-fed her bites of a grilled cheese sandwich dipped in tomato soup.

Ivy had her hand up to her mouth politely as she chewed. "You did?"

"Mmhmm. The 1000 steps."

"I haven't been in a while," she mused. "It's pretty up there, isn't it?"

"It is," Logan agreed.

A beat of silence.

"Rome almost died."

I snorted at the memory and Logan's face split into a wide smile.

"What?" Ivy laughed.

Logan sighed. "I wanted to do a pack date up there but I don't know if he'll survive doing it again."

"He's more of a sprinter," I explained. "Endurance is not his strong suit."

"Really?" Ivy looked confused. "It didn't seem that way when he spent the entire day—"

She promptly shut her mouth as she realized what she was saying. I smirked, knowing exactly what day Rome had been good with *endurance*.

"Guess he has to be *really* motivated," I teased her and she went even pinker.

I could already see the tightness draining from her the longer we spoke. Logan had also washed a bowl of grapes and I offered her one. My dick liked the way her lips closed over it a little too much.

Ivy fidgeted and shifted her weight in the water. She wanted to protest. Insist it wasn't necessary. I gave her a stern look and she released a soft sigh, sinking a little more into the bath as she opened her mouth for the next bite.

When she finished everything she thanked Logan and he kissed her forehead. He told her she did a good job, making her extra flustered before he left with the empty dishes.

I lifted her arm out of the water, cradling her hand between both of mine. My thumb carefully explored the back of her hand until I found the correct spot, a little left of the webbing between her thumb and index finger. I applied a solid pressure and Ivy let out a small whine.

"Acupressure," I explained softly. "This point helps reduce stress and tension." I massaged in circular motions for a couple of minutes. I watched her brow unfurl, the lines on her forehead smoothing out.

Next point. Heart 7. I turned her palm upward, tracing along her wrist until I found it. Right along the crease, almost directly in line with her little finger.

"This one is for anxiety and has calming effects."

Her breathing grew deeper, steadier, the longer I massaged it.

"Where did you learn this?" she asked me quietly.

"My mom." I continued to apply the same circular pressure. "I grew up watching her use these techniques on herself all the time."

She swore by it—still did—but as an adult I wondered how much of it was because we couldn't afford to see a doctor back then.

I found the last point I had in mind. On her palm, nestled in the muscle at the base of her thumb.

"And this one is for . . . ?"

"Lungs mainly," I explained. "But also immune system support."

Logan returned and his eyes widened. "Her scent. She's so . . . relaxed."

Ivy was a gooey dollop of satisfied omega. "Mmhmm," was all she was able to manage.

It was very difficult not to laugh at her cute expression. I watched as it turned serious, her eyes liquid with vulnerability.

"James, I really didn't know what I was missing out on until I found you all."

I leaned over the edge of the tub and kissed that shaky lower lip until she was clinging desperately to me. A small hand began to sneak its way toward the edge of my shirt. I stopped her before she managed to worm her way underneath.

"Soon," I said against her lips.

Ivy huffed adorably.

"Let me have some fun first." I stood up, guiding her to step out of the bath. Logan had returned and grabbed a towel ready for her.

It was a shock to my system to watch the water sluicing off her naked body. Dripping down her soft curves. Big blue eyes and nothing else. I swallowed, my cock thickening even as Logan wrapped her up. He swiped the corner of the towel across her face, catching stray droplets.

I grabbed a small vial of massage oil and Logan raised a brow at me. "More?"

"A different kind this time," I said lightly.

His eyes flashed hungrily. "Bedroom it is."

It really was very nice having packmates that understood.

"On your front," I murmured, pushing lightly on the small of her back. Once she had settled on the bed, I repositioned the towel over her lower half, covering her up.

I had a feeling she was going to be begging us to rip it off very soon.

Logan had pooled some oil in his palm and passed it over to me to do the same. The citrusy, earthy blend mingled with Ivy's natural perfume as we massaged it into her skin. Logan ran calloused palms along her legs and thighs. I traced the graceful curve of her spine before fanning out with overlapping palms across her back.

It was relatively innocent. Until it wasn't. Logan grazed her inner thigh. I caught the edge of her breast with my thumb.

Ginger, cinnamon and brown sugar overtook the scent of the oil. Ivy twitched, her hips fidgeting and seeking relief.

"This is *fun* for you?" she asked, her voice strained with need.

No, it was utter torture.

But worth it.

"Very fun. Turn over for me, sweetheart," I said lightly, as if my cock wasn't aching to be freed. Like every muscle in my body wasn't taut and waiting to rip that towel off her so I could bury my face in her juicy pussy.

Ivy wasted no time flipping over. A little shimmy into her new position and the towel slid low enough that I could spy the top of her mound.

"Why don't we get this out of your way," Logan murmured.

Fuck. My control was shredding. Her peaked tits, that plump bottom lip, the little dip to her tummy. Her thighs fell open slightly and I could see her clit. Swollen and pink, begging for a taste.

"Do you need more oil, James?" Logan asked.

This alpha had to be inhuman.

Well, if he wasn't going to stuff her full of cock yet then I had to wait too. Painfully. Hard as fuck. We poured more oil and went back to work on her. Up her arm. Across her torso, between her breasts. Everywhere but those rosy little nipples, no matter how much her chest rose trying to coax my hand there.

Logan wasn't even hiding that he was only focusing on her inner thighs and lower abdomen anymore. He circled closer and closer to her slick folds until her hips rose off the bed.

"If you're trying to punish me for what I did"—Ivy sounded like she was struggling to form words—"it's working."

I leaned over her, holding myself just out of reach of her lips and a soft little whine escaped her. "Tell me what you want then," I said, lightly running my fingers down her throat.

She looked down at Logan. Back up at me. "I want to be with you both," she whispered.

My hand inadvertently tightened. I released my hold immediately but her hand flew up, placing my hand back on her throat.

Fuck.

"Tell us exactly what you mean by that," I demanded, my voice deepening the longer she let me hold her down. "We need to hear it."

Her other hand curled around my wrist too. Suddenly I was the one being held captive, falling endlessly into her infinite, trusting eyes.

"I want to have both of you. At the same time."

Our noses were almost touching now. "Logan in your pussy. And I'm going to take your ass," I said explicitly.

Her chin rose. "Yes."

My thumb skimmed the hollow of her throat. "Have you ever . . ."

"No."

"I'll go slow."

Crazy how the tiniest smile could possess me so thoroughly.

"I know. I trust you."

She was giving me everything. Yet when I kissed her, I was certain *I* belonged to *her*.

Chapter 31

IVY

I DIDN'T HAVE A SINGLE INHIBITION LEFT.

I propped myself up on my elbows, brazenly watching James and Logan strip. My mouth went dry as James reached behind his shoulder blades to pull a fistful of his shirt forward. The careful way he folded up his glasses and placed them on the bedside table. His stiff cock, curving upward, the head a deep pink. I wanted to stick my tongue in that little slit until precum spilled out of it for me.

My gaze swung across to Logan. His bicep flexed as he undid his belt with one hand, never taking his eyes off me. It whipped loudly through the air as he pulled it through the loops and my pussy clenched instinctively in response.

That was so unfairly hot.

A faint smile teased his lips. He was reading my mind and I was going to combust at any moment now.

I admired the dark hair across his chest and belly, trailing down to his cock hanging between his legs. The velvet skin was stretched tight over his hard shaft, veins pulsing along the heavy length.

Logan sank down on the bed and I immediately clambered all

over him. I was slippery all over and he kept losing his grip as he tried to grab hold of me. He finally got a good palmful of my ass just as my oiled breasts glided over him.

"I'm in heaven right now," Logan groaned. "I swear to god I'm in heaven right now."

The bed dipped as James joined us. He traced the arch of my back and my hips rose in the air. He yanked me toward him, dragging me further down Logan's body. Putting me in the perfect position to wrap my hand around my alpha's cock. I teased and stroked, enjoying every muttered curse I could draw out of him.

My movements stuttered at the first lick of James' tongue on my pussy. I immediately pushed back, wanting more. The bath, being fed, *two* massages—it had been the longest foreplay session in existence and I needed to come badly.

"That feel good?" Logan asked affectionately. His big hand braced around the back of my neck. He guided his cock toward me, letting the engorged head rest on my bottom lip. I opened my mouth obediently, trying to focus as James used his fingers to slide apart my pussy lips. The sensations ensnared me as he lapped at me. Drawn out. Wet. His warm breath fluttered over my sensitive flesh. I cried out and it allowed Logan to slide his cock past my lips.

He stretched and filled my mouth. My jaw slackened, my tongue swirling. I tasted salt and sweat, each steady inhale full of his resinous, forest scent. The craving grew, even as he pumped in and out of me, fingers digging into my hair.

Lips closed over my clit and sucked. Lightly at first, testing, and then voraciously like he couldn't get enough. I bucked and I took more of Logan than I thought was possible.

"You have to come for him." Logan caressed my hollowed out cheek. "Give him all the slick he needs to get you ready."

It had never been something I was interested in (why would anyone put it *there*?) but here I was, *anticipating* it. *Craving* it.

I shuddered and came all over James' face, chin, wetness dripping down the muscles on his chest. Logan cradled me close against his body. Soft kisses peppered all over between murmured praise.

Logan hiked my legs around his hips, spreading me wider than before. A second touch—two exploring fingers—grazed my back entrance and I jumped.

"I'm going to take my time," James promised.

It was hard to silence nerves. "I know."

"Relax." Logan blended both command and purr and I melted for them both.

Logan's cock was thick against my stomach, the heat of it making me leak slick copiously. Down my thigh, down *his* thigh, my pussy begging and ready and empty. James stole it, snaking upward, his fingers coated as he started to work it into my ass. I felt him add the massage oil too, silky and warm as it eased me open. Kisses from my alpha grounded me as the sensations changed. Discomfort, a low burn, a stretch that turned pleasurable. James was careful. Patient. I wasn't sure how long I lay over the top of Logan, being kissed and stretched and dripping, dripping all over them.

I had gradually moved up Logan's body, his length slipping between my thighs. The ridge of his crown lined up with my clit, too perfect and too delicious, my pussy lips hugging his shaft. I started to ride it, wanton and needy, burying my face into his chest.

"Take what you need." Logan's breathing was shallow as he guided my hips. "We want this to be so good for you."

I looked back just in time to catch James spreading my wetness over the head of his cock, stroking it along his shaft. He lined himself up and I lifted my hips higher, eager and ready for him. Even after preparing me there was still a sting as my body adjusted to the foreign sensation.

"Breathe, gorgeous." James kissed and stroked and *adored* me. "You're doing so well."

God, how far did he have to go? I didn't think I could take any more yet he kept going, so much deeper than what his fingers could reach. Strange how I could feel full yet empty all at once. The pressure was different and my pussy clenched with need, my clit humming desperately for attention.

James kissed my shoulder as he finally bottomed out completely inside me. No space left between our bodies, his cock nestled entirely in my ass.

"You feel so good," he groaned. The sheets curled into his fist and I felt his labored breath over my sweat-lined skin.

He began to move and I cried out with surprise. The pleasure was different but just as good when he pulled out. James was being so careful, so slow that I began to push back against him. Meeting his thrusts, wanting him to *own* what I'd just given him. James fucked me until I was moaning into Logan's shoulder. The alpha held my hair and took in my scent deeply from my neck. *Reckless.* I was a pheromone bomb, trying to drive them to lose all control.

The notch of Logan's cock against my entrance made me gasp. His arm between us, a question in his deep blue eyes.

"Yes," I begged. "I want you too, alpha."

Gravity did all the work. We got the right angle and somehow he fit. Inch by inch. Gradual. Blinding.

My world imploded as Logan thrust inside me just as James receded. I didn't know what I needed more—both of them filling me at once or the tandem rhythm of never being without a cock. Was it heresy to want both? I was hallowed and unholy all at once, feeling the lick of pleasurable flames all over my body and only wanting more.

The air filled with their grunts, curses and wet hedonistic sounds as my body adjusted to their rougher pace. James pulled out until only his tip was inside me. A hard smack as he filled me to the root, his pelvis flush against my cheeks. I rode against the unyielding muscle of Logan's perfect alpha knot, careening toward another orgasm.

"Fuck. You were made for us, weren't you?"

"So fucking perfect. Look at you riding our cocks, gorgeous."

I screamed into the sweaty fuzz of Logan's chest hair as I came. I felt suspended on invisible strings as they took over.

Use me, mark me, come for me.

"More," I whispered.

I kissed the vein pulsing in Logan's strained neck as he threw his head back with gritted teeth.

"Harder," I urged them.

James sank his teeth into my shoulder—not to bite but to muffle the sounds pouring from his throat as the first lash of heat spilled inside me.

"God, I can feel you," I choked out. Throbbing and pulsing, his uneven thrusts growing wetter with each sticky load of cum.

But it wasn't enough. "I want your knot, alpha," I said, staring into Logan's feverish, glassy eyes.

Logan's snarl was guttural and deep as he drove into me with a single, forceful push. He smothered my sharp cry with his kiss and I whimpered, fluttering around his knot and earning his cum deep in my pussy.

James withdrew slowly and I could feel his release sliding out of me. There was no hiding what we'd just done. A natural rush of embarrassment surged up and Logan noticed.

"You're ours," he said resolutely.

"Ours to take care of in every way you need," James continued, lips seeking all the sweet spots up my back. "Do you understand?"

It was becoming impossible not to believe them.

I nodded, finding it easier than words. Logan rolled us onto our sides and James wrapped himself around my back.

I was safe here. Safe with them.

I could let go and they would catch me.

"Pack," I whispered. Saying it out loud made me feel weightless.

Logan kissed my nose. "Glad you're finally getting it, princess."

Chapter 32

IVY

"James ran a bath for you, didn't he?"

My blush gave me away.

"He's good with those," Rome said affectionately. He continued drawing lazy designs along my arm where Logan's shirt had fallen off my shoulder. After his knot had gone down he had insisted on putting me in his clothes before we fell asleep.

James and Logan were snoring lightly beside us. Rome had come home late last night, squeezing into what little room he could find on the bed. I had climbed gracelessly over James so I could reconnect with my other alpha in the quiet hours of the morning.

"Where were you?" I asked, combing his rumpled hair through my fingers. There was a sleep line from the pillow across his perfect arched cheekbone.

I liked seeing him like this.

His mouth lifted wryly. "I'll show you later."

"I—" I blinked as I got stuck, unused to expressing how I felt so plainly. "I missed you," I said simply.

The effect was instantaneous. His eyes softened into an open vulnerability as he pressed his forehead against mine.

"God. I missed you too, Ivy."

Simple words shrank weeks of distance between us.

He kissed my fingers. "I know you want to keep things professional at school and I agree," Rome began. "But I really want to—"

"Yes."

He looked taken aback.

"But you don't even know what I'm—"

"Yes. Just yes, whatever it is."

Rome's eyes narrowed. "You've given me a lot of power right now."

I smiled. "I know."

"I could use it for evil."

"You won't."

He sighed. "Now you've ruined it and summoned my conscience."

He was so adorable I had to kiss around his neck until I found the spot that made him let out a high-pitched squeak.

"I only wanted to walk into school holding your hand," he said, trying to sound serious as he protected his neck from tickles.

I squidged the tip of his nose with a finger and he huffed at the indignity. "I'd like that."

ROME WALKED ME ALL the way from my car to my classroom, head held high and yes, holding my hand. I don't know if he was envisioning a crowd of gasping, fainting, clapping onlookers. It was very early and Bruce was the only one who saw us. The crusty old maintenance man didn't give us a second glance but Rome stared him down like a viper.

"What's wrong?" I asked, realizing he had fallen out of step with me.

"He shouldn't have left the door unlocked last night," Rome hissed.

"I told him I would lock up when I left. Don't blame a man who is mentally sipping piña coladas on a beach in Florida," I chided him. "I could've convinced him to let me set off a firework display and he'd tell me to try to keep it down."

I went to open the door of my classroom and his hand shot out and stopped me.

"What is it?" I said with a confused laugh.

He shuffled his feet. "Before you go in . . ."

"Yes?" I prompted, growing more suspicious.

"I was in a . . . er, different state of mind last night when I found you." His eyes were frantic, unable to meet mine. "Know that I had the very best intentions and I'll help you revert it all back if you hate it."

"Hate . . . what?"

Rome winced as I pushed the door of my classroom open.

My first thought was that Bruce must've finally oiled the hinges so it didn't squeak anymore.

My second thought—far more poignant and life-altering—was that this was a kind of love meant for me and me alone.

The space posters I had wanted to put up but hadn't gotten around to thanks to my below average height and lack of a ladder were on the wall. Exactly where I had envisioned them. There were perfect piles of flash cards, freshly laminated. Books sorted back into their tubs. Stationery caddies neatened and color coded.

I stared at Rome as realization dawned on me. "You fixed the door too, didn't you?"

"Er, yeah. Just a bit of—" He mimed a spraying motion, his voice trailing off nervously before stuffing his hands back into his pockets.

I walked a slow circle and noticed how *clean* everything was. Every table had been wiped down, the shelves dust-free. My finger inched a drawer open and found the inside immaculate.

"How long did this take you?" I whispered.

Rome scratched the back of his head. "Several hours, I think? I mean, you three had been passed out for a while."

My supply cupboard wasn't completely restocked but it was certainly fuller than it had been yesterday. "Where did you get all this stuff?" I asked. "Nothing would've been open last night."

"I stole it from the other teachers."

I slammed the cupboard shut, standing in front of it with my arms braced as if I was expecting a police sweep. "You *what*?" I hissed.

Rome was unrepentant. Growing with confidence as he realized that I did not in fact hate what he had done. He held his hand, one finger raised. "Jeff had *stacks* of construction paper in his office. Why? What the hell does he need it for? The man's favorite activity is finding new ways to delegate his job."

He continued ticking off more fingers. "I'm pretty sure Tom meant to order sports tape, not masking tape, so I did him a favor taking them off his hands, really. I hit as many classrooms as I could for a few spare pens and pencils from each so I don't think anyone will miss them. But look how many you have now!"

Rome uncapped one of my whiteboard markers. "You have the same amount of whiteboard markers but I swapped the ones that were drying out with fresh ones." A hasty scribble proved his point.

"Swapped with—"

"The teachers who always manage to weasel out of bus duty."

Revenge *and* organization. Was there no depth to the ways this man could make me swoon?

"I have to admit, I was a bit spiteful with Robyn's classroom. That was personal. She owed you for the IEP so I took your payment in the form of Post-it notes, brown kraft paper and reward stickers. Hardly an even trade, but the best I could do." He sniffed disdainfully. "Plus, it's only temporary until all the donated supplies come in," he added easily. "You'll of course get first dibs and everyone else can share the rest among themselves."

My head was spinning, overloaded with information. What donated supplies? I was still trying to process that my desk was dust and fingerprint-free.

"Oh! I also want to get you a plant." He clicked his fingers and pointed at an empty spot on my desk. "Right here. Got any preferences or are you happy for me to surprise you?"

I stared at him. My beautiful, lovely, thoughtful alpha.

Then I burst into tears.

"Baby." Rome rushed over and enfolded me in his arms. "No, I didn't mean to make you cry."

I only sobbed harder.

"I only wanted to show you that I can help. I'm *happy* to help." He wiped the tears away and kissed me despite my unfortunate state.

"I'm sorry," I blubbered. "It seems so stupid that I-I pushed you away when you . . ." I gestured helplessly at my surroundings.

"It's ok," Rome soothed me. "You've gotten used to not asking for help. We didn't show you that we could. But now that you know . . ."

"I'll ask for it when I need it," I promised.

I saw the glint of hope. It was a big thing and we both knew it.

Small steps. Relearn. Rewire.

You're no longer alone.

This would only make me a better teacher. And as I fought a fresh surge of tears, a better omega for my pack.

"Wait . . . did you say something about donated supplies?"

Rome's grin was incorrigible. "You'll see." He checked his watch. "Oh, would you look at that? I have to get my room ready."

He kissed me thoroughly, dipping me into the most ridiculous bend. I was left dizzy and disoriented, clutching my desk like a high society lady thoroughly ravished by a rogue. I had collected myself and dulled my perfume with a fresh application of No-NonScent Deodorant by the time my students arrived. They loved the classroom—how could they not?—and I fought the urge to cry all over again.

My omega was chirpy with delight that things were fixed with my pack. She was a very one-track minded instinctual being and was looking forward to a regular supply of alpha knots again.

My conscience, however, still had some serious repairing to do.

I was busy composing the perfect apology text to the girls during recess when Jeff knocked on my door. And immediately opened it before I even had a chance to answer.

"Ivy! It's a madhouse. Obscene is what it is! I need you to—"

"No."

I didn't even look up from my phone. Did I put too many exclamation marks? Could I replace a couple of them with emojis? But what emoji? I deleted my last line with a frustrated exhale. This was harder than I thought.

"Ivy, are you even listening to me?"

"Hmm?" I finally looked up at my principal, all red-faced and sweaty with outrage. "I'm on my break, Jeff."

"B-but—"

"Is it something that only *I* specifically am able to do because of my extremely individual skillset?" I asked, blinking at him earnestly.

He sputtered like a rusty clunker. "That's not the point, you—"

"That sounds like more of a *you* problem, Jeff." I turned away, already losing interest.

I pursed my lips thoughtfully. A good charcuterie board solved a lot of things. I should invite the girls over along with my apology.

"I . . . how can you . . . why are you . . ." Jeff stamped his foot. "I can't believe this! If you think I won't remember this when performance reviews come around, you are sorely, *sorely* mistaken!"

He slammed the door shut and I collapsed in my seat, the adrenaline of standing up to him draining rapidly out of me.

My heart was pounding. There was still a section of my brain screaming at me that this was going to backfire in a big way. My students would suffer. I would be tossed out to the curb, pelted with rotten fruit and vegetables by the entire school.

But I was determined to drown it out. I reminded myself that my academic results and overall positive outcomes spoke for themselves. That's what really mattered. Not . . .

I glanced out the window and saw Jeff trudging in the snow, yelling at a group of eighth grade boys building a gigantic snow penis complete with plucked shrubbery sticking out of the humongous balls.

That.

He'd handled it fine on his own. He just didn't want to.

Feeling even better about my decision, I sent off my text to the girls' group chat.

> I'm so sorry about how our coffee catch up went. I know you were all just looking out for me. Let me make it up to you, please? My place whenever you're all free—there's a grazing board with your names on it.

A flood of gratitude swamped me as the replies came in thick and fast.

LUCY
There's nothing to forgive!

OLIVE
We'd love to come over. Saturday?

SUMMER
I like brie

LUCY
Summer!

SUMMER

Maybe some prosciutto too

Brie and prosciutto coming up

Emotion welled up in my throat.

Love you girls.

I hugged the bombardment of emojis to my chest.

Caitlin was a simple fix. After all, having spats came hand-in-hand with sisterhood.

I'm a bitch

CAITLIN

It's ok. I'm clueless. See you next dinner?

Of course

CAITLIN

Sweet

I already knew my parents would only care that I was feeling better but I wanted to apologize regardless. Mom picked up almost immediately when I called.

"Ivy! What a pleasant surprise. I never would've expected to see your name pop up. Aren't you working?"

Oof. A gut punch of self-inflicted guilt. A daytime *weekday* call was shocking to her.

"Yes, but I'm on my break."

"Wonderful, honey. Let me put you on speaker—I'm repotting

my herbs. These poor dearies are not liking their new spot. I'm going to have to move them back beneath the kitchen window even though your father will *never* let me hear the end of it about how they're in the way."

Another stomach lurch. I probably would've gotten frustrated that she was talking too long about something that was irrelevant to me when I could be working.

I had to do better.

"Mom. I'm really sorry. About the other night." My voice cracked and there was zero chance she wouldn't notice.

"Oh, Ivy. Hun." I heard a metallic thunk as she set down her gardening tools. "Are you doing better? That's what matters to me."

"Yes." A wobbly smile formed. "A lot better. I . . ." Deep breath. In and out. "I was thinking of asking my pack if they'd like to come to dinner. But I wanted to make sure you and Dad were fine with it first."

Mom inhaled sharply.

"Ivy Noelle Winter, your mother needs a *warning* before you give her a heart attack!" she wheezed. She sounded like she was running. Or at least trying to. I could picture her, hair flying, arms flapping as she bumbled through the house. "George!" I heard her screech for my father. "Can you cook for seven next time the girls come around?"

"Seven?!" he hollered back. "Are they dwarves?"

"Ivy and her pack and us, you big dolt!"

There was a long pause followed by a significant amount of scuffling before my dad's gruff voice came through.

"This pack. They treating my girl well?"

I fought the urge to roll my eyes and smiled. "Yes, Dad. Very well. Better than I treat them, really."

"That's how it should be," he sniffed. "All right. Maybe I'll smoke a nice brisket for them. Make a homemade spice blend. And better wood chips than the ones I got last time, that was a disaster—hey!"

Mom snatched the phone back. "We'd love to have them over," she gushed. "Ask them and let us know when."

"I will," I said warmly, before asking how her morning was going.

By the time recess was over, I had done no work. But I had never felt better about how I'd spent my time.

There was one more bridge I had to repair, but I knew it was going to be on *his* terms. I didn't expect him to show his face around me for a while and I completely understood.

But when I saw Felix two nights later, sleeping on the cushion Carmen put out for him in the window of Mariposa Market, I took my chance.

I purchased his favorite gourmet treats, made my way over to him and gave the bag a light rustle. One eye popped open, assessing me like a majestic sleeping dragon. He shut it promptly, his purr taking on a growly, unimpressed undertone.

"I'm really sorry, Felix."

Both eyes open now. Thin slits judging me.

"I know you were only trying to help."

His huff spoke volumes. *You should've been grateful, you silly twit.*

"You really do know better."

One orange-y ear perked up immediately. Felix frowned, annoyed that his true feelings had been betrayed.

"Not just in this instance. In all things, really."

I was really laying it on thick but I thought it was needed.

Felix uncurled himself, stretching his whole body out. His claws popped out before retracting as he shook himself off and leaped down from his cushion.

"You wanna come stay with me tonight?" I offered.

His tail swung lazily. *I thought it was obvious? Do you want me to reconsider?*

"My pack will be in my nest too, if that's all right with you."

I swore I saw a hint of a smile that he hid with a light headbutt of my legs. He padded over to the entrance of the market and sat waiting for me. I let out a sigh of relief, following after him.

I think everything was going to be all right after all.

Chapter 33

IVY

LOGAN'S CHEST WAS SUCH A NICE PILLOW.

Was it sacrilege to feel good on a Monday morning? I felt wonderful. I carefully untangled my legs from Rome's behind me. He was the little spoon to James' haphazard embrace. They were so perfect together I found myself biting down on James' bare forearm out of sheer affection. I pulled back with a breathy squeak.

Still asleep. Whew.

I slithered as slowly as I could out of the nest so I didn't disturb my sleeping pack. One last lingering glance—Logan's butt was partially on display and just lovely—before I slid on my slippers and made my way to the kitchen.

My breakfasts were usually something quick like toast but I actually had proper groceries in my fridge after we shopped over the weekend together. I got to whisking eggs and frying up some bacon. Breakfast wraps sounded good, especially since Logan could take it to go as he had to leave earlier than the rest of us.

"What are you doing?"

I shrieked and nearly sent scrambled eggs flying over my shoulder. Logan only found my lack of awareness funny. "Not used to having people around your home?" he asked, hugging me from behind and helping me set the pan back in the middle of the burner.

My heart was beating a million miles an hour. "Not big alphas who are much stealthier than they appear," I grumbled.

He started to kiss my neck and I was instantly putty. "Why are you cooking breakfast for us?" he murmured.

"Well, it was supposed to be a surprise for all three of you," I said, feeling reluctant to leave his arms to go fetch wraps from the pantry. "But help me surprise Rome and James instead?"

One last lingering, scent-marking kiss. "That I can do," Logan rumbled before pulling away.

I liked the newness. This break in my routine. The domesticity of wondering if we should add some garlicky sautéed mushrooms along with the spinach and cheese. But old habits die hard and Logan did not miss my repeated glances at the TV. He gave me a questioning look and I tucked my hair behind my ear self-consciously.

"I usually have my baking show on in the background when I cook or do chores," I admitted sheepishly.

Logan flicked his chin at the screen. "Put it on. It won't wake them."

Rome made fun of James for sleeping through anything and was oblivious to the fact that he was just as bad.

It was an episode I had watched many times before, washing over me like comforting white noise. Logan, however, almost burned the bacon because he was so transfixed.

"God, how are they going to turn this around? There's fifteen minutes on the clock and the cake needs *twenty*."

I giggled and took the spatula from him.

Logan and I folded wraps together, one of us a little more efficient than the other.

"Can we watch this later tonight? After dinner?" he asked once we were done. "I can't believe I have to leave for work in ten minutes."

He looked so forlorn I had to kiss that downturned mouth.

James and Rome were finally up, rubbing sleep out of their eyes as they stumbled into the kitchen. I finished off my wrap and held the plate out to them.

"You made breakfast?" Rome asked, a little line forming between his brows.

"*We* did," I corrected, pointing at Logan disappearing down the hallway to get dressed.

"Wake us next time so we can help."

"Mmmm . . . no," I said and earned myself a pinch on my butt followed by a sizable grope.

James had no such qualms, already midway through his wrap. "We slept in. Gotta get into the shower," he said before devouring the rest in one gigantic bite.

Ooh. The first hurdle in trying to streamline four individual morning routines. "*I* need to shower," I said.

Rome's mouth flattened. "Me too."

"Not me." Logan was back and ready for work. "I shower at night. Can't be getting in the nest covered in dust and grime or whatever I've picked up that day."

He was *so* dreamy.

Logan kissed me good-bye, cradling my face in both his hands and leaving me with enough of his brisk evergreen scent that I got a little head rush.

"So . . . all three of us need to shower?" I asked, trying to pat my hair back into place.

James licked his bottom lip. Slowly.

"We can't have sex in the shower. We'll be late," I said, putting my foot down.

He blinked so *innocently* like I was the perverted one. "I don't know where you got that idea from, Ivy. All I was going to ask was if you needed to wash your hair today."

Incorrigible, up-to-no-good *deviant*.

"I do."

James turned to Rome. "Rock paper scissors. Whoever wins gets to pick soap or hair."

My hands flew to my hips. "Excuse me?"

Rome already had his fist in his palm. "Rock, paper, scissors, *shoot*." He won, crushing James' scissors with his rock. "I want soap."

James laughed. "I wanted hair anyway."

"Look at that, we didn't need to play at all," Rome chuckled before turning to me. "Come on, Ivy. Let's go."

My shower was extra long that morning. James jumped in first, shampooing my hair with the most spine-tingling head massage before conditioning my ends. He cleaned himself in a minute flat, before swapping with Rome. I was soaped so thoroughly I was starting to wonder why on earth I said we weren't allowed to have sex.

"Because we have work," Rome said, kissing the tip of my nose.

Right. That.

I was in the middle of applying my makeup but went to see James off at the front door. He gave me an amused smile as I zipped his coat up for him over his scrubs.

"Send me cute pics?" I requested, rising on my tiptoes to kiss him. Fingers crossed for a huge bunny or a litter of puppies he would struggle to hold all at once.

"You got it." James winked. "Selfies all day long."

He was such a—"Get out of here!" I scolded him, pushing him out the door.

Rome was waiting for me on the couch to finish getting dressed. "Ready?" he asked, looking up from his phone. Our bags were already neatly lined up by the door.

"Yes." I smiled. Only one car today. The thought set off a flutter of wings in my stomach. We drove in a comfortable silence and walked into school hand-in-hand in plain sight of the few giggling students milling in the schoolyard.

"Ivy!"

Our administrative assistant Cora had her head stuck out the office door, waving frantically at me. The sweet but bumbly lady only had two settings—calm and sheer panic.

"Cora? What is it?"

She sighed defeatedly. "Lord, just come and see. It's like a gosh darn warehouse threw up in here."

Rome and I exchanged a glance and followed her into the building. Boxes. Piled at least three high and barricading the way for anyone larger than a field mouse.

"The deliveries started this morning and they have *not* stopped."

A UPS man chose that moment to appear and Cora wailed like he'd brought her a severed head.

Rome tried to look for a label. "Who are they for?"

"Heyyy, Mr. C."

A nervous Robbie popped up out of the box mountain. "Half of these have my name on them," he said, scratching his head sheepishly.

"The donations are here already? That was quick. I can take it from here." Rome patted a relieved Robbie who was very happy to scamper off.

I hadn't quite believed it when Rome told me what he and Robbie had done. But I couldn't deny the literal mountain of evidence before me. It wasn't like we'd only received boxes of crayons either. There were some serious tech and sports brands who had contributed. A notable publishing house. I had a feeling there was still more to come.

"I want to make sure you get everything you need," Rome said quietly, his arm around my waist and squeezing my hip.

Getting even a small portion of these donations was beyond what I could hope for. "Let the department heads catalog this and decide how to divide it up. I don't need more than my share, Rome."

A couple of the boxes had been opened, perhaps by a nosy Cora before she realized she could not keep up with the influx. I spied a fancy ergonomic chair cushion that my omega was very interested in.

"Except this. This is mine." I grabbed it and held it to my chest.

Rome tucked my hair behind my ear and kissed me. "You deserve it. Best teacher ever."

"Ok, let's not get carried away now."

His hug was frighteningly smushy. "Say you're the best," he teased me.

"No!"

"Rome!"

For once I was grateful for Jeff's flustered appearance. "Why am I getting emails from the Future Fitness program? The Brighter Paths Project?" Jeff waved his phone in Rome's face. "SGS has been on the waitlist on some of these programs for *months* and suddenly they're emailing me and mentioning *you* of all people!"

Rome for some reason thought it was a good time to ignore Jeff completely and tilt his head toward me. "Did I tell you Robbie made a second video for me?" he said out of the corner of his mouth.

"I-I don't really keep up with that sort of thing," I said faintly.

Jeff cleared his throat impatiently.

"This is a good thing. Isn't it, Jeff?" Rome said sternly.

"Well yes, but there's *protocols* and—"

"You're welcome," Rome said briskly. "You'll reply to those emails today? I'm looking forward to being more supported from now on."

All semblance of fight and authority drained from Jeff like the slow wheeze of a deflating balloon.

"You two are a menace," Jeff muttered before storming off.

Rome turned to me. "Did you hear that?" He closed the gap

between us, the air between us igniting with his indulgent wine scent. "We're a menace, Ivy."

"That is . . . *entirely* you," I said, trying not to breathe him in. "Now let me go to class before you make me perfume." I swatted at him, using my cushion as a shield from his *alphaness*.

"All right," Rome said mildly. He stepped back and waved at me. Next moment I was in his arms giving him a proper good-bye.

"Um . . . bye," I whispered. My face was a furnace. We were not alone and my omega had *strong* opinions about leaving him.

He laughed affectionately. "Have a good day, baby." He stole one more kiss before sending me on my way, staying back to help Cora figure out how to best get the donations out of the office.

I got six selfies from James throughout my day. Smiling ones, slightly coy behind his hand ones, mirror ones. After opening the seventh one that was clearly a thirst trap designed purely for me (his arm took up half the image!) and decided enough was enough. I crouched down in front of the tank and got a photo with Fish James.

> he's cuter

JAMES

> hmm maybe spanking is my new kink

I hastily reapplied my deodorant and decided not to make the mistake of texting James during school hours again.

It felt unnatural to close my laptop at the end of the day rather than gearing up for more work. I tidied my classroom, prepared the materials for tomorrow's lessons and nothing more. There was still a part of me that felt guilty, that insidious little voice telling me all the ways this was going to backfire for myself and my students.

I breathed it in and let it go. As much I could anyway. Baby steps.

Rome said he'd come by once school was out but there was no

sign of him. Rather than sit around and chance being lured into doing more work, I made my way to the music room. The slowly descending sun cast an encore of golden light across the snow, a familiar evening chill starting to creep into the wind swirling around me.

Even peeking at Rome through the little window in his doorway was enough to make me smile. He was moving chairs around and I could see the seating arrangement for a band taking shape. New instruments gleamed from their racks lined up neatly along the wall. He'd put the grant money to good use and I was so proud of him.

I knocked lightly. His face brightened and then dropped like the swoop of a rollercoaster.

"Sorry, Ivy. I forgot I moved band practice to tomorrow morning. It always takes me more time to set everything up," he apologized with a sweep of his hand at a pile of still collapsed music stands.

My bag dropped from my shoulder. "Tell me where things go. Then we can get home faster."

The way he made me feel with a single look was radiant. Rome was in front of me, drinking me in, leaning in like he was going to kiss me and—

"No. We can't." His outstretched hand curled into a fist instead. All control mixed with regret that he could not ravish me in his classroom. I giggled and he coughed, embarrassed by his momentary lapse into instincts. "Help me sort this sheet music out into different parts?" he asked, pointing at a stack on his desk.

"Of course."

We made it home before the sun set. It felt like a win and I nursed the glow it gave me secretly in my chest.

Chapter 34

LOGAN

Rome and James were on a date, an early Valentine's Day for just the two of them. We would celebrate tomorrow as a pack at the festival. I loved the time we spent together but I was half feral knowing I had Ivy all to myself tonight. It was impossible to keep my hands off her. Opportunistically grazing her cute little butt whenever I moved past her in the kitchen. Kisses on her neck as we cooked dinner together. She shivered once and I draped my shirt over her shoulders.

Seeing her swamped in my clothes automatically made my dick hard.

It was affecting her too, her sugary gingerbread sweetening as we ate dinner in front of the TV. I let my legs fall open innocuously, my knee touching hers.

There was an instant bloom of needy omega pheromones.

I think the last thing Ivy wanted to hear when I finally carried her to her nest was, "I want to take my sweet fuckin' time with you."

"No, Logan. Please," she whined. Back arched, pussy hot against my thigh.

I deserved some sort of trophy for my control.

I had her naked for me, spread so prettily in her nest. Kissing that pink soaked pussy like I had all the time in the world. My mouth moved over her folds, tongue swirling softly all over. Slanted kisses with her clit between my lips.

"What are you . . ." She inhaled unsteadily and tried again. "Why are you . . . doing it like that?"

My fingers spread her open. I traced her entrance with a long, lingering swipe.

"All . . . slow." Her voice was barely a squeak. "It's like you're, *god*, making out with my pussy."

"That's because I *want* to make out with your pussy," I growled. I spat on her perfect cunt, slick mingling with saliva until we dripped down into her nest as one.

She was a mess. *My* mess.

Twitching and bucking and moaning as I enjoyed the fuck out of tasting her.

Her thighs tried to clamp over my ears as she came but I held her down, feeling her needy little hole flutter. I let her soak my beard with her slick before diving deeper, wanting one more orgasm from her. Hungry for it, *starved* for it. Her tits filled my palms and I rolled her nipples lazily with my thumbs until I got what I wanted.

I'd like to think I'd come a long way from Ivy's heat spike when I shot my load prematurely.

"*Please* let me have your cock."

"Soon."

I slid up her body. Kissed her and let her taste herself on me. My cock was aching, branding her, streaking fluid across her stomach. I filled her with two fingers and she threw her head back. Frustration and pleasure rolled into one.

"*Logan*."

I hooked against that spot inside her that made her gasp.

"One more, princess."

She squeezed me so tight as she came. Slick pooled in my palm, down my wrist. My other hand circled the head of my cock with my thumb and index, choking the blood flow.

Don't fucking embarrass yourself again, Logan.

That little distraction was all it took. My head wandered for a brief second and I was on my back. Ivy lined herself up and sank down all the way to my knot.

"Fuck! Oh jeez."

She was panting. Fingers digging into my chest. Bliss written all over her face. "How does it feel this good every time?"

I wanted to know too.

I watched her ride me. Bouncing, everything bouncing, driving me fucking insane. But it was nothing compared to that little smile tugging up the corner of her lips.

She loved this. Loved my cock.

Shit, it was hers. She could have it whenever she wanted.

I ran my hand down between her breasts. My palm stopped at her belly, fingers splayed wide.

I imagined it feeling round. A little firm beneath my touch.

It was a fatal thought. Dam bursting, instincts overriding, need overflowing.

I couldn't stop picturing myself filling her full of my cum. No suppressants, no birth control, full-blown heat. Days of nothing but rutting her. *Breeding her.* Pushing anything that spilled out back inside her cunt where it belonged.

I wanted her pregnant. Carrying *our* child. Growing our pack family.

Fuck Logan, don't say it.

I bit my tongue as I pulled her down on my knot.

And I came harder than I'd ever come before.

Chapter 35

LOGAN

ROME

Presents exchange at the festival?

I glanced down at Ivy snoozing against me. The nest had felt oddly empty last night.

She's still sleeping. But sounds good.
We'll meet you there at 11.

JAMES

Stanley might run me out of town if I do my
present in public

What the hell had he gotten her?

JAMES

Just kidding
sort of

Starlight Grove's Valentine's Day festival was, in Stanley's words, the "crown jewel of New England's February festival season."

I dunno. Seemed like red decoration suppliers made a lot of money off us.

Ivy was excited though, bouncing on her heels in the circle of my arms. She wanted to wait for Rome and James to arrive before exploring. But I could see that brain of hers calculating the exact route she wanted to take.

"Ivy!"

Rome had an alarmingly large bouquet of roses. James had coffee which seemed much more useful.

But I suppose the roses were more of a surprise for Ivy, who gasped, hands flying to her face. "For me?" she squeaked.

Rome laughed and kissed her hello. Bending her backward like a snapshot from a Hollywood film. "For you," he said grandly, once she had collected herself.

Ivy nearly toppled off balance from the bouquet and Rome had to take it back for the time being.

"This is from all of us. Happy Valentine's Day, gorgeous." James kissed her too—suspiciously chaste, in my opinion—and when he stepped back there was a small velvet box in her hands.

Ivy opened it, eyes widening at the gold watch lying inside. Swiss. Classic. Expensive as all hell but it was worth it.

"Oh. That's so pretty," she whispered, tracing her finger along the edge of it.

She wasn't a big jewelry person but this felt perfect for her. James helped her put it on and then couldn't resist being . . . *James*.

"I got you this too," he said offhandedly.

A little handmade-looking book passed between them. Ivy's brow furrowed as she flicked it open. "A coupon book?" A couple more pages and her eyes widened before she clapped it shut against her chest.

"James, why are these all coupons for . . ." she looked around furtively making sure no one else could hear. "*Pussy eating*," she hissed.

"Think of it as a present for both you *and* me."

"Oh my god."

I snorted. "Princess, I've got you covered with a lifetime supply already."

"Shh!"

Her face matched the paper hearts strung up everywhere.

"Well, I have a present for all of you too." She straightened her big blue coat, trying to wrest some semblance of decorum back.

"What? You didn't have to get us anything," Rome protested.

Ivy waved an envelope in his face. "Too late," she crowed. She slid it between his coat lapel and sweater and jumped back.

Rome extracted it with an affectionate shake of his head and opened it. His head snapped up from the unfolded pages. "Ivy, what is this?"

I took it from him, my brows shooting up.

An itinerary for five nights at Moonfall Valley in the summer?

The sleepy little town several hours away was known for many things. A sprawling winery, artisan cheesemakers and scenic drives. I also had a sneaky suspicion the famous chocolate factory was a big part of why she'd picked it.

She'd noted potential stops and activities for each of us. A local blues lounge for Rome. A list of thrift stores James might be interested in. I don't know why seeing my name next to a steakhouse dinner hit me so hard. Her neat little handwriting—*really good reviews, not too upscale.* I found myself again beside a morning hike in a national park. I smothered a smile behind my palm at her note—*maybe leave Rome with James.*

Ivy was organized, meticulous and endlessly dedicated to her work. Now she'd turned those skills to making us happy.

"The dates will work for all of us." Ivy was talking a mile a minute, clearly nervous. "Rome and I will be on summer break. Logan, I spoke to Lars and he's happy to take any emergency jobs that pop up during that time. Oh and James, your coworker Mark always stays in town because his parents like to come visit around that time so hopefully if you put in your holiday request it'll be accepted."

Thoughtful. Down to the last detail.

Ivy looked down at her boots, digging her toe into the frozen ground. "There will still be times during the school year when it will be hard for me to make time for us. Even with all the extra support I'm getting." She gave Rome a grateful smile. "But I-I wanted you to know that I'll never stop doing my best to make this pack my priority."

I don't know how she managed to make calling us "a priority" sound so romantic.

We hugged her close and thanked her. Kissed her until her pupils were a little too wide, hair tousled from wandering hands. Townspeople pretended not to stare at us and hid it badly.

"I'm really grateful you went out wandering in that blizzard, princess," I murmured. "Even though I never want you to ever do anything like that ever again," I added as a stern afterthought.

Ivy smiled and stroked my beard affectionately. "I don't think Mother Nature needs to do any more matchmaking with me."

STANLEY MADE US WEAR costumes in the Cupid's Counsel tent.

There was a reason Cupid rhymed with stupid.

The elastic of the barely fitting cheap feathered wings dug into my shoulders. Humiliating *and* painful.

Ivy was cute as fuck though. Not only did the wings fit her perfectly but she had a foam bow and arrow with a love heart on the end. She swung it in James' direction and he clutched his chest like he'd been hit before lunging in her direction and smothering her giggles with kisses.

Unfortunately, our first 'client' walked in before they could do anything to get us banned from volunteering in the future.

Turned out the rest of us were dead weight anyway because Rome managed to do our job all on his own. He got a couple disagreeing about what time they went to bed to realize the conversation they had before they fell asleep was really what they were trying to preserve. He sternly made a hard-mouthed husband admit he messed up chores on purpose so he could stop being asked to do them. Ivy was very unimpressed during that one.

Little Eleanor wandered in right near the end of our shift. Rome listened patiently as she launched into a *lengthy* explanation of why mermaids were real. Eventually her frazzled mother found her and escorted her out apologetically.

I admired him. I was grateful for the way he'd brought me into the fold. He was the reason Ivy was coming home earlier, chattering a mile a minute at the dinner table about the changes she was already seeing at school.

James whipped a blanket out of nowhere and laid it over Ivy's knees. He had a knack for pre-empting what she needed. Getting that squeaky, red-cheeked laugh out of her that was only for him.

What did I have to offer her?

I held her tighter against me, relieved when her gingerbread scent warmed up and sweetened.

Keeping her omega content was the least I could do until I figured my shit out.

Fifteen year old Amir came in right as we were handing the reins over to Ivy's friend Olive and her pack. The young man was shaking like a leaf and panicked at the sight of so many alphas. "I'll come back!" His voice warbled as he tried to exit.

Easton was having none of it, throwing his arm around the kid and almost bringing him to his knees. "I'm here to help, buddy! Tell me everything."

"Well, um, there's this girl in my English class . . ." Amir dodged all eye contact as he recounted his failed attempts to even speak to his crush. Poor guy.

I wordlessly handed my wings to Lars. The big blond giant was going to struggle fitting into it as much as I did. He looked down at it and sighed.

"The things we do, huh?"

"Yup."

Easton was dispensing some seriously alarming advice. "Amir, you remind me a lot of myself. When you know, you know, right? The secret to getting with your one true love is stalking. Find out her schedule and follow her to every class," he said magnanimously.

Luckily Olive was there to set him straight. "Do *not* listen to him! That is illegal behavior!" She tugged on his earlobe disapprovingly.

"Ow! Worked with you, didn't it, baby?"

I shook my head. That pack had to be chaos. Ivy had already ducked out of the tent and I followed her.

My blood ran cold when I saw that she wasn't alone.

This. Fucking. Guy.

I thought Ivy's ex only returned to Starlight Grove over Christmas. So why the fuck was he here?

Hated the sight of him. Hated that he existed. Hated that he was breathing the same air as Ivy and I wasn't allowed to crush his windpipe for it.

I couldn't hear what he was saying. That big fucking mouth of his curled into a smirk. But that wasn't why there was a red haze clouding my vision.

I watched the way his words made her shrink. Her shoulders caved in, scent souring. Making her believe she was less than the fucking miracle she was.

I was going to jail for murdering Sean Prior tonight.

Chapter 36

IVY

"Attending the Valentine's Day festival alone, Ivy? Again?" Sean gave me a pitying look. "Where's your pack? Shame. I really thought you made it work this time."

The shock of seeing him back in town trapped every screamed protest in my throat. Why was he here? His presence unearthed so many awful feelings I'd been working so hard to process and let go of. All I could do was curl up defensively, wishing he would disappear.

The touch of a hand on the small of my back sent warmth rushing back into me.

Logan.

"Problem?" he bit out, tucking me protectively into the circle of his arm as he loomed over Sean.

"Of course not." He was slimier than a frog. "I can say hi to an old friend, can't I?"

I choked, unable to stomach such a bald-faced lie.

"Sean was just leaving," I said, finding strength in Logan's presence.

"I was. Laura's been talking *nonstop* about this festival. Can't resist spoiling her." He grinned, showing far too many teeth.

An old version of myself may have thrown him a *how nice* or *lucky her* out of politeness.

"Bye Sean," I said flatly instead.

We watched him leave, just as Rome and James joined us.

"What happened?" Rome was immediately on high alert. He cupped my face in his hands as he scanned my features.

"Nothing. A ghost from the past who won't move on," I sighed wearily.

Stanley's timing was impeccable as always, waltzing over before Rome could press me for more details.

"Ivy, you *must* come help Rosie with the love letter station," he cried.

Caving to Stanley was not ideal, but Rosie was a sweetheart. I was happy to help *her*.

I mouthed a quick apology to the guys as I followed our impatient mayor. James pointed at the food pavilion. "We'll wait for you there!"

Poor Rosie was struggling big time with the wax seals, her table a veritable graveyard of ruined envelopes.

"Ivy, I'm hopeless," she wailed.

The chronically clumsy omega had burned herself twice and I already knew Char and Gavin were going to absolutely lose it when they found out.

"You're not hopeless, you just need someone to show you how to do it properly," I assured her calmly, slipping into teacher mode. "Like this, see?" I showed her the best way to angle the glue gun filled with wax over the letter until a circular blob bubbled up. Then I quickly pressed the design into it to form a near perfect round seal.

Rosie blinked. "Damn, you made that look so easy." She tried again and whooped when she succeeded. "This booth is kind of sweet, isn't it? I like hearing the nice things everyone is writing to each other. I'm having a lot of fun," she beamed. "Minus the, er, burns," she added sheepishly.

"We should take turns running it then. I'll do it next year and you do the year after," I offered with a smile.

"Deal."

I left a much more confident Rosie behind and went to find my pack. As much as I loathed to compliment Stanley, the Valentine's Day festival was a fun day out, regardless of your relationship status. The town square was a pink and red fever dream. Kenny was wandering around selling candy heart shaped balloons, holding so many I was worried he would float off into the sky. At least he was sparing us exposure to his questionable hot dogs.

Carmen and Marisol always ran the kissing booth with their dogs dispensing sloppy smooches. I waved excitedly at Lucy and Summer at their 'Love Potion' booth. Summer would have poured enough liquor into that gigantic glass bowl to take down a linebacker and Lucy looked like she had taste tested it a little too well.

I craned my head around the large statue of Starlight Grove's founders, trying to spot my pack.

"Ivy."

An arm looped aggressively around my elbow, pulling me behind the tall marble block. Soap. Laundry. Starched and overpowering.

Why does this keep happening to me?

"What is your problem, Sean?" I snapped, my patience wearing out.

His demeanor was so different from earlier. He was squirrelly and agitated, his lips pressed so tight they almost vanished. "Do you think things could've been different, Ivy?"

"What are you talking about?" My unease skyrocketed as he stepped closer, backing me up against the statue.

He ignored my question. "I always wondered, you know. What it would've been like if we had bonded."

Screeching sirens blared loudly in my head. "You're *married*, Sean," I emphasized. Where was Laura?

Sean ran his hand angrily along the short bristles of his hair. "What's different this time? Why are you happy being an omega with them and not with me?" he asked bitterly.

I was caught like a deer in the headlights. I didn't have a good answer for him. "It's in the past, Sean."

He stepped even closer. "You want me to fight for you? Is that what your omega needs? An alpha who can show you who you belong to?" His hands hit the side of my head, trapping me.

"Sean, you need to back the hell—"

Five fingers closed hard over my throat, his cheek sliding roughly against mine. *Scent-marking me.* The prickle of his uneven facial hair was like needles, his breath shaky and putrid.

"God, you smell so fucking good." He shuddered. His powdery scent swamped my senses horribly. "I haven't knotted anyone since you, Ivy."

I shoved at his chest. "Get off me!"

He looked rabid, on the verge of losing control.

"We were doomed from the start, Sean," I rebuked him. "I could never be with someone who expected me to give up what I loved for them."

His caustic laugh sliced through me. "*Please.* You think they're going to put up with that for long? They're a *pack*, Ivy. They're going to want you tending to their needs constantly the way an omega should. On all fours, where you belo—"

I slapped him. Hard. The sharp sound reverberated like thunder.

"Never speak to me again, Sean," I said fiercely. "Don't even look in my direction. If you see me on the street, you turn around and walk the other way. Do you understand?"

I was done giving him my politeness, my time, my *town.*

He panicked, realizing he had gone too far. "Ivy, wait—"

I walked away, not wanting to waste another second on him. His scent was all over me and I could feel myself losing it. My bravery. My conviction. Strength drained out of me, each step shakier than the last. I needed my pack. I needed their scents to erase him. I hiccupped, trying not to cry. Each breath I took felt like an invader in my lungs.

Rome was the first one to see me.

"Ivy. *Baby*. God, what happened to you?" He took in my ashen face and uncontrollable shaking.

"H-he scent-marked me," I sobbed. My backbone had completely disintegrated and I was reduced to a blubbery mess.

The immense spike in alpha aggression almost drove me to my knees. Instead of being cowed, my omega relished it. *Reveled* in calling her pack to war.

Show him who you really belong to.

"I'm gonna kill him," Logan snarled.

Rome's fist curled. "He's dead, Ivy. That fucking asshole is leaving town in a body bag."

I think both of them were completely serious.

James held my face in his hands. It was hard to focus on him, my head was in shambles. "You can't stay here any longer, can you?" he said softly.

I was torn between wanting justice and needing to get Sean's scent off me.

"Lucky you have two alphas, then," James said wryly.

Suddenly I was in an alpha sandwich. I huffed their scents desperately. A long comforting drink in the quiet shade of a rising forest. Some of the nausea lifted.

"James and I will get you home first," Rome promised from behind me.

Logan lightly traced the exact spot Sean had marked me. "Let me take care of him for you." He said it so sweetly, yet it was probably the most dangerous I'd ever seen him.

"No actual murder," I whispered. I felt like it was *really* needed to clarify that. "Don't do anything that will get you arrested."

Sean wasn't worth that.

"Of course not, princess. Only what he deserves."

I gazed into the burning eyes of my big, protective alpha and nodded.

Chapter 37

LOGAN

I snapped into action, turning to Rome and James.

"I'll be home when I'm done."

I left my pack to care for our omega and went hunting. My vision narrowed, my senses honed on a singular task. I was a bloodhound for a pissant, spineless alpha.

There he was. All five foot eight of his scrawny self trying to leave the festival. I watched him grow frustrated when his wife wanted to stay before he stormed off on his own. *No murder*, I reminded myself while daydreaming about how crisply his nose would break under my fist. I watched him make it to the footpath beside the houses nearby and visibly relax.

Idiot.

I stalked after him, fuming that his head was still attached to his body. An orange, white and black streak raced past before circling back and flanking me.

"Are you coming to help?" I asked the unruly furball bounding at my feet.

A low hiss. Guess that was a yes.

"Don't get in my way."

That earned me a blistering look. Felix bared his pointy little teeth and raced back toward the festival crowd.

Whatever. I ignored the twinge of disappointment. Beheading Sean wasn't a team sport.

Each one of my strides encompassed three of Sean's hurried, pathetic steps. He completely lacked situational awareness and only noticed me when I was practically on top of him.

"What the—"

I strangled the rest of the words from his throat with a sharp yank of his collar. Grabbing him on the back of his neck like an errant pup.

"You scent-marked my omega," I growled.

"Fuck, it was an acci—"

I shoved his lies away, enjoying the gurgling sound he made as he choked on his own spit. Ivy's handprint was a slash of red across his face like a brand.

She should never have had to do that in the first place.

I got a better grip on his shirt, twisting the fabric around my fingers and tightening the collar around him like a noose. One fierce curl of my bicep and I was lifting him, squealing, into the air.

We were right in front of Mrs. Cassini's house. Her high hedges were her pride and joy. She could be found regularly trimming them to perfection, perched on her ladder in her floppy sun hat no matter the season.

I planted Sean deep into them. Threw him, really. As high as I could reach. The dense foliage swallowed him up, only his head and limbs partially sticking out. Stuck like a pinned bug on a card.

I made a mental note to apologize to Mrs. Cassini later.

"You have a wife. *Children*," I reprimanded him. "Get your fucking shit together."

His actions were so far beneath what it meant to be a good alpha. Sean flailed and sank even deeper.

"Never come back here again." My alpha dominance had never risen so quickly, so easily before. *For Ivy.* Her name pounded in my ears like drums of war. "If I get a single whiff of you, I will string you up on the flagpole in front of the whole town."

His fear was a fine wine on my tongue.

I surged at him and he flinched. Eyes pinwheeling, sweat beading his clammy brow.

My voice took on a sinister edge. "If you don't want to answer questions about why you keep getting put in high places you can't get down from, you will *stay the fuck away from her.*"

Sean made a pithy, warbling sound. "All right! Fucking hell, I hear you. Can you get me down now?"

I laughed darkly. "No."

"What on god's green earth . . . is that Sean Prior?"

There was the unmistakable click of a camera shutter. I spun around to see a throng of townspeople gaping at Sean. Stanley was complaining to his husband Harry about rowdy visitors disrespecting the wholesome festival ambience. A tipsy Lucy and Summer golf-clapped appreciatively. Marisol raised her phone higher, zoomed in and took another photo.

Felix stood at the head of them all, a fearless leader. I had no idea how he managed to corral everyone so quickly.

His tail flicked imperiously. *You're welcome.*

Sean wasn't likely to show his face around here anytime soon. I'd have to stock up on Felix's gourmet treats.

But I had a more important mission first. Get back to my omega and make sure she knew she was ours.

Chapter 38

IVY

BEING HOME WAS ALREADY EASING THE SHAKES IN MY HANDS.

But it was also creating a new set of problems. We weren't in the fresh air anymore with the winter breeze. There was no mistaking Sean's scent, lying on top of my own like a stain. Rome was struggling, wanting to be there for me while his alpha rattled the cage of his control.

James had a soapy washcloth for me and I scrubbed my face hard to get the worst of it off. I caught the briefest glimpse of my reddened cheek in the bathroom mirror before Rome was on me, kissing and scent-marking me over that spot.

"Rome," James said warningly. He tried to ease his alpha back and an animalistic snarl tore from his throat.

"It's ok." I wasn't afraid. He needed this badly. I lifted my chin to expose my neck and Rome crushed me against the wall. Intoxicating me with his scent until I could barely stand up.

"Sorry." Rome shuddered. One last little lick before he drew back.

I was woozy like I'd drunk several wines on an empty stomach. I took his hand and deliberately laid it on my breast. He growled, closing the distance between us again. There was so much desperation in his kisses. Messy and rough, alternating between my lips and my cheek. I breathed his name and he swept me up and carried me to my nest. Undressing me layer by layer and marking every inch of exposed skin.

"Where else did he touch you, baby. Here?" Rome stroked my arm.

I'd been wearing my big coat. Sean hadn't gotten anywhere close to leaving his scent there.

Yet my preening, attention-seeking omega had me biting my lip and nodding.

Rome's eyes flashed. "We can't have that, can we?" The rough slide of his jaw along my arm made me whimper. Mulled wine sharpened, a red spill across starched white tablecloth. All the phantom memories replaced with my alpha's touch.

There was the hushed sound of clothing falling and zippers being undone. I was soaked in layers upon layers of Rome's scent, but it was only a part of what I desired.

"James." I stared down at him. Gorgeous, dark-haired, giving me the full brunt of his beautiful brown eyes without glasses. "You too, please."

His scent was less potent but that didn't mean I didn't need it too.

James gingerly cupped my jaw and scent-marked me with his cheek. They were so different. Rome's complex scent a punch of spice and citrus but James a glowing comfort. Melting me from the inside out, taking all the edge off my lingering anxiousness.

"Keep going."

James kissed the corner of my lips gently before giving my cheek another swipe. Unsure at first, his courage growing with every little response my body gave him. His cock was rising, pressing against me. The skin stretched over his shaft silky smooth as it rolled against my hip. A second set of lips, hungrier and pleasure-seeking, closed over the hardened bud of my nipple.

"Taking good care of you, I see, princess."

I gasped at Logan standing at the foot of the nest. Blue eyes piercingly bright as he raked them over us. He pulled his shirt over the back of his neck and my mouth went dry at his wide chest and thick arms. He made quick work of his pants before climbing into the nest, James and Rome shifting to make room.

"What did you do to him?" I managed to ask between his kisses. I needed my brain to work for a few more seconds before I lost myself in him.

"Stuck him in Mrs. Cassini's hedges."

Rome snorted.

"Everyone saw him and he'll need help getting down."

James guffawed.

I couldn't think of a worse humiliation for a man so rigid in his ideas of designation. His perception of himself as an apex predator thoroughly shattered in an instant.

I drank in the sight of Logan. My heart fluttered, lovestruck by this alpha who had defended me.

The strangest compulsion to bite and mark him overwhelmed me.

Logan was oblivious as he swept my hair to the side. He ran his nose along the slope of my shoulder, scenting for remnants of Sean.

"They got it all already," I assured him.

"I hate that it even happened," he said gruffly. He marked me as well, adding his pine scent to the blend of Rome and James. I jolted as a hint of his sharp canines scraped against me.

I carded my fingers into his dark golden curls. "You need more of your scent on me?" I asked softly.

He groaned hot into my neck. "Always, Ivy. I don't think you understand how feral you make me feel sometimes."

"Then come on me," I blurted before I could lose my nerve.

I didn't think any of our hearts beat in that singular moment.

"Are you serious?" Rome rasped.

I draped myself over him, burrowing into his chest as Logan curled up close behind me. It was easier if I didn't look at them so I couldn't feel self conscious about what I was saying.

"Yes. Anywhere you want," I whispered. "I want to know I belong to all of you."

A roughly torn *fuck* was the only warning I got before Logan thrust into me. My sticky panties shoved to one side, hips caught between his huge hands. Aggressive and urgent, unable to hold himself back anymore. He surged forward relentlessly, forcing my slick channel to stretch to accommodate his girth. Rome drank my whimpers and moans as Logan fucked my pussy like he owned it.

I threw my arm out to steady myself and James caught it. He pressed a kiss into my palm before moving it south. Over the ridges of Rome's tattooed chest, the bristle of black hair leading south to his cock. James wrapped me around our alpha, guiding my movements up and down. We stroked him together, his wet head sliding against my wrist.

But it was still three against one. A set of fingers rubbed my slippery clit, kisses overlapped. Wine, chocolate, pine until I was soaring. My orgasm rolled over me in waves, the aftershocks rippling with every additional thrust of Logan's cock. I tried to clench my thighs together but I couldn't hold back the slick trickling out of me.

"Up you get, princess." Logan was still rock hard as he slipped out and positioned me on top of Rome. He maneuvered me so easily, it was heady how strong he was.

Rome teased his tip against my entrance, running the ruddy head along my swollen folds. "Come sit on your alpha's cock, baby," he purred.

I let my hips fall, feeling him fill me and press against the spot that made bright white glaze my vision. My breasts filled his hands, squeezing and pushing them together.

"You're so good to us, aren't you?" Rome continued. "Look at what a mess you made of Logan."

Logan's stiff cock bobbed at eye level, shining wet with my release.

"Wasn't it nice of him to put your piece of shit ex in his place? Make sure to thank him by cleaning him up like a good girl."

I took Logan into my mouth, eliciting a hiss of pleasure from between his teeth. My tongue traced the ridge of his cock head, swiped along the underside and lapped at the precum that spilled over. His knot was half-swollen, the skin tanner than the rest of his shaft. Mesmerized, I licked him slowly there too and a deep groan burst from his chest.

Rome stroked down the curve of my back. "You love taking such good care of your alphas, don't you?" He thrust up into me and I pitched forward, taking Logan deeper down my throat. "I can feel how wet your sweet little pussy is." Another blunt thrust. "Do you need James and I to fuck it together?"

The idea sent blood roaring through my ears. *Taking all of your pack at once.* "Is that . . . even possible?" I rasped, voice raw from Logan's cock. "How will you both fit?"

A strangled cry rushed out of me. James' tongue, right where Rome and I were joined. His hands on my ass, spreading me so he could plant himself deeper. Somewhere in the recesses of my mind was a panicked voice telling me I couldn't possibly let him put his face *there, like that, from that angle* but then his eager moan vibrated straight to my clit.

"Oh my god." I collapsed against Rome's hard chest. "*James.*"

He added a finger, then another. Plunging in and out of me alongside Rome's cock. I felt him rise, curling over my back to kiss my shoulder. "You were made for us, gorgeous."

He pushed his cock against my entrance. *Too much. Not enough.*

More. Less. My desire conflicted with what I thought I was capable of. James coached me through a deep shaky breath until the head of him slipped inside. They let me settle and adjust to the stretch with a flurry of kisses. Logan guided my mouth back onto his cock as James worked himself further into me.

"Eyes on me, princess."

I lost myself in the icy blue of Logan's eyes.

"Beautiful," he murmured, threading his fingers through my hair. "You look like ours."

Imagining how I must've looked made my pussy gush slick. James finally stuffed me full, his hips against my ass. Two cocks, impossibly hard, hot and throbbing inside me. They began to move, both of them groaning as they slid against each other.

"Fuck, she's gripping us so tight." Rome set the pace, thrusting against both of us as he rocked me over both their lengths. I clenched around them, hurtling closer to the edge at an alarming speed.

"God, that's so fucking good." James buried his forehead into my shoulder, letting Rome take over.

I didn't know if I would survive this. The pleasure tightened low in my belly, coiling and coiling until I was dizzy from it. I gave myself over to them, letting Logan fuck my throat and tell me how well I was doing.

"Oh fuck, I'm gonna—"

James' words devolved into moans as he squeezed my hips, shoving his cock in as far as he could go. His cum pooled inside me in a flood of heat. It set me off too and I cried out, everything inside me unraveling and spiraling undone.

"Shit." Rome's neck strained, the veins stark as he reached the point of no return. He pulled me off both of them and threw me down onto my back. He looked divine, a fierce dark-haired alpha god. Sweat gleaming off the designs on his skin as he stroked his cock furiously with a mix of James' cum and my slick. I arched my body, wanting to present and please him. He shot a hot rope of cum across my stomach. Then another. Painting lines of milky white release all over my body.

Logan kneeled down, his large hand bracing my jaw and throat. He turned my head to the side and his cum landed right over where Sean had marked me. Possessive. *Hot.* His fist was a blur as he squeezed every drop onto my face.

"Fuck, look at you."

He ran his palm down my body, smearing his and Rome's combined release into my skin. He collected what puddled in the dip of my stomach before hooking inside my sensitive pussy to collect James' too.

"Open."

I stuck my tongue out obediently and let him push two fingers into my mouth. Licking and swallowing everything he gave me. Logan did this several more times, until I felt his alpha's satisfaction that I was properly marked.

I didn't even realize James had left until he returned with warm washcloths. The three of them cleaned me tenderly, leaving so many kisses on my bare skin I felt like I was floating in their affection.

The four of us huddled close, legs over under, arms thrown about, not caring who was touching who. Rome's purr rumbled gently against me as Logan stroked my hair with lazy fingers.

"We're going to bond you one day," Logan said quietly. "Start a family with you. Love you for the rest of our lives. I hope you know that."

The feeling in my chest grew too big, too fast. I quickly swiped away the tear that spilled from my eye.

"Baby—"

"No, it's good," I reassured Rome quickly. "But you know me. I want to plan what our future looks like. Start hunting for a pack house. Decide when would be a good time to go off suppressants and birth control."

Logan's grip definitely tightened at that.

"A bond is permanent," I said softly. "I don't want to rush it."

I knew they were perfect because they didn't get upset. They didn't even seem surprised.

"But I know this pack is my forever." My voice shook but I kept going. "I love you. *All* of you."

James beat the alphas, diving forward to kiss me first. "I love you," he said fiercely. "I love this pack. We're a family because of you."

Rome was looking at me like I'd made the sun come up. "You're my home, baby," he said simply. "Of course I love you."

Logan nuzzled his beard against me. "I love you, sweet girl." He chuckled. "I'm going to spend a lot of time deciding where to bite you." His mouth ghosted over my neck. Down the slope of my shoulder. The top of my spine. "I was waiting for you before I even knew you were meant to be mine. What's another year or two?"

Before long the feather-like kisses turned more serious. We gave into the temptation stoked by small touches. Thighs pushed open, James between them. Logan in me, under me. Rome's husky voice melting me with praise. Knotted and purred to sleep, licked and kissed awake. It was like that all night, and in the quiet between, we repeated all our promises and engraved them into our future.

Chapter 39

IVY

IT WAS NOT MY FIRST TIME RUNNING INTO A BENNETT ALPHA in the wine aisle of Mariposa Market. But I was certainly surprised by the timing of this encounter. *And* of the alpha.

Chester Bennett was a smaller version of Logan (not hard to be) with extra laugh lines and peppery gray hair.

"Do you have a favorite?" he asked me with a warm familiarity, nodding at the rows of bottles.

"Um." I was off kilter. I pointed to the only wine in front of me I'd tried before. "That one."

He whistled. "Good choice. This was the one you sent with Logan when he met Glenna for the first time, wasn't it?"

So it was. That felt like a lifetime ago. I nodded dumbly and he plucked it off the shelf.

"Am I not meant to be *officially* meeting you in," I blurted, glancing at my watch, "fifteen minutes?"

He smiled at me like he had all the time in the world. Aged, weathered hands turned the wine over so he could examine the label. "You are," he finally said.

Mom and Dad hosted our pack regularly at dinners now. I'd met James' mom and Rome's family pack over video call already.

James' mom called me beautiful about seventeen times. Right at the end, she asked if Rome still had his tattoos. I thought she was kidding but James told me later she was not. "She calls me her almost perfect son-in-law," Rome said matter-of-factly.

Rome's family took a lot longer, as every single extended member insisted on getting their turn. His grandparents on his dad's side were the most memorable, extremely sweet while also insisting that they could tell Rome wasn't eating enough. There was going to be some sort of care package coming our way despite the many *many* times we insisted there was no need.

Logan's dad was the last one for me to "meet," even though it was purely a formality. I'd known him for years as a fellow resident of Starlight Grove.

Chester gave me a sidelong smile. "I asked Logan to come by early to fix something in the attic and then snuck out."

No wonder Logan had apologized for not being able to head over together.

"You wanted to see me . . . before?" I deduced.

An ancient, lived-in kind of grief settled into his features.

"I never thought this day would come, Ivy. Meeting his omega," Chester clarified. "I worry so much about him. Worried that I ruined him with my own grief. It took me years to . . . well, you know."

"Yes," I said softly.

This version of Chester was very different from the Chester I remembered growing up. All of Starlight Grove knew how much he struggled after losing his omega, trying to raise his son through his tumultuous teenage years. Piecing together a version of his life he never expected to have, all while trying not to fall apart.

It had left its indelible mark on Logan. My quiet, closed-off alpha who had not realized how much he needed us all.

Chester faced me. His eyes were so similar to his son's. "Is he a good alpha to you?" he asked thickly.

"The best," I promised. "He's loved with us."

"Good." He sniffed and his eyes shimmered. "That's all I want for him."

It was an odd place for such an emotional declaration. We sat in the moment, the silence alive and mossy between us.

"Do you think he might be your scent match?" Chester finally asked.

Scent match.

It was an outdated term. To describe a magical feeling of compatibility, the secret locked away in how you responded to another's scent. I understood why people wanted to believe in it.

"He could be," I said, not wanting to shatter an old man's hope. "It doesn't matter either way. He's the one I want. They all are."

Chester nodded, satisfied with my answer. His back straightened, eyes dancing with humor once again. "Well, I better get back. Look forward to meeting you in fifteen minutes." He mimed zipping his lips and left.

I bought my wine and stepped outside the market. We had had a decent snowfall that day and it settled plush and powdery over the whole town. Despite the occasional car driving by and the people about, there was a deep blanket of quiet, the snow swallowing up all sound.

I stared up at the clear, twilight sky. Thinking about scent matches.

It was a lovely, farfetched idea. That I was made for them and they for me.

The stuff of fairytales, surely.

But I thought of Rome spending his whole life searching for a home until he found one with us. James' overly large heart needing an entire pack to care for. Logan and I, orbiting like distant satellites almost our whole lives, colliding like a supernova only when we were both ready.

There wasn't a single aspect of my life that wasn't embraced whole-heartedly, not a part of me they didn't love.

Fated. Written in the stars.

Could it be?

I was beginning to think there was more truth to it than I'd ever thought possible.

Chapter 40

FELIX

My paws were silent as I padded along the sidewalk through my town. Shops were starting to close. Lights flickered off followed by the metallic scrape of doors being locked. The occasional townsperson stopped to greet me and scratch my head.

I indulged them. Let them bask in my presence while I was feeling generous.

Two shops remained open. Side-by-side, soft light emanating from their windows and spilling out onto the snow. I drew closer, rising up onto my tiptoes to see who could still be working.

Hmm. It was the smiley omega who always rubbed our cheeks together when she hugged me. The one who worked with people's clothes, flittering around and sticking needles in them. I liked her despite how high-pitched and nonsensical her words became when she got near me. Her scent reminded me of the first perfect romp in a garden after a cold winter.

I hopped down and sauntered next door. It was the shop filled with flowers I was not allowed to eat or roll around in. The beta who occasionally smelled of the sea was inside, sweeping up fallen petals.

Interesting.

The telltale chime of the market door opening tinkled on the other side of the road. The shy teacher omega stepped through it. I watched a radiant smile light up her ordinarily reserved face as she stared up at the falling snow.

It was all thanks to me. I was enormously talented.

I gave the two lit-up shops one last glance and went to choose a house for the night.

Epilogue

JAMES

I YEAR LATER.

I WONDERED WHAT WOULD HAPPEN FIRST—IVY'S HEAT OR the alphas spontaneously going into rut.

They were insufferable on the plane. I seriously considered tossing water over all of them to stop the endless scent-marking. Ivy had stopped taking her birth control a month earlier and the alphas swore her scent was even sweeter.

You'd think they would've adjusted by now.

Rome laughed at me when he realized I had packed cards. "I love that you think we're going to play Big Two."

He wasn't even hiding how dangerously close his hand was to Ivy's crotch.

"It's for after her heat! We're going to be here for two weeks," I grumbled.

We had been looking forward to this Indonesia trip for many reasons and every new development only fueled our growing anticipation. The sight of the heat resort tucked away like a secret. The luxurious villa with a nest filled with scent-neutralized bedding. The twenty-four-hour room service menu.

Ok, I was the one most excited for that last one. But I was not going to have the heat-brained stamina of an alpha and was looking forward to a 3:00 a.m. ice cream on the veranda.

The expansive glass doors of our villa opened out to a private beach. The resort designers understood very well that alphas would not take kindly to anyone getting a glimpse of their omega.

Case in point: Ivy in a tiny bikini sauntering toward us, sipping a fruity cocktail. Pink lips puckered around the straw and her pert little nipples taunting me beneath the thin material.

Holy shit. I adjusted myself. We should spend every winter in a tropical paradise so I could get this view regularly.

Ivy set her cocktail down daintily, pretending she did not see Rome on the verge of coming in his pants. "I didn't take my suppressants this morning. Or yesterday. I wonder how quickly my heat will start?" she asked, biting her lip coyly.

"Fuck." Rome surged up off the sun lounge and pulled her into his lap.

I was not expecting him to whip his hard cock out, yank her bikini to the side and plunge himself knot-deep into her. Ivy moaned, her tits jiggling and threatening to pop out of her miniscule excuse of a top entirely.

"God, you're so fucking wet already," Rome groaned, rifling her over his cock like a man possessed.

Logan looked incensed. "I'm still putting on sunscreen! Hold the fuck up," he said, angrily swiping his arms as he watched them from the shade of the villa. "If you make her come without me, I swear to god—"

"She can have more than one!" Rome hollered.

I sighed and went back inside to get a stack of towels. Hopefully the alphas would remember to shower thoroughly because Ivy would be upset if there was sand in her nest.

IVY STARTED SHOWING SIGNS of going into heat very rapidly after that.

She went from flirty to determined, stealing all our clothes and disappearing into the nest. "It's not ready yet!" she yelled through the door when we knocked.

Rome and Logan nearly bowled each other over when her little face peeked out.

"Can I—*ow*, I mean, *we* come into your nest?" Rome asked, rubbing where Logan had elbowed him.

Ivy nodded, the picture of demurity.

The nest was already beautiful and luxurious but she had made it her own. The gauze-like canopy enclosed us in and our scents were already lingering in the cozy space. I smiled, recognizing the pillow arrangement that matched the one in our pack house back home.

"Such a pretty nest, omega," I praised her the way I had read about in *Your Omega's First Heat* articles.

Logan pulled her close, his broad hand across her stomach. "Everyone's going to know," he murmured.

"Know what?" she asked, her voice breathy.

"That we went away and fucked until we put a baby in you."

Clearly he did not read any of the links I had sent him.

Rome tipped her chin up. Her eyes were already dazed. "Do you like the sound of that, baby? All of us filling you up with our cum over and over for days?"

Oh, so they were trying to *jump start* this heat. Got it.

"We won't come anywhere else," Logan purred. "Not in your mouth, not on your pretty tits, not anywhere you beg for. It's going deep in your pussy every time."

Ivy wavered on the spot, squeezing her thighs together. The bloom of gingerbread-scented slick was unmistakable.

I pushed past the alphas to check on my omega. Her skin was hot, a tiny sheen of sweat already forming across her forehead. "I love you, gorgeous," I said affectionately, before she would lose herself to her heat.

Her expression softened. "I love you too."

"Are you ready?"

Ivy carefully removed my glasses and set them aside. "Take off your clothes," she said with an impish grin. She rose up onto her tiptoes and whispered in my ear. "I'm so ready to bite you."

I was instantly hard.

Lots to do this heat.

Ease her need for knots.

Make sure she ate and drank.

Bond each other.

Fuck a baby into her.

I couldn't fucking wait.

We thought *we* were the ones with a breeding compulsion. But Ivy in heat eclipsed us entirely.

Rome was passed out after countless rounds of knotting. Ivy showed no signs of flagging, her spread thighs hooked over Logan's elbows as he pounded into her. But it wasn't enough for her. She was taking greedy pulls of my cock at the same time, stroking my shaft far too expertly.

"Ivy." My abs strained from the effort of holding back. "I'm too close, wait—"

"In me," she ordered me.

I glanced at Logan, who was still very much fucking her.

"Come in me," she demanded, oblivious that her request was difficult to fulfill considering her pussy was already occupied. Ivy twisted her fist over the drenched head of my cock. *Fuck*, I wasn't going to last.

I wrenched myself from her grip and stumbled down to her pussy. A couple of quick pulls and I unloaded all over her, my cock twitching with each hard spurt. My cum covered her clit and dripped obscenely down over her folds.

"Push it in her," I panted at Logan.

Logan withdrew from her clinging pussy, his length shining with her slick. He grasped his cock by the base and collected the sticky white fluid with the tip. "You want this, greedy girl?"

Ivy let out an eager little whimper, lust etched across her flushed face.

A rumble of satisfaction curled out of his chest. "You're too pretty to pull out of," Logan purred before he shoved his cock deep.

"Knot. Alpha, please, I need—"

"I know." He held her protectively, his tender kisses incongruous with his rugged strokes. "I'm right here with you."

He locked his release and mine inside our beautiful omega.

How is this my life?

I collapsed against the wall of pillows surrounding the nest. Ivy made a beeline for my lap. I sighed a tired noise of defeat, stroking her hair as she suckled my softening cock clean. She was chirpy with happiness, rubbing her nose on my inner thigh and kissing me all over along the muscle there.

Suddenly there was a jolt of pain, and the sensation of being caught by *teeth*.

"Fuck, Ivy," I cried out, my body jerking violently.

But then I felt the bond form. It was different from Rome's. He roared through me like a wildfire but Ivy held me in the palm of her hand. The rightness was staggering, like she had found a carved-out recess inside me I didn't know existed and filled it with her light.

"I wanted to keep you." Ivy blinked up at me, the sweetest omega in the entire world. All instinct and all love at the same time. I didn't even care that she'd done it while locked with Logan. This pack, this heat, these building blocks of family, it made sense like nothing else did. My lips found hers, a little too warm and tasting of all of us.

I was already hers, anyway.

Epilogue

ROME

THE NEST WAS THICK WITH OUR SCENTS. INTERMINGLED spices, sugar and Logan's resin beneath it all.

I was knotted with Ivy but her face was still twisted with need, a crimson flush beneath her freckles.

"More, alpha," she whined, trembling as her heat instincts wracked her. If Logan had been awake he would've been sliding his cock past her lips already.

Instead, he was practically comatose. Lying on his back in a big, fucked-out heap, tucked in neatly with a light sheet by James. I dimly recalled James informing me we had been at it for over twenty-four hours already. The rut haze had been a complete blur. We must have gotten some sleep somewhere in there while Logan kept going.

I rubbed her swollen clit until she convulsed around my knot. My cock defied all reason and got harder, precum bursting inside her.

"God yes," Ivy panted, scraping her nails down my back trying to draw more out of me.

Fuck, maybe we shouldn't have made such a big deal out of breeding her.

A familiar hand squeezed my ass. "I know how to make you come over and over in her."

The bond between James and I sizzled with dark, thrilling heat. We were pretty set in our dynamic but every now and then this side of him came out. I loved exploring the shift, the raw edge it gave the fucking.

And how hard it made me come.

I kissed him hard, moving down to scrape my teeth over my bondmark on his neck. "You wanna fuck your alpha?" I breathed into his ear.

"I want to give my omega what she wants." He gripped my hair roughly in his fist. "*And* I want to fuck my alpha," he taunted me.

Any remaining blood in my body rushed to my cock and knot.

James began lubing me up and working himself inside me gradually. A couple of inches. Another squirt of lube. Even deeper.

"He's making you feel good?" Ivy asked, pushing aside my sweat-soaked hair.

"You both are." I muffled my grunt in her neck as James filled me completely.

Jesus Christ, there was nothing like this. The slickest, hottest little pussy wrapped around my cock and knot while James pounded that crucial spot inside me. I was a groaning, cursing mess. Ivy whimpered beneath me as my knot shifted and ground along her inner walls with each thrust.

The pressure built and built in my spine. My balls drew up tightly and I exploded hard, pumping Ivy full of my release. She shuddered with every spurt, hugging me tightly against her.

"I love feeling you, alpha," she said, the affection in her voice like honey.

Fuck, I was hopelessly gone for her. If she needed all the cum my balls could produce until they dried up like raisins she was going to get it.

"Did you fill up our omega like a good boy?" James asked, nipping at my ear with his teeth.

"Yes," I managed to answer. Would I survive both Ivy and James? Maybe not but *he died doing what he loved* made for a solemn eulogy.

James pulled out almost all the way before fucking himself back into me hard.

"Think you can do it again?"

I was high off heat pheromones, walking the fine line between rut and rationality, set on fire by my bond. There was no chance of my cock going down.

"Slower." I entwined all three of our hands together. "Let's make this last as long as possible."

"James?"

"Showering, baby."

I couldn't decide what moments I liked best. The wild abandon of primal heat fucking or these little periods of calm where Ivy ate sliced mango from my hand. James returned, toweling off his hair and handing out water to us.

Ivy thanked him and drank slowly. She gave me an uncertain, sidelong glance.

"Are you going to bond me soon?"

Somehow I was fucking her again, licking up mango juice from between her breasts. I could hear James laughing that I was somehow still raring to go after the last couple of hours.

If my omega didn't want me to have a refractory period then I wasn't fucking going to have one.

Ivy was giggly and sweet and breathy beneath me, indulging all my nips and scent-marking. I fucked her in slow, rolling strokes, thinking about all the fun places I could bite her. On her inner thigh, to match the one she gave James. Her soft little boob was enticing too. Maybe even her butt if she would let me.

But that jumping pulse by her throat was a siren call for my alpha. The thought of seeing my bond mark poke out from beneath the collars of her cute sweaters made my pupils dilate.

"You're mine."

I licked and kissed that delicate spot until her gingerbread spice overwhelmed me.

"Please—"

My teeth sank into her graceful neck and the bond awakened between us in an instant. The perfect, lilting counterpoint like a love song I would always carry. She brought a depth and beauty into my world so powerful it ached.

"Rome."

I didn't even realize my face was wet. She swiped the tears off my cheek.

"You're mine too."

She smiled her perfect smile and claimed me right back.

Epilogue

LOGAN

Ivy had bonded Rome and James. I could still scent the blood in the air as Rome lay passed out in the nest, Ivy's teeth marks visible on his neck. James had mumbled something about needing to stave off dehydration, leaving a bottle of water near me before falling asleep next to his alpha.

Ivy had completely worn them out while I slept and still needed more. I couldn't even wrap my head around how this was physically possible because her little hand sought out my cock greedily, trying to stroke me to hardness.

I grasped the back of her neck. "Present, omega," I said, letting a hint of my alpha bark slip through. She went liquid and submissive under my touch, ready to be taken care of. She lowered herself obediently. Pushing her ass high into the air, resting her face on her crossed arms.

She made such a pretty picture, on display for me like that. All puffy and reddened from hours (*days? Who knew anymore*) of fucking and knotting. Drooling slick in anticipation of more. I notched my cock at her entrance and her pussy lips parted to engulf the head of my dick.

I sank in the rest of the way. Her hot little cunt throbbed like a heartbeat around my cock. Fuck, I loved heat sex. My heart dropped at the thought of not having another heat for a while if we got her pregnant. Then my cock kicked back awake at *that* thought.

We wanted kids. Plural.

Maybe we'd get to have lots of heats while we tried for them.

I looked down at the remnants of my pack's cum streaking my shaft as I fucked her. Who were we kidding? There was no fucking way she wasn't pregnant after this. Every single time one of us had come it had been inside her, just like we promised.

Ivy was making wispy, breathy little cries beneath me. Her scent was happy and eager. All sugar and spice and butter melting on my tongue and driving me wild.

God I loved her. Loved that she trusted us with her heat, her future, her heart.

My palm slid lower, between her shoulder blades. A slight press drew out a needy moan. The sound undid me. I envisioned my teeth in her neck and felt woozy from the immediate head rush.

If I bit her there, it would be unmistakable to any alpha that it had been delivered like this. Holding down my presenting, submitting omega while she took my cock.

"Do it, alpha."

How did she—

I struck hard and fast, biting her across the nape of her neck. The copper tang of blood filled my mouth and a primal surge of alpha dominance crashed through me like a freight train.

Mine.

As quickly as my animalistic urge had risen, it was washed clean away by the first careful, unfurling sensation that could only be *her* in my chest.

The bond.

It felt exactly like her, distilled down as pure as possible. The sparkle that lit up her eyes when she was happy. The tilt of her head that accompanied her affectionate smile. The wholesome, selfless way she loved us all.

"Ivy, I—"

"Shh, I got you."

I choked back the rise of emotions swelling rapidly upward. She found my hand, my large one engulfing hers yet I was the one who felt held and safe. She lifted my wrist to her mouth and I felt the sharp sting of her teeth. There it was. Her triumph. Her satisfaction.

I was so fucking lucky.

"Knot me," she whispered. "And stay with me just like this."

I shut my eyes tight, and locked us together completely as one.

Epilogue

IVY

I WAS KNOTTED WITH A DOZY ROME. LOGAN WAS SLEEPING too, his wonderfully resonant purr filling the whole nest. James was cuddling me, feeding me strawberries and indulging my fussiness over only wanting sweet, cold things. Our new bond was alive and thrumming between us, so his exasperation over my unbalanced nutrition was very obvious.

"James."

"Yes, sweetheart."

"I think winter is my favorite season."

He looked pointedly at the palm trees swaying outside. The bright tropical sun beating down on the hot sand. Then back at me with his eyebrows raised.

"Right season, wrong hemisphere," I said, undeterred. "Still counts though."

James popped a strawberry in his mouth. "Any season with you is my favorite."

He took in my grimace and laughed, unfazed that he had not stuck the landing for once in his life.

"It's true though. Best year ever." He kissed my hand.

I felt like the entire world looked forward to spring. But winter was the moment right at the top of a held breath. I sensed the anticipation in all our bonds. Of beginnings and possibility.

I let James feed me another strawberry and wondered if we would have a little boy or girl.

The End

ACKNOWLEDGMENTS

EMILIA!! AUTUMN TO MY WINTER, SPRING TO MY SUMMER, design queen to my meme machine. It's been amazing to lift each other up, celebrate wins and problem solve together. I'm so proud of what we've created and couldn't imagine doing this with anyone else. Best shared universe partner ever and most excellent snow sensitivity reader. I can't believe we have to get tattoos now.

Patrice, our agent, for dreaming even bigger for Cozyverse than we ever thought possible. Some of those emails didn't even feel like real life. We feel incredibly lucky to have you in our corner.

Kate and the Putnam team, thank you for your giddy excitement and the way you've embraced this series and *us*.

Thank you to my team of readers who helped me beta read, sensitivity read and give me insight into the world of teaching. Elyse, Sara, Amara, Emmi and Elizabeth. My indie editorial team of Kai and Chelsea. I would not have been able to tell this story without you.

Anna for our gorgeous covers and for drawing such cute cats we had to include one.

And finally, thank you to every single reader who supported us. Those who reviewed, recommended, created content and showered this series with love. I think you all have a touch of Felix magic.

WANT MORE COZYVERSE?

A Pack for Autumn by Emilia Emerson

A Pack for Spring by Emilia Emerson

A Pack for Summer by Eliana Lee

On a station platform, with nothing to read,
and a four-hour train journey stretching ahead of him...

That's where the story began for Penguin founder Allen Lane.
With only 'shabby reprints of shoddy novels' on offer,
he resolved to make better books for readers everywhere.

By the time his train pulled into London, the idea was formed.
He would bring the best writing, in stylish and affordable
formats, to everyone. His books would be sold in bookstores,
stationers and tobacconists, for no more than the price
of a ten-pack of cigarettes.

And on every book would be a Penguin, a bird with a certain
'dignified flippancy', and a friendly invitation to anyone who
wished to spend their time reading.

In 1935, the first ten Penguin paperbacks were published.
Just a year later, three million Penguins had made their
way onto our shelves.

Reading was changed forever.

—

A lot has changed since 1935, including Penguin, but in the
most important ways we're still the same. We still believe that
books and reading are for everyone. And we still believe that
whether you're seeking an afternoon's escape, a vigorous debate
or a soothing bedtime story, all possibilities open with a book.

Whoever you are, whatever you're looking for,
you can find it with Penguin.